that's NOT what happened

that's
NOT
what
happened

KODY KEPLINGER

SCHOLASTIC PRESS / NEW YORK

Library of Congress Control Number: 2017060501

ISBN 978-1-338-18652-9

10 9 8 7 6 5 4 3 2 1   18 19 20 21 22

Printed in the U.S.A.   23

First edition, September 2018

Book design by Mary Claire Cruz

Dear Reader,

I'm not sure who's going to read this. I'm not even sure if anyone should.

But after everything that's happened, I needed to write it all down. Because even with the answers I've gotten over the past few months, I'm still feeling just as lost as I did three years ago.

You know part of the story already. In those first months after the massacre, there were news specials, articles, an hour-long TV documentary, and even an episode of a popular teen drama based on the events at Virgil County High School. And, if you've been to any Christian church in the past three years, you've *definitely* heard of Sarah McHale, the Girl with the Cross Necklace. The girl who died defending her faith.

My name is probably less familiar. Even if you'd heard it at the time, you've almost certainly forgotten it by now. But I was Sarah's best friend. I was one of the girls in the bathroom with her the day she was murdered. And I—Leanne Bauer—am one of the six witnesses who survived the shooting.

So much of what you think you know about that day is wrong. The stories have been twisted, tweaked, filtered through a dozen different lenses.

For a short time, all eyes were on Virgil County. Everyone wanted a piece of the tragedy. But within a few weeks, the reporters and camera crews were gone, on to another story.

And we, the survivors, were still here, still sorting through the rubble. Because while the twenty-four-hour news cycle may have moved on, our stories had only just begun. And now they were tangled into a knot of fact and fiction.

Some of that, at least when it comes to Sarah McHale, is my fault.

Virgil County is going to be in the news again soon. People will start remembering our names, looking at our stories. Only, the stories that are out there are wrong. I thought it would be a good idea to gather the pieces of the truth, for all of us survivors to share what really happened to us that day and after. But after the last several months of digging into the truth, I'm starting to think that maybe I was wrong.

Maybe some truths are better left buried.

So I'm writing it down. Everything that happened this spring, everything I've found out. I'm going to piece it all together and maybe—hopefully—when I'm done, I'll know what I should do.

XXX

I wake up every morning with death on my mind.

Most of the time it's this steady, existential hum, easy to drown out with a little bit of effort and daily medication. Until the end of February that is, when the hum starts to build, growing louder and sharper and impossible to ignore, leading up to The Anniversary. On that day, it's a thudding bass, a violently crashing crescendo pounding through my skull.

This year, the third anniversary of the shooting, was no different. I didn't get up until a little after eleven, and even then, I was exhausted from a night of awful dreams. There was already a chain of text messages on my phone.

Beware the Ides of March. Is everyone okay this morning? This was from Ashley Chambers, who is always the first to check in.

There were six of us who witnessed the shooting directly and survived. Before that day, we'd barely known each other. I mean, some of us had classes together. We knew each other's names. Virgil County is tiny and rural, after all. But we'd hardly interacted before that day. Since the shooting, though, we've all kept in touch.

Well, five of us have.

Eden Martinez and Denny Lucas had already replied. I'm all right. I hope everyone else is okay today and Okay over here. Take care today.

I typed out my own response, Still here. Glad to have you guys, before scrolling to the top of the chain and looking at the names of the recipients. I knew the ones I'd see there—and the one I wouldn't—but its absence still made my stomach twist with guilt.

I put the phone aside and pulled on a hoodie and some jeans. I couldn't eat anything. Not that day. I knew if I did, it'd just come back up. I'd learned that the hard way on the first anniversary. And then again on the second. So I went ahead and brushed my teeth and washed my face. When I was done, I walked into the living room and, through the front window, saw a boy sitting on my porch steps.

He was hunched over, his back to me. Dark auburn curls poked out from under his black beanie. I opened the front door, but he didn't turn to look at me.

"Hey, creeper," I said. "How long have you been waiting?"

Miles Mason looked up at me then, with his half-closed hazel eyes that always make him look sleepy. "Only a few minutes," he said. Or mumbled. Miles almost always mumbles. You probably saw the one and only TV interview he did after the shooting, where the reporter had to keep asking him to speak up. "Just texting everyone back. We're picking up Denny, right?"

I nodded and he stood up, following me down the steps to my truck.

Despite only doing one interview, everyone who followed the shooting remembers Miles. His story got a lot of attention after. He was "the unlikely hero." Seriously. That's the wording several articles used.

As the stories told it, he'd thrown himself on top of another student who'd already been injured, shielding her from any more bullets. The media made a big deal out of the fact that, prior to that day, Miles was on the verge of being expelled.

In the words of his grandmother, he was "a bit of a troublemaker."

In the words of one national publication, he was "the sort of young man you might expect to be pulling the trigger, not protecting his peers."

I'm not even kidding. That's a direct quote from some journalist who thought it was an okay thing to say, only two days after this fifteen-year-old had survived a nightmare.

Miles has never liked talking about any of that, though. Not even with me.

I unlocked the truck and we both climbed in. We didn't turn on the radio. We just listened to the white noise of the engine as we rolled down the empty streets of our neighborhood. It was midday. Everyone was either at work or school. Normally I would have been a fidgety, nervous wreck about skipping classes. I would have been paranoid about someone seeing my truck and telling my mom. Unlike Miles, I've never been much of a rule breaker.

But no one expected me, Miles, or Denny to go to school that day. No one would punish us or even mention the fact that we'd skipped. Everyone knew it was impossible for us to step foot in that school on the fifteenth of March.

It took us about ten minutes to get to Denny's house. He was waiting outside, sitting on the porch swing, with his yellow Labrador guide dog, Glitter, lying at his feet. He stood when he heard us pull into the driveway, and once I'd parked, Glitter led him right to the passenger side of the truck, where Miles already had the door open.

"It's tight quarters," I said as Denny began to pull himself into the truck. "We're gonna have to snuggle."

"Why does Miles always get to be in the middle when we snuggle?" Denny asked with mock outrage. "Not fair."

Miles slid across the bench seat, positioning himself so he had one leg on either side of the gearshift. The whole left side of his body was pressed against me. I shifted nervously, trying not to worry about what he might be thinking about us sitting so close. Instead, I looked past him as Denny hoisted himself into the truck and allowed Glitter to hop up onto the floorboard, where she sat between his knees.

"You know, Lee," Denny said, yanking the door shut, "if you're going to chauffeur me around, you're gonna need a bigger vehicle. I'd like to request a limo. One of those stretch Hummers."

"Yeah, I'll get on that," I said. "As soon as you can pay for it."

Denny grinned, and for the first time that morning, I felt this fleeting moment of calm.

Of the survivors, Denny was probably the most photographed and interviewed. He's a cute, slightly chubby black kid who's been blind his whole life. After being shot in the arm, he had to go through a lot of physical therapy to relearn how to use a cane. The media made a big deal out of this, emphasizing his blindness over and over. As if that was his defining characteristic.

The truck took off and we headed straight for the county line. We were getting as far from this town as possible.

I reached forward and turned on the radio, trying to drown out the Death Drum in my head, but even blasting one of my mom's old Nirvana CDs couldn't overpower the intrusive thoughts.

I should be clear: It's not that I *want* to die. Those aren't the kind of thoughts I have to fight. The opposite, actually. Even on a good day, there's this quiet anxiety, bubbling just under the surface, reminding me that with every second that passes, I inch closer to the end of my own existence. Reminding me that I have no control over when or where or how I will die.

On bad days, like every anniversary, that bubbling boils over.

Every turn I made, I imagined another vehicle speeding toward us in the wrong lane. Every bridge we crossed, I imagined collapsing and plunging the three of us to our watery graves. When we stopped at a gas station to fill the tank, I found myself repeatedly checking over my shoulder, convinced someone would approach me or the cashier inside with a weapon. And when some guy pulled up in a Chevy and slammed his car door, I nearly jumped out of my skin.

I saw death *everywhere*.

So we drove out to the middle of nowhere. Down a dirt road and back into some woods about an hour outside of Virgil County. It was a place we'd found two years ago with Eden. That first year, we'd all piled into her mom's van and driven until we found a spot where no one would look for us. We'd been back every year since, with a few scattered visits here and there when things got too rough. Ashley had come with us a few times, too—before her daughter, Miriam, was born. Now she had a family, and Eden was off at college. It was just Miles, Denny, and me.

I drove slowly. The road is so rarely used that it's nearly grown over, and that day, it was scattered with branches that had fallen during the last big storm. The truck bounced over thick roots until, finally, we reached our spot, deep in the trees. I knew we were in the right place because on our first trip here Miles had carved a large "6" into one of the tree trunks.

Though only five have ever been to this place.

I cut the engine and we climbed out. The air was chilly. A typical midwestern March. You could see the promise of spring beginning to bloom, but the biting breeze wasn't quite ready to let us go. Still, we piled into the bed of the truck, sitting on the tailgate.

Denny took off Glitter's harness. "Let me know if she goes off too far, okay?" he said as the dog started walking around in the grass, her nose pressed to the ground.

"Sure," I said.

For a while, we didn't say anything. Just sat there, listening to the sounds of the woods, watching the yellow dog roam through the trees, on the trail of some mystery scent. We've all learned how to sit in silence with one another. The quiet, at least when we are together, is safe. Even when we did start to speak, we kept our voices soft.

"Three years." Denny let the words out with a sigh.

"Yep," Miles said.

I was thinking about our text messages from earlier. About that missing name. I thought about it a lot. About how we should've been six instead of five.

About Kellie Gaynor.

I guarantee you don't recognize her name. It hardly ever got mentioned outside of Virgil County. But she was the other girl in the bathroom with Sarah and me. I hadn't seen her in years.

Every time I wanted to say something about her, the questions got lodged somewhere in my chest, pushed down by the weight of guilt. I wanted to ask then. To find out if Miles or Denny had heard from her. If they ever thought about her or if it was just me.

I even managed to open my mouth, to suck in a breath. It was a quiet sound, but Miles heard it. Or maybe he could just feel it. Sometimes it seems like he can sense things about me. Like he's aware of my every move, breath, blink, and he knows what each of them means. Honestly, it's both comforting and startling. And the way he looked at me then, like he was ready to hang on to my every word, made my heart stop for a second. His sleepy eyes made me forget what I was going to say.

Denny, who was sitting on my other side, hadn't noticed.

"You know," he said, readjusting the dark sunglasses he wore. "No one will remember the shooting once we graduate."

"What?" I asked, glad to look away from Miles for a second. Though I could still feel him watching me. "Of course they will. Everyone remembers."

"No, I mean . . . No one who was actually there, who remembers what happened, will be there after we're gone. We're the last class. The last survivors. Once we're gone, everyone at VCHS will only know what they heard or saw on TV. It'll just be a story to them."

I sat there for a minute, letting this sink in. I'm not sure why, but it had never crossed my mind before. He was right, though. In a couple months, the three of us would graduate. We'd been in the freshman class when it happened and soon we'd be gone, and the only students at Virgil County High would be the ones who had heard stories, the ones told over and over in our town, on the news, at church. Students who know just as much about the massacre as . . .

Well, as you.

And there is so much that you—and they—don't know. So many stories that had gotten mixed up, confused, or misrepresented. Even I didn't know how much at the time.

"Huh," Miles said. "I can't decide if that's a good thing or bad thing."

"Me neither," Denny agreed.

But *I* knew. Because the thought of us leaving that school and our stories leaving with us, of really and truly letting those halls be filled with the twisted versions of what happened that day, it made me feel sick.

Miles put a hand on my shoulder. "Lee, you okay? You look a little . . . You all right?"

I nodded, because I didn't trust that I could open my mouth without throwing up.

"It's just today," Denny said. "Today is always bad."

"Yeah," Miles agreed. "Always."

They were right. That day was always painful. And I'm sure it always will be. But sitting there, all I could think was that it was probably even worse for Kellie Gaynor, wherever she was.

And that was my fault.

The school didn't reopen until the August after the shooting. There were a few camera crews waiting outside, ready to film our return, but not as many as you might expect. It had been five months, and other tragedies had pushed Virgil County out of the mainstream news cycle.

I was glad there weren't a lot of cameras, though. I didn't want my picture all over the news. Especially not that day, when I wasn't even sure if I could walk into the building without having a panic attack. That would have become a headline in a matter of hours. "Virgil County High School Survivor Has Meltdown Upon Return to Site of Brutal Massacre." I'd be some poor tragic figure that the country pitied for a few days. I didn't want anyone's pity.

I didn't think I deserved it, either.

Mom had someone cover her shift at the store that morning. I think most of our parents took the day off. Everyone wanted to be the ones to drop their kids off for the first time. Some even walked them inside, like it was the first day of kindergarten.

"I can go in with you," Mom said when we pulled into the parking lot. We watched as a senior boy, sticking close to his dad, entered the building. "I can stay if you need me to."

I shook my head. "No. That's okay."

As much as I was worried about freaking out when I tried to walk inside, I knew without a shadow of a doubt that my mother wouldn't be able to handle it. Sometimes, it feels like what happened that day hurts her more than it does me. Which, in those first few months after, often left me furious. Like she was making my pain about her. I knew that wasn't her intention. I knew that I was being too hard on her. But there were moments when I wanted to scream at her. To tell her she didn't have a right to cry or to panic or to have nightmares. Because *she* hadn't been there.

"Are you sure?" she asked, and I could already hear the quaver in her voice. "Lee, you don't have to go if you don't want to. I told you. We can look into homeschooling or find somewhere else—"

"Mom."

I'm sure she was trying to help, but I found these feeble offers more frustrating than anything. She worked far too many hours to even consider homeschooling me, and unless we moved—which we definitely could not afford to do—there were no other options. VCHS was the only high school in the county.

And anyway, it wasn't as if changing schools would fix anything. The shooting was going to haunt me, no matter where I went.

"I'm just worried. You got so upset when we did the walkthrough with the detectives. If you don't want to go back in there—"

"I'm going to be late."

I grabbed my backpack and climbed out of the car, slamming the door before she could say anything else. The sound made me flinch, and I felt a pang of guilt. I'd been slamming doors a lot that summer. But as bad as I felt, I knew I wouldn't apologize.

I kept my eyes trained straight ahead, away from the media parked on the school's front lawn. All of my focus was on the door. The same one I'd burst out of five months earlier, smeared in my best friend's blood.

I swallowed hard as I followed a group of upperclassmen inside. This may sound absurd, but part of me expected the place to look different somehow. Like we'd walk in and see the signs of the shooting everywhere. But it wasn't like that. Everything in the front hall, the cafeteria—it looked exactly the same as it had the previous semester, before it all happened. It was clean and decorated with Virgil County colors—green and gold—and everyone was running to their friends, hugging and laughing, like any normal first day of a new school year.

You'd think that'd make it easier, but it just felt wrong.

I'd been back here once before that day. Some of the witnesses had come in over the summer to help the detectives map out exactly what had happened. But the school had been quiet then. Nearly empty. And it had been possible to pretend, at least for a few minutes, that I was somewhere else.

But this, it felt too normal. I found myself scanning the crowd for Sarah, as if I expected to see her waiting for me, the way she had been every other morning I'd walked into this school. Her bright purple backpack slung over one shoulder, a Pop-Tart in hand. And she'd always have an extra one for me, because she knew I skipped breakfast in favor of sleeping in.

Of course, Sarah and her backpack and her Pop-Tarts weren't there. So I just stood in the middle of the cafeteria with no idea what to do or where to go.

That's when I saw the plaque, a large, shiny black square hung up on a pillar in the center of the room. It was the only real physical change to this part of the school, and I almost hadn't noticed it. I took a few steps forward, looking up at it, and wishing I had the strength not to.

The plaque was engraved with their names. All nine victims, listed in alphabetical order. I took them in one at a time, even though I already knew them by heart.

Kevin Brantley

Brenna DuVal

Jared Grayson

Rosi Martinez

Sarah McHale

Richard McMullen

Thomas Nolan

Aiden Stroud

Essie Taylor

And beneath their names was a quote from Emily Dickinson: *"Unable are the loved to die, for love is immortality."*

I hated that quote, because it was a lie. Even if love were immortality, I couldn't help thinking that eventually everyone who loved you would be dead, too. And then what did any of it matter? It didn't. Quotes like those were just there to make the living feel better. Another way to help us ignore the fact that oblivion was inevitable.

I shook my head, trying to quiet the intrusive thoughts. But I couldn't bring myself to turn away from the plaque.

The shooter hadn't been listed among the dead. He wasn't named on any of the other memorials around town, either. From what I'd gathered, that had been a heated controversy over the summer. There were people who had suggested including him. He was just a kid, after all. Sixteen, a junior. In some ways, they argued, he was a victim, too. A victim of bullying, of his own brain, of a gun-obsessed society. As if any of that mattered. This was the *one thing* that wasn't about him or why he did it. This was about everyone else, about the damage he had done.

Several of the parents had objected, and I was glad. I didn't want his name up there. I didn't want it anywhere near Sarah's.

"Lee," a voice said behind me. I looked over my shoulder and found Miles, dressed in his usual black T-shirt and worn-out jeans. For a second, we just stared at each other. Despite everything that had happened over the summer, it felt odd to talk to him on school grounds. It was the sign I'd been waiting for, the one that proved just how different things were now.

After a second, he shrugged and gestured for me to follow him. We wound our way through the packs of students, over to the side of the cafeteria, where Eden Martinez and Denny Lucas stood with their backs against the wall. Eden had a hand in her hair, pulling at the dark, wavy strands, and she looked a little green, like she was on the verge of being sick. Denny still had a cane then, and he was clutching the rubber grip at the top with both hands, like he was ready to use it as a weapon if he had to.

"Lee and Miles coming up on your right," Eden told him.

"Hey, guys," Denny said. "Weird day, huh?"

"The weirdest," I said.

And maybe the strangest part was standing with those three. We were an odd group with almost nothing in common. Eden was a year ahead of Denny, Miles, and me. And before the shooting, we'd all hung out in very different cliques. But they were the only people I *could* be with. The only group I really felt a part of anymore.

Ashley had graduated in May, finishing most of her classes from the hospital and at home. She'd sent us all a text message that morning, wishing us luck and letting us know we could call if we needed anything. I wondered if she felt lonely, if she wished she could be there with us instead of just watching brief news clips of us walking back into the school. Or maybe she was glad she never had to return. I wondered how I would feel in her position, as the only one of us not returning to VCHS.

Or, not the *only* one.

I glanced around, looking for a flash of blue-black hair or a skull-patterned backpack.

"Who're you looking for?" Miles asked.

"Kellie," I said.

"Kellie Gaynor?" Eden asked. "You didn't hear?"

"Hear what?"

"She moved." Eden lowered her hand from her hair and began picking at her fingernails instead. "Her whole family did. My abuela saw them packing up a van a few days ago, and now there's a For Sale sign in front of their house."

"What?" The word came out as a cough. My throat felt tight all of a sudden. The way it does after I've been stung by a bee, before Mom gets out the EpiPen. I tried to breathe through it, but overhead, the bell rang, sharp and loud, startling all four of us. Which didn't help.

As swarms of students flooded past us, heading to their classrooms, I reached out and grabbed hold of Eden's arm. She jerked back at first, curling in on herself. Then we both mouthed quick apologies.

None of us like to be touched without warning, even by our friends. It was worse back then. Any sudden movement felt like a threat. We all had to learn how to be careful with one another.

When the ringing had died down, I managed to squeeze out a few words. "Kellie . . . Kellie is . . . ?"

"She's gone."

Later, in an assembly, our principal didn't talk about the new zero-tolerance policy for violence. Or the various civil suits being filed against the school. Instead, he focused on the one positive thing he could find.

He told us that, to the school board's surprise, every student who had been in the freshman, sophomore, and junior classes the previous year had returned to VCHS, and our incoming freshmen class was the largest in the school's history. We'd all come back to our school, he said. We weren't going to let fear or hate win, he said. This was our home, he said.

Here's what he didn't say: *Almost* every student had come back.

Every student but one.

X X X

I spend a lot of time googling the massacre. It's something like a hobby. Or maybe an addiction.

It started about a month after the shooting, on one of the many nights when the thought of sleeping in my dark bedroom was too frightening to fathom. I'd walked down the hall, to the living room, and logged on to the desktop for the first time in weeks. Mom had mostly kept me away from any media, but I'd picked up things here and there from the other survivors. And I wanted to know what people were saying about Sarah.

One link led to another and another and another. With every article or blog post, I became more anxious, more panicked. My heart was pounding and there were tears pricking my eyes. But I couldn't stop clicking. I knew I needed to. I knew it wasn't good for me. But I was in a spiral that I couldn't break free from.

Eventually I ended up reading a series of message board posts about the shooting and how it was a conspiracy. There were dozens of commenters, trying to show "proof" that none of it had happened. That this was just the government trying to trick us so they could take everyone's guns away. And all the teenagers running out of the building—including me—were just crisis actors. "It's so obviously fake," one comment said. "Use common sense, America."

. . . obviously . . .

. . . common sense . . .

My mom found me at six a.m., staring at the monitor with red eyes and tears streaking down my face.

"Lee, what are you doing?" she asked.

"How can they say this?" I asked her, my throat aching. "They say it didn't happen. How can they say that, Mom? Why would they say that?"

"Oh, Lee baby—"

"Why would they say that?!" I shoved the desk much harder than I meant to, violently enough that the monitor slid back and smacked loudly against the wall. Which only made me start to panic and gasp between sobs.

Mom stayed home from work that day and called my psychiatrist. We decided to up my medication and increase how often I was seeing my therapist. Mom also put a limit on how much time I could spend on the internet and only let me use my phone when I was leaving the house without her, though I usually just snuck on while she was at work or late at night. It made me miserable, but I was obsessed, and I knew how to clear a search history.

If you're wondering where my dad was for all of this, then we have something in common. My dad was never really in the picture. He got my mom pregnant when she was a teenager and he was in his early twenties. He took off before I was born, and the only contact I ever had with him was the child support checks the court ordered him to send. After the shooting, I'd kind of thought he'd show up. Like maybe hearing that his daughter had been part of something so horrific would spark some sort of paternal instinct. It didn't happen, though.

My mom has always had to be both parents. Sometimes I wonder if that means she felt the pain of what happened to me twice as much. I think I was angrier at him for that, for not being there to be a partner for her when I was at my lowest, than I was at him for being such a deadbeat in the first place.

Not that it matters anymore. He died two years ago in a car accident. I only know this because he left some money for Mom and me in his will. I guess some part of him did feel guilty. It wasn't a ton, but enough to help pay for part of my college tuition.

Anyway, my father isn't important. He wasn't there. Mom was. But as hard as she tried after that morning, she couldn't keep me off the internet forever.

Three years later and I still frequently find myself on Tumblr pages and message boards, reading posts about the shooting from people who didn't have to live it. Most people have stopped talking about it by now. It's old news. But there are still some dedicated bloggers who write about VCHS almost daily. Some of them are true crime junkies. Others have formed what I can only really call a "fandom" around the shooting.

Fandom may sound like a strong word, but I'm not exaggerating. There are memes and fan art and—I'm not kidding—*fan fiction* about the massacre. Sometimes the focus is on Sarah or Miles. Mostly, though, it's about the shooter.

I'm not going to mention his name anywhere in this letter, by the way, if that's what you're waiting for. There's enough out there about him already. I won't be adding to it.

Anyway, as angry and disgusted as it all makes me, I still lurk on a few different forums and websites, checking them at least a couple times a week. The more anxious I am, the longer I spend online. And, of course, anniversaries are always the most anxious days. So when I got home on the night of the third anniversary, after spending as long as I could in our secret place in the woods, it was no surprise that I found myself heading straight for the computer, even when I knew I shouldn't.

It was late. Mom was already in bed. And there was no chance I'd be sleeping that night. So I logged on and went straight for one of the most active VCHS massacre forums.

I expected to see the usual: debates about old conspiracy theories, discussions about why the shooter might have done it, that sort of thing. There hadn't been any news on the shooting in years, so the same things tended to be discussed over and over again, just by new voices.

This time, though, there was something new.

The top post was from a regular poster with the username VCHS_Obsessed. He'd written a short message, Hey, guys, have you seen this? Below was a link to an article. The headline made my stomach flip over: "School Shooting Victim's Parents to Pen Daughter's Inspiring Biography."

At the top of the article was the picture of Sarah, the one everyone knows. It was her class photo from freshman year, the one printed in the yearbook just two months after she died. The one that still stares out at Main Street from the sign in front of Virgil County Baptist Church.

That picture is the reason I drive home the long way after school. Because I can't handle seeing my best friend smiling at me, her red hair worn in two braids, making her look even younger than she was, her brown eyes wide and bright and completely unaware of what was to come.

And, of course, the necklace. I'd seen this photo enough times to know that some sort of digital editing had been done to make it stand out even more—that little silver cross dangling from a thin chain. It rested against her chest, right above the collar of her lavender T-shirt. That stupid necklace. It wasn't even the one from the crime scene. The *famous* necklace. But people see this photo as evidence. It makes them feel sure they know who Sarah was.

Here's the thing, though: She'd only worn the necklace on class photo day because her grandmother had given it to her for her birthday, and her mom thought it would be nice to have it in the picture. Sarah almost didn't do it—for the simple, silly reason that she liked gold jewelry more than silver—but in the end, she wanted to make her grandmother happy.

I wish she'd taken it off. If she hadn't worn it, then . . .

But I'm letting myself off the hook too easy.

Because she did wear it. And now everyone knows her as Sarah McHale, the Girl with the Cross Necklace. Everyone believes she's something she wasn't. That she died for something when she didn't. But that necklace isn't to blame.

I am.

I scrolled past the picture, guilt already creeping up from my stomach and into my chest. I couldn't bring myself to do more than skim the article. My hands were shaking and my eyes kept flitting around the screen, unable to focus on the same spot for more than a few seconds. But I got the gist of it.

Sarah's parents were going to publish her biography. They had found her old diary and wanted to use excerpts as they told the "inspiring story of their daughter's refusal to deny her faith, even in the face of death." The book had sold at auction, to a publisher paying six figures. And there was already interest from Hollywood in adapting Sarah's story to film.

"It's been three years since she was taken from us," Ruth McHale was quoted as saying. "It's been difficult. Some days, my husband and I have just felt like we couldn't keep going. But God has stood by us. Lifted us up when we needed Him most. And I know that what He wants is for us to keep Sarah's memory alive. To make sure no one forgets what a brave girl she was, and how dedicated to her faith. We should all hope to be as strong as Sarah."

I read that quote over and over, feeling sicker each time. I was feeling too many things at once—anger and sadness and guilt.

And dread.

Because if this was really happening, if there was going to be a book and possibly even a movie, that meant people would be looking at Virgil County again. The massacre would be on the news. The stories would get rehashed and repeated. Everything the world got wrong the first time was going to be pushed to the surface again. As if living with the real memories of that day wasn't bad enough, the twisted version was going to haunt me, too.

And it would be even worse for Kellie.

I just barely made it to the bathroom before my stomach gave way and the fries I'd eaten on the way home from the woods came back up. I was a fool to think it was safe to grab dinner from a drive-thru, that this might be the first anniversary without vomit. But no. I was three for three.

I flushed the toilet and sat back, leaning my head against the wall as I breathed slowly. Our house is small and the walls are thin, so I wasn't surprised when I heard Mom's bedroom door creak open down the hall.

"Lee?" she asked, her voice still slurred with sleep. "Everything okay, baby?"

She wasn't a light sleeper before the shooting, but since then, every little sound, every sign that something might be wrong, and she's up. Sometimes, like when I'm having nightmares and she is there to shake me awake, I'm grateful. Usually, though, I'd rather be alone, without the pressure of knowing I'm worrying her.

"Fine," I said. "I'm okay, Mom. You can go back to bed."

"All right . . . Don't be up too late."

"I won't. Good night."

Her door creaked again, but I didn't hear it latch, and I knew she was leaving it cracked. She'd be awake until she heard me go to bed.

I sighed and got to my feet. My empty stomach was still churning as I brushed my teeth. I headed down the hallway to my room, where I changed into my comfiest pajamas. Not that it mattered. There would be no rest that night.

I'd been staring at my ceiling for a little over an hour when my phone chimed with a text message.

You awake?

I typed back a quick response. What do you think?

Outside?

Too chilly. You can call though.

A second later, my phone rang.

"Hey," I said.

"What're you doing?" Miles mumbled on the other end of the line.

"Nothing. You?"

"Just watched a documentary on YouTube."

"About?"

"The stock market crash of 1929."

"That sounds . . . *greatly* depressing."

"Wow. Denny doesn't even make jokes that bad."

"Hey."

He chuckled, and the sound ran through me like a sip of hot chocolate on a cold winter night. I rolled onto my side and curled into a ball, knees pulled to my chest, phone still pressed to my ear.

"Tell me about it."

"You . . . want me to tell you about the Great Depression?"

"Yes."

"What about it?"

"Anything," I said. "Just . . . talk. Teach me something."

I could hear his hesitation before he sighed and said, in that mumbling, almost-slurred speech of his, "Okay, well . . . the stock market crash began on October twenty-fourth. It was right at the end of the twenties and . . ."

I closed my eyes and listened as he rambled, going off on soft, slow-spoken tangents and sharing a handful of anecdotes from other books he'd read or films he'd seen.

Most people would be surprised to realize how much Miles knows about history. Considering his poor grades and that he had to repeat sophomore year, it may not seem in character, but ever since we started hanging out after the shooting, he's been really interested in it. You can ask him about almost any point in American history and he'll go on for hours. This from the boy who answers in monosyllables half the time.

I'm not that interested in history. It's just never really

intrigued me the way it does other people. But I took comfort in listening to Miles. I love hearing it when he gets worked up or passionate about something. Admittedly, it's just a small inflection, a tiny lift to his voice that I like to believe no one besides me notices.

I let him go on about the Great Depression for hours. I didn't tell him about what I'd just learned regarding Sarah and her parents. I didn't say much at all, really. Just slipped in questions or comments here and there so he knew I hadn't dozed off, so that he'd keep talking.

I *needed* him to keep talking.

If he stopped, I worried about the places my mind might wander. And I hoped it was helpful for Miles, too. I couldn't be the only one in need of a distraction until this cursed night passed.

He kept going, right up until the first hints of morning appeared through the blinds of my bedroom window.

"I should probably go before my mom gets up," I said. "School is going to suck today."

"Yeah," he agreed. "But at least we got through it. And we have another year before the next one."

"Yeah." Though I tried not to think about what I would be doing this time next year, about the prospect of the first anniversary spent far away from other survivors. Away from him. "Thank you," I said after a minute of silence. "For staying up with me."

"Not like I was gonna be able to sleep, either," he murmured. "Just hope it wasn't too boring."

"You're never boring." I cleared my throat. "I have to go. See you at my truck in a couple hours?"

"Sure."

I hung up the phone and rolled onto my stomach just as my mom's alarm started going off in the next room. I squeezed my eyes shut and tried to slow my breathing. She'd poke her head in soon to check on me, and I didn't want her to know I'd been up all night.

If I could ease her worry, take away even just a tiny fraction of it with a lie, I would.

These little lies kept us both sane.

X X X

I did *try* to tell Sarah's parents the truth after the shooting.

It was late July, about two weeks before the school reopened, and the McHales had invited me for dinner at their house.

I hadn't wanted to go, honestly. Not because I didn't like the McHales—they'd been a second family to me since I was seven and first slept over at their house. Chad, Sarah's dad, had played board games with us for hours while Ruth, her mom, baked cookies and made us laugh with silly jokes. Then they'd invited me to church with them the next morning. I'd said no. I hadn't packed church clothes in my overnight bag, and I was embarrassed. They dropped me off at my house on their way to Virgil County Baptist, but Ruth told me that their house was mine now, too. It was the first of dozens—maybe even hundreds—of sleepovers. I was in their home nearly as much as my own. Sometimes it felt like I saw Ruth and Chad more than I saw my mother, who was working two jobs at the time. And almost every week, that offer to attend church with them was made. They never tried to pressure me or make me feel guilty when I said no (and I always said no), but the door stayed open.

I loved the McHales. I still do. Though I doubt they feel the same now.

But that night—the night they invited me for dinner—would have been my first time seeing them since Sarah's funeral. My first time in their house since the shooting. And the idea of walking through their front door without Sarah waiting on the other side, of sitting on their couch without her flopping down next to me while she apologized for accidentally spoiling an episode of our favorite TV show that I hadn't gotten to yet, of walking past her bedroom and knowing no one had slept there for months . . .

I didn't want to go.

But I also didn't want to hurt their feelings, and in the end, my need to be polite overruled all my other instincts.

"We're so glad you were able to come see us, Leanne," Ruth said, spooning mashed potatoes on a plate before passing it to me. "We wanted to see how you were doing before you head back to school. To catch up. I'm not sure we've ever gone this long without seeing you. The house doesn't feel quite the same without you and . . ." She trailed off. Her eyes, the same wide, round shape as Sarah's, dropped to the table, as if she were suddenly interested in the pale yellow tablecloth.

"It's been a quiet summer," Chad agreed.

"The, um . . . the mashed potatoes are delicious," I said, chewing on my bottom lip. I hadn't actually tried them yet. I'd been sliding them around on my plate with the tip of my fork, willing myself to develop some sort of appetite.

Ruth probably saw right through me, but still she said, "Thank you, sweetie."

I'm not sure any of us lifted a bite to our lips as the silent minutes crept passed. Forks scraped against plates, and Chad sawed away at his pork chop for so long that, by the time anyone actually spoke, it had been cut into pieces no bigger than my thumbnail.

"I hear Ashley Chambers is out of the hospital," Ruth said. "Have you seen her, Leanne?"

"Um, no. I mean, not recently. I saw her in the hospital a few weeks ago but not since she came home."

"She's a sweet girl," Chad said. "I heard she got engaged to that Osborne boy. Oh, what's his name? Help me out, Ruth. Jennifer and Don's son. The one with the freckles."

"Logan," Ruth said.

"That's it. Logan Osborne. Good kid. Do you know him, Leanne?"

I shook my head. "No. I think he graduated before I got to VCHS. I didn't even really know Ashley until . . . recently."

"She's a good girl, that Ashley," Ruth said. "So is her sister, Tara. She's a little younger than you and Sarah, I think. Their family has gone to our church for years. Those girls were always so sweet to Sarah. I'm so glad they'll both be there this Sunday when we announce the billboard."

"Billboard?"

Ruth glanced at Chad. "Well, it was supposed to be kept quiet until Sunday but . . . You know that highway you take out of town if you're headed toward Evansville?"

I nodded, dread already bubbling in my stomach.

"Several churches around Indiana worked together to raise money so we could put up a billboard for Sarah," Ruth said. "Right on the highway. It'll have her picture and her favorite Bible verse. To remind everyone who sees it what she stood for."

"What we should all stand for," Chad said.

"Isn't that wonderful, Leanne? Sarah did always want to be famous . . . Leanne, sweetie, are you okay?"

I was standing, without even realizing what I was doing. "I need the bathroom." And before she or Chad could say another word, I was running through the living room and down the hall, speeding through the house I knew as well as my own, until I reached the bathroom and shut the door behind me.

I leaned back against the door, pressing my hands to my eyes and breathing in and out slowly. I felt like my heart was going to burst out of my chest. Like my body had suddenly turned on me and was actively trying to destroy me from the inside.

Panic attack, I told myself. *You're okay. It's just a panic attack. Not even a bad one. Just breathe.*

When it had passed, I moved to the sink, running cold water over my hands, then splashing it onto my face. When I looked up into the mirror, there was a split second where I swear I was looking into the past.

Sarah was standing behind me in a dark green dress—the one she'd worn to our eighth-grade end-of-year dance. Her long red hair fell around her shoulders in loose, beachy waves. She'd learned how to style it that way from a YouTube tutorial. And now she was wielding a curling iron like a weapon as she tried to turn my limp, dark brown hair into something stylish. That was back when my hair fell nearly to my waist. I'd chopped it all off a few days after the shooting because I couldn't get it clean enough. No matter how many times I washed it, I was sure I smelled the blood.

I could almost hear Sarah's voice, a giggle laced through her words as she asked, *"Do you think Richie will be there tonight? Do you think he told anyone we made out?"*

Then the scene vanished—if something that was never there can really vanish—and I was staring at my pale reflection, all alone.

I had to tell the McHales the truth. I'd been putting it off for weeks, but now, after hearing about the billboard, I knew I couldn't procrastinate anymore. I couldn't let them continue to believe this lie. This stupid rumor that seemed to have come out of nowhere.

Besides, Sarah wouldn't have wanted this. Yes, she wanted to be famous, but she wanted to be a model, not a martyr. Especially not a false one. And as much as I love Ruth and Chad, they didn't really know her. Not as well as they thought they did. They had no idea that she was secretly dating Richie McMullen because she wasn't technically allowed to have a boyfriend. They'd never believe that she let him get to second under the bleachers at a football game at the beginning of freshman year. Or that she smuggled makeup to school and put it on in the bathroom before class. Or that she once kneed a boy in the crotch and told him to go to hell after he called me an awkward freak.

The Sarah I knew wouldn't want the class photo she hated plastered on church signs all over Indiana, let alone a billboard. She wouldn't want to be remembered this way.

And she wouldn't want someone else—like Kellie—to suffer because of it.

Which meant I was the one who had to tell them the truth. Because I was the only one who could.

I splashed a little more water on my face, took another deep breath, and opened the door. I walked down the hallway with as much determination as I could muster. I wasn't going to over-think it. I wasn't going to babble. I was just going to tell them what really happened in the bathroom that day.

But before I could make it to the end of the hallway, I noticed that Sarah's bedroom door was open and Ruth was standing inside. Just . . . standing. In the middle of the room. Her eyes fixed on one of the posters taped to the walls Sarah had insisted they paint purple when she was eleven.

I was so startled that I almost tripped over my own feet as I came to a stop outside the room. Ruth must have heard me, because she turned toward the door and gave me a small, tired smile.

"Leanne," she said. "I was coming to check on you and I got . . . distracted." She sighed and turned to glance around the room again. "I haven't been able to touch any of her things. Not even to clean it up." She gestured to the dirty clothes strewn all over the floor. "Sarah never liked to pick up after herself. It drove me nuts, but I just haven't been able to . . . I probably sound silly, don't I?"

"No," I said, stepping slowly into the room. "You don't."

I don't believe in ghosts or hauntings or anything like that. But being in her room, with all of her things just where she'd left them, like she'd been there just that morning . . . it was eerie. Almost otherworldly. The room still smelled like her. Or, mostly like her. Like lavender shampoo and vanilla candles mixed with dust and time. It was unsettling, but the idea of touching it, of changing a single thing from how she'd left it, was so much worse.

This room was sacred. Hallowed ground. It was the room where, when we were eight, Sarah first declared that I was her best friend and made me pinkie swear we'd never be without each other. It was on that hideous lime-green rug where I'd let myself cry for the first time about my dad and wondered what was wrong with me that he didn't want to know me. Eleven-year-old Sarah had hugged me and told me it was his loss and who needed him when I had her? And I was sitting on that bed, just a few weeks before the shooting, when I told Sarah I thought I might be asexual. She hadn't known what that meant. I hadn't really understood it well at the time, either. But she squeezed my hand, a quiet gesture of support, and told me she'd do some googling later. That was Sarah. I knew she'd stick by me, even when she didn't understand.

Being in that room made me realize how much I was still grappling with the idea of a future without her.

"She left some stuff at my house the weekend before," I said, crossing my arms over my chest. I was shivering, though it was late July and the air conditioner was turned down low. "Just a T-shirt and a hair clip. I'd put them on my desk so I could bring them to her, but I kept forgetting and . . . they're still there. I haven't touched them. It feels like if I do that means I really can't actually give them to her again and I just . . . I'm sorry. You probably want me to give you those things. I should've—"

"No, sweetie, no." Ruth swiped the back of her hand across her eyes. There were tears slipping down her face, and her mascara had started to run. I'd never seen her less than perfectly put together until that moment. "You keep those. Sarah was as much your family as ours. You meant the world to her, you know."

I know what you're thinking: That was when I should've told her. If I meant so much to Sarah, I owed it to her to tell the truth about how she died. It's what she would've wanted. Believe me, I was going to. The words were on the tip of my tongue.

But then Ruth had turned away from me. She walked to the window, staring out at the small, fenced-in backyard where Sarah and I used to have water gun fights as kids, where we'd dragged out old sleeping bags and slept beneath the stars in the summer.

Ruth was seeing a whole different set of memories as she wiped her eyes again.

"I just have to keep reminding myself that God has a plan," she said. "And this . . . this was His plan for her. As much as Chad and I miss her, we know she was His servant. She was here to remind us all of what a good Christian should be. Her story will inspire so many people. I have . . . I have to remember that."

The way her voice cracked, the way her hand shook as it rested on the windowsill, it destroyed any resolve I thought I had.

"Oh, dear," Ruth said. She sniffled and then cleared her throat before turning back to face me. "I'm so sorry, Leanne. I didn't mean to turn into such a mess. I was coming to check on you, after all. Are you feeling okay?"

"Yeah." I coughed, then let out a slow breath as I lowered my arms to my sides. "I'm fine. Let's just go finish dinner."

She nodded. "Good idea. Chad will eat all the mashed potatoes if we don't stop him."

We both knew that wasn't true, but we let ourselves believe it anyway.

Sometimes it's okay to believe things that aren't true. Sometimes it's necessary. At least, that's what I told myself. Unlike the McHales, I wasn't religious. I didn't believe in an afterlife. Once you were dead, you were gone. You stopped existing. Sarah wouldn't have wanted to be remembered for a lie, but she was gone. She didn't know that this was happening. She didn't care. And her parents, they needed that lie.

That lie was holding them together.

They needed to believe that their daughter died for *something*. That in her last moments she was strong and brave, and not a scared little girl clutching her best friend's hand in a bathroom stall. I couldn't take that from them.

I knew the harm this lie was doing. I knew about Kellie Gaynor. But the McHales were like my family, and I'd barely spoken two words to her in my life. So, I chose to let them believe.

I chose to stay silent.

"You look like crap."

I sat down at the computer next to Denny's, not even looking at him as I typed in my school password and asked, "How would you know?"

"I don't. But it seems like a safe guess."

It was the day after the anniversary—the day after I found out about the McHales' book—and Denny and I had a study period. Some seniors preferred to spend the hour in the library, but most of us flocked to the computer lab, where we didn't so much study as play games on the handful of websites the school hadn't managed to block from the server yet.

This is the *new* computer lab. After the shooting, the old computer lab was emptied out and turned into an overly large storage room, where no one but the occasional unlucky faculty member would have to venture. There was a big fundraiser and a new computer lab was built, tacked somewhat awkwardly onto the opposite side of the building. It was nice, though. There'd been enough donations that the school was even able to buy thirty new computers. That was a big deal in a small, rural high school like ours. The ones we'd had before were ancient, slow, and prone to randomly shutting down without warning.

Denny, in particular, was a fan. The new computers were compatible with updated, better screen-reader software, which made getting work done—or, as often was the case, playing games—much easier.

"Let's be honest," I said. "The only one here looking good is Glitter."

The Labrador looked up when I said her name. She was lying next to Denny's chair, her leash tethered to the leg of his desk. She gave a couple of quick tail wags before lowering her head back to the carpet.

"Yeah, well." Denny pulled a set of earbuds from his pocket and began untangling them. "Unlike you and me, she slept like a baby last night. And snored. Did I tell you she snores? *Loudly?*"

"Maybe it just sounds loud to you because you're blind and have better hearing than the rest of us," I said, knowing it was the kind of thing that would get under his skin. Over the past couple years, Denny has told me dozens of stories about ridiculous things people said to him or believed about blind people. The idea that he had superhero-like hearing seems to be the most common misconception.

"Ha-ha," he said. "You want to be an actress, right? Stick with drama. Comedy isn't your thing. Speaking of that, though." He'd just gotten the earbuds untangled and was plugging them into his computer so he could use the screen reader. "I have a favor to ask."

"A favor that involves me being an actress?"

"Not that. About me being blind. And . . . the anniversary. I was going to ask you yesterday, but it just . . ." He shrugged. He had one earbud in now, while the other dangled in midair. His fingers zoomed across the keyboard, though the monitor was blank. He always turned it off so our classmates wouldn't look over his shoulder while he worked. I didn't blame him. Our classmates were nosy, and neither of us liked when people stood too close behind us.

"What's up?" I asked, already wary. I was trying really hard not to think about the McHales or Sarah or the book. I wanted to keep my head down, pretend none of this was happening, and make it to graduation, when I could get out of this town, move across the country, and make a living being someone else. Talking about yesterday's anniversary wasn't going to help with that.

I know I was being selfish. I was also lying to myself. If the McHales really published that book about Sarah, there would be no escape. For me or anyone else.

I wondered if Denny had heard the news. He didn't know the truth about Sarah and Kellie. No one did, except me, but I imagined he probably wasn't keen on the shooting being all over the media again. And God forbid a movie actually got made . . .

"I'm applying for scholarships," he said, snapping me out of my thought spiral. "This one I'm working on requires a letter, explaining to the committee why I deserve the money. I talked to Mr. Halpern in the guidance office, and he thinks I should write about—"

"The shooting."

"Ding ding."

"Well . . ." I sighed. "He's not wrong. Being a VCHS survivor would definitely get the committee's attention." I'd done it on a couple of scholarships myself, and I knew exactly why Denny seemed hesitant.

"Yeah, and I'd be a fool not to use it." He grimaced. "I feel gross even saying that. But anyway. I wrote the letter and it . . . went in an unexpected direction."

"That sounds ominous."

"I think it's good, actually," he said. "It's not what they'll be expecting, but I think it's something I needed to write. I don't know. I sound ridiculous. But I was going to see if you'd read it over to make sure it's not too . . . accusatory?"

"You're worried that your letter to a scholarship committee is accusatory?"

"You'll see what I mean when you read it," he said. "*If* you will. And I hope you will because Miles isn't exactly my top choice for a proofreader."

"Hey, now," I said. "He's going to pass Senior English this semester with at least a C."

"Only took him two tries."

We ignored the real reason Denny wasn't asking Miles to

read the letter. Miles has never liked talking about the shooting. I mean, it's not as if the rest of us are eager to chat about it over snacks or something, but it has always been different with him. Any mention of the details of that day and he just shut down completely. And we didn't push it.

"Deanne said she'd read it, too, but I'd really like the perspective of . . . you know. One of us."

Deanne is Denny's older sister. She was a senior when the shooting happened, the same age as Ashley. She'd been in a classroom under lockdown, on the other side of the school, so I understood what Denny meant. Deanne was great. She'd give good feedback. But she wasn't really there. She wasn't one of us.

"All right," I said, trying not to let the reluctance leak through my words. "Email it to me. I'll read it tonight."

"Thank you, Lee. You're the best." He popped in the other earbud and went back to typing. "Maybe I should've led with that instead of telling you that you looked like crap, huh?"

"Maybe."

A minute later, the letter was in my inbox. I went ahead and opened the document since I had nothing better to do and, no offense to Denny, I wanted to get this over with. It was . . . not what I expected.

Denny's letter changed everything for me. It was the catalyst. The thing that made me do all of *this*. You can decide whether that's a good thing or not.

Dear Ms. Mulgrove and Members of the Horton Scholarship Committee,

As part of your application materials, you requested a letter explaining why I should receive a scholarship from your organization. I thought about this question a lot, about what I could say that would make me stand out from the rest of the applications you've read. I know one story I could tell. It's the story everyone expects me to write in these applications and essays. And I've written and deleted that version several times.

I'm assuming the committee has already reviewed my application. If so, then you know a few things—I'm black, disabled, and from Virgil County, Indiana. And a bit of googling will reveal some pretty embarrassing YouTube clips from the local news, where fourteen-year-old Denny talks about the shooting and relearns how to use a cane during physical therapy.

So the story you probably thought you'd find when you opened this letter was something inspiring. Poor kid from tiny town, blind since birth, survives school shooting and now strives to rise above— or something like that. But that's not my story.

I mean, I guess it is—all the pieces are right—but it's also *not*. The facts are there, but the framing is all wrong.

So, instead of giving you the expected version of this letter, I'm going to give you the less inspiring but more honest version. And then I can tell you why I still deserve this scholarship.

Even before the shooting, I stood out at VCHS. I was one of only two black kids in a mostly white school (the other being my older sister), and, on top of that, the only blind kid. And people didn't really know what to make of either. My classmates weren't so bad. I'd known most of them since first grade, and, yeah, some were racist assholes (sorry, I probably shouldn't say *asshole* in a scholarship letter) and some liked to steal my stuff and hide it since I couldn't see. But at least they were up front about it. And my peers also weren't scared to ask questions, "Is this racist?" and "But how do you do this if you can't see?" being the most common. It could get exhausting, yeah, but it was better than the teachers.

The teachers just made weird assumptions or said really awkward things. Like the English teacher who told me how "well spoken" I was after I gave a presentation on *Lord of the Flies*. Or the band instructor who begged me to join because he was certain I'd have musical talent. Because I guess every blind guy with dark skin might as well be Stevie Wonder or Ray Charles reincarnated. (I don't have any musical talent, by the way.) Oh, and let's not forget the social studies teacher who asked me if I'd "seen the news," then immediately stuttered out an apology before changing "seen" to "heard." And all of this was on top of the assumptions they made about what I would and wouldn't need help with in class. Because asking me directly was an outrageous concept, I guess.

There was one teacher, though, who *didn't* make me want to smack myself in the forehead with my own cane. And that was Essie Taylor.

Ms. Taylor started teaching the computer science classes at VCHS my freshman year, and she was amazing. She was young and funny and smart and, yes, I definitely had a crush on her. But don't worry. This letter isn't going in some weird, pervy direction. Ms. Taylor was my mentor and nothing more. And I wasn't the only one who adored her. For a lot of us nerdier types, Ms. Taylor's computer lab quickly became our second home. We spent every lunch, every free period, every chance we could get in her classroom. It was our geeky haven.

It obviously did not stay that way.

One of the reasons I loved Ms. Taylor—on top of her just being awesome—was that she knew her stuff when it came to tech. These days, assistive tech for blind folks is kind of amazing and, for some, life changing. Sure, screen readers are great—I use one every day—but it goes way beyond that. Did you know there are devices you can hold up to an item of clothing and it'll tell you what color it is? There are apps that allow you to take a picture of something—like a label or even just a random object—and within seconds, you'll get a voiced response telling you what the picture was of. And they can get really specific, too. Once I snapped a photo of my guide dog and I got "adult yellow Labrador on blue blanket." There are video games for blind people, where the gameplay is entirely audio driven. There's so much out there.

But there could be more.

Ms. Taylor was the first one to suggest I try building an app. She sent me links to articles and podcasts and helped me brainstorm ideas. She even said that if I finished it by the end of the semester, she'd count it as my final project. She made a nerdy freshman believe he didn't have to wait until he grew up to start doing the things he dreamed of.

And then the shooting happened.

Ms. Taylor's class was an elective, which meant there were students from all grade levels, but mostly freshmen. It was also a very small class. Most kids at VCHS preferred to take Ag classes, so there wasn't even a dozen of us in the first period computer applications class. I was sitting near the front of the class with my friends Jared Grayson and Rosi Martinez.

Jared was a stealth nerd. He acted like your typical midwestern farmer's son, but in reality, he knew more about video games than anyone I knew. He didn't just play them—he knew all about the different developers, what engines they used, and graphics. He'd go on forever about graphics and frame rates, not seeming to grasp that the blind kid didn't really care about that stuff.

Rosi, on the other hand, was *not* a nerd. She was on student council, sure, but she was also freshman homecoming queen and the only underclassman to get picked for VCHS's cheerleading team. But we'd become friends earlier that semester when she'd offered to tutor me in Spanish if I helped her with Ms. Taylor's class.

For me, the weirdest part of thinking about that day is remembering how *normal* it started. It was toward the end of the period and most of us had finished our classwork (building a database) and the room was a mix of chatter and keyboard clicking. Like it always was.

"I'm really excited about the new Age of Dragons game, but I can't decide if I want it on PC or console," Jared was saying. "It'll look way better on PC, I know. It's supposed to look amazing in 4K. But my computer's been running slowly lately, and I'm worried it'll lag. It'll probably run better on my console, but it won't look as good. I mean it'll look *fine* but not with the kind of resolution you can get on a PC. But also—"

"Denny," Rosi interrupted. "I'm trying to find a birthday present for my abuela. If you were a seventy-year-old woman, would you rather get a comfy sweater or a pretty necklace? Keep in mind I'm broke, so it'll probably be coming from Walmart."

"Hey," Jared said. "We were talking over here."

"No, you were talking," Rosi said. "And Denny doesn't care about what resolution you play your stupid game in. He's blind."

"Yeah, but he *really* cares about what you buy your grand-mother," Jared retorted.

"He does. Because he's a thoughtful guy. Unlike some people."

"I'm thoughtful!"

"Now *kiss*," I said. Because to this day, you cannot convince me that those two weren't in love with each other. Yeah, they argued constantly, but whenever the other wasn't around, they pined. The only thing Jared talked about more than video games was Rosi. She wasn't quite as transparent, but I knew her. She liked him. Even if she would never admit it.

"Okay, guys," Ms. Taylor said. Her voice came from the front of the room, just a few feet from where Jared, Rosi, and I were. "The bell is going to ring in a few minutes. Please don't forget to log out and . . ."

Her voice trailed. I don't know how to explain this, but I could *feel* everyone's attention shift. I remember the sound of a collective gasp, but I'm not sure if that really happened or if my brain just planted it there, because it seems like what *should* have happened.

This loud, popping sound started, and there was yelling, and two hands—one on either side of me—grabbed me by the arms and yanked me down, out of my seat and onto the floor. It was so fast that I bumped my forehead on the edge of the desk. For a weird second, I thought this was some sort of bizarre revenge from Rosi and Jared for teasing them. But that didn't explain all the loud noises, or why they'd be climbing under the desk, too, legs tangling with mine.

People always assume those few minutes of chaos were the scariest of my life. They weren't, though. They were the most confusing. I hadn't seen ███ standing in the doorway with a gun. I didn't know what the popping sound was. I just knew it was *loud*. I raised my hands and pressed them against my ears, sure it would pass in a second and someone would explain.

I felt Jared slump against me, and I lowered one of my hands to ask him what was going on, but he didn't answer, and I figured he couldn't hear me over the noise. Even when the bullet went through my arm, just below my elbow, it didn't register. I felt the pain and I knew I was bleeding, but I still couldn't connect the dots. Maybe it was shock or adrenaline or just denial, but I wasn't scared. This was school. I didn't need to be scared.

Then the popping got farther away. I heard it echoing in the hallway outside the computer lab, heard a voice on the intercom telling teachers to go into lockdown. I knew something was wrong then. We'd been doing lockdown drills since first grade. And yet, as crazy is this is going to sound, I *still* didn't get it. I remember sitting there, under my desk, my arm bleeding, and wondering why I hadn't heard Ms. Taylor shut the classroom door yet.

And then there was quiet. The heaviest kind of quiet. I don't know how else to explain it. But it was so quiet that I wondered if all the popping had messed with my eardrums. I reached over to where Jared was leaning against me and nudged him, but he just slid limply down, away from me. I thought he'd been knocked out. Maybe he'd hit his head, too. I could feel a knot forming on mine, and I was thinking that I'd give him and Rosi crap for jerking me down so fast later.

Then I heard someone moving across the room. And breathing. I don't usually notice how people breathe—being blind doesn't mean you have superpower hearing—but this was fast and loud. And in a room this quiet, it was alarming.

"Hello?" I said, because I really couldn't think of anything else to say.

"Hush." The voice was sharp and ragged and I didn't recognize it, which seemed kind of weird. I thought I could recognize the voices of pretty much all of the people in that class.

Then there was more shifting and what sounded like someone crawling toward me. I wondered why anyone would crawl in a classroom. Were we supposed to crawl during a lockdown? Was that part of a drill I had missed? I know all of these thoughts probably seem strange, but at the time, nothing was making sense.

"Stay quiet," the voice said, much closer now. "I heard sirens. The cops should be— Oh no, Rosi."

"What?" I asked. "Why are cops coming? What's wrong with Rosi? What's going on?"

But the girl—it was a girl's voice—just kept repeating "Oh no, oh no, oh no" in a broken whisper.

I found out later that that girl was Eden Martinez, Rosi's cousin, and she was saying "oh no" because Rosi was dead. I'd never even heard Eden speak before that day. She's quiet and reserved. Basically Rosi's opposite. But suddenly, we were the only two people alive in that classroom.

I didn't know that then. It was after the cops came, after I was put in an ambulance, after I learned that the pain in my arm was a gunshot wound. I didn't know the full extent of what had happened until I was safe and sound in a hospital room with my parents and sister.

Shortly after that, the camera crews showed up. There must have been a dozen news stories and TV segments about me over the next few months. I wasn't just the blind kid anymore. Now I was the blind kid who survived a mass shooting. And with that came this assumption that, somehow, my story was the most interesting. Or the most tragic. Like things must have been so much worse for me because I was the disabled kid in that computer lab, scared and lost in the chaos.

But I don't think that's true.

Don't get me wrong. I'm not saying the shooting didn't affect me. I lost my two best friends and my favorite teacher. Physical therapy and relearning to use my cane again sucked. And I still jump at loud noises and sometimes have nightmares and all the things you might expect. But I can't help thinking I got off relatively easy compared to the others. Because I didn't have to *see* any of it.

Look, you don't have to see things to be traumatized by them—I know that, obviously—but most of the pain and horror for me came in the aftermath. It came from learning what had happened. I didn't have to witness it the way others did. I didn't have to see the bodies of my friends. To this day, I don't know where Rosi or Jared or Ms. Taylor were shot, and I don't want to know. The other survivors didn't get that choice.

I have the option to stay in the dark.

So I don't really feel like the tragic, inspirational figure everyone wants me to be. If anything, I feel like a fraud. I've spent years feeling guilty about not being in more pain. Which is pretty screwed up, if you think about it.

I don't think I deserve this scholarship because I'm a black kid from a poor community who was born blind and then survived a shooting. I deserve this scholarship because of my ambition and talent.

Because while I was never able to get a grade for that app I was making freshman year, I did make others. For now, they are pretty basic—no overnight successes—but they are all accessible for people with visual impairments. And I have ideas for more. And one day, I really think I could change the game when it comes to assistive tech and accessibility.

Not because I want to inspire people—I'm pretty tired of being "inspiring" at this point—but because I could help people. And, yeah, let's be honest. For selfish reasons. I'm tired of being Denny Lucas, the blind VCHS survivor. I'm ready to be Denny Lucas, Tech God. Or, at the very least, Denny Lucas, the guy who makes really cool stuff.

I know there's a good chance I've disappointed you here. But I'm hoping that won't keep the committee from seeing why I should get this scholarship. I have big goals. I am driven and ambitious, and I know that with a bit of financial help, I could do some really awesome things.

So I am asking you to please consider my application. Not because of who I am or what I've been through—but because of who I could be in ten or fifteen years. I know I have potential and that I will use the money well. I hope you feel the same way.

Sincerely,
Denny Lucas

X X X

Denny's scholarship letter blew my mind.

I don't know why, but until I read his words, it had never occurred to me that any of the other survivors were struggling with how our stories were being told. I was so wrapped up in my guilt over what had happened with Sarah and Kellie that I'd never even considered the other narratives being spun. Knowing Denny had his own frustrations about how the world saw him made me feel less alone, but I wasn't sure if it made me feel *better*.

What I did know was that I had to tell him the truth about Kellie and Sarah. Since reading the news about the McHales' book, I'd felt constantly on edge, a buzzing hive of anxiety, and if I didn't confide in someone, I thought I might burst. Now I was sure that if anyone would understand, it was Denny.

"I read your scholarship letter," I told him over lunch the next day. We were sitting at one of the small round tables on the edge of the cafeteria, one that made it easy for me to see all of the exits. Miles was sitting next to me, his head resting on a thick book he'd been lugging everywhere for the past week, with his eyes closed. I wasn't sure if he was awake or not. During our lunch hours, Denny and I usually did most of the talking.

Well, *Denny* did most of the talking.

"On a scale of one to ten, how brilliant am I?" Denny asked. "One is brilliant. Ten is brighter than the damn sun."

"Negative four," Miles said, not opening his eyes.

Denny laughed. "Accurate. But really. How bad is it, Lee?"

"It's good," I said. "It gave me a lot to think about." I hesitated as I speared a small piece of the greasy school pizza with my fork. (Yes, I eat pizza with a fork. You are free to judge me. Miles and Denny have already informed me of just how unacceptable this is.) Just before I put the fork to my lips, I added, "I was actually hoping to talk to you more about it after school."

"You mean like give me notes or help me edit it?" he asked.

My mouth was full, so I nodded, then remembered he couldn't see me. I'd known Denny for most of my life and been friends with him for the past three years. It was embarrassing how often I still made little mistakes like this. I chewed and swallowed quickly, then answered, "Yeah. Something like that. I can give you and Glitter a ride home after school if that's okay."

"*Okay?* That'd be *great*," Denny said. "Any day I don't have to worry about maneuvering Glitter around a school bus is a good day." He reached down to where the yellow Lab was lying next to his seat. She lifted her head, pushing her nose against his palm. I watched as he ran his hand backward across her muzzle and to the top of her head, where he began scratching her ears.

Then I felt a pair of eyes on me.

Miles had lifted his head, and he was raising a questioning eyebrow at me.

"You . . . don't mind taking the bus home, right?" I asked.

He shrugged. "It's fine." But he didn't take his eyes off me. He knew something was going on. Or else I would have just asked him to tag along for the extra stop on our way home. He didn't ask, though. I'd known he wouldn't.

But Denny did.

That afternoon, when I parked my truck in his driveway and proceeded to sit there quietly for a minute, not sure how to begin what I wanted to tell him, he did the work for me.

"I'm going to guess this isn't about my letter."

"What?"

He lifted a shoulder. "You told Miles to take the bus home. It's not hard to figure out something is up, because my scholarship letter doesn't warrant this kind of secrecy. So what's going on?"

I let out a breath. "It is sort of about your letter, actually," I said.

"Really? Crap. Now I'm worried."

"Don't be," I told him. "At least . . . not about your letter. It's good. Really good. And it made me think about some stuff . . . about the shooting."

"Oh," Denny said. "Well, this sounds like it's going to be a pretty heavy conversation, so I vote that we get out of this truck, raid my fridge, and head to the backyard so Glitter can take a break while we talk."

"I can get behind that."

Ten minutes later, with sodas and a bag of freshly popped popcorn in hand, Denny and I were making our way through his house and toward the back door. Glitter was out of her harness now, closely following behind Denny, with her eyes fixed on the bag of popcorn.

"Glitter, please stay out from under my feet," he said as she bumped up against him. "She's trained not to expect food from people, and usually she's good about it, but I swear, she loses her mind over popcorn."

"Can you blame her?"

He laughed. "Not really. Popcorn is God's food."

"Did you know Miles hates popcorn?"

"Does he? I think I might have to end our friendship over that. Shame. I was starting to like him."

He navigated through the house smoothly, without the help of Glitter or the cane he used before getting her back in the fall. The only sign that he couldn't see was the way he occasionally held out a hand to find the wall he knew was close by. When we reached the back door, he unlocked it with one hand and pulled it open. He'd barely pushed on the screen door before Glitter bolted past him, out into the fenced-in yard, nearly knocking Denny off his feet.

"God, Glitter," he said, holding back a laugh as he stepped out onto the little wooden deck.

Glitter was already running around the yard in large circles, a tennis ball that had seemingly appeared out of nowhere clutched between her jaws. Even though I've seen her like this plenty of times since Denny got her, it's always startling. She's so calm, so focused when her harness is on. Denny says it's like her business suit. When it's on, she knows it's time to be professional. But the second it's off, it's time to party.

We sat down on the steps, the warm bag of popcorn between us.

"Okay," he said, carefully popping the tab on his can of soda. "Now that we have our supplies, tell me what's going on."

I heard a light tapping sound on the wooden planks and it took a minute to realize it was my foot hitting the bottom step, bouncing with nervous energy. Talking to Denny seemed like the right thing, like I might finally be able to get this off my chest and tell someone who would understand. But now that I was here, with him ready to listen, I felt like I might combust from the anxiety.

"Lee? You okay?"

Spit it out, I told myself. *Just say it. It's time to say it.*

"It wasn't Sarah's necklace."

The words came out in a rush, a single, shaking breath.

Denny just sat there for a second, a fistful of popcorn frozen in midair, halfway to his mouth. Slowly, he lowered his hand. "Wait . . . what?"

My leg wasn't the only thing shaking now. My hands were, too. I folded them tightly in my lap. "The necklace they found in the bathroom, it wasn't hers. I don't know how that rumor got started, but it wasn't Sarah's. And she never said anything to *him*. Not a word."

"Are . . . Sorry, but are you sure?"

"Positive," I said. "I don't know what else happened in the bathroom. I don't know what really happened with Kellie. But the story about Sarah isn't true."

"Wow," Denny said. "That's . . . wow." He shook his head. "Why are you telling me this now?"

"Your letter got me thinking," I said. "About all the misconceptions people have about the shooting. About us. I guess for a long time I thought it was just me—just Sarah's story that people got wrong. But I don't think it was. I know it's different, what you were writing about, but . . . I don't know."

"It is different," he said. "But I think I get what you're saying."

"And then I was thinking about what you said on the anniversary," I continued. "About how when we graduate, the last people who were really there will be gone. And everyone at VCHS will just be going off of what they heard or saw on the news and . . . and that'll become fact. And then the McHales' book will be coming out . . ."

"I heard about that," Denny said. "Have you told them about this? About Sarah?"

"No." I chewed on my bottom lip, my stomach writhing with guilt. "I almost did. A few years ago. But I . . . I felt like I would've been taking something away from them. Like they really needed to believe the story. I couldn't bring myself to do it."

"That's tough," he said.

"I know it's three years too late, but I've got to do something.

I just keep thinking about Kellie. I don't know what really went down with her in the bathroom that day, but she was right that the Sarah thing didn't happen. And you remember what happened to her. I didn't do anything then and I know I should have. I need to now. I just don't know who to tell. Or how."

"You didn't even tell Detective Jenner?" Denny asked. "When he questioned you after?"

"I hadn't heard the story yet when I talked to him. I just told him the basics. That *he* came in, that we were in a stall, and that he killed her. When Detective Jenner tried to ask me more, I . . . I started having a flashback and freaked out, so we cut it short. He probably would have asked me about the necklace if I hadn't. I don't know. I screwed this up bad, didn't I?"

"You were a fourteen-year-old who'd just seen her friend killed. I think you can be forgiven for being a mess afterward."

I wasn't sure I could, though. Not when it led to someone else getting hurt.

"Maybe Detective Jenner is a good place to start," he suggested. "No matter what you decide to do next, he should know."

I let out a long breath. I was sure Denny was right—if anyone should know, it was the officer who had investigated the shooting—but he was also one of the last people I wanted to see. He entered my life during its darkest days, when I was barely sleeping, having frequent panic attacks, and still trying to find the right dose of medication. I've come a long way since then, but I still feel like I'm walking along a tightrope. One misstep, one wrong move, and I could go spiraling back to where I was three years ago.

Denny couldn't read my mind the way Miles could, but it didn't take a telepath to know what I must've been thinking in that moment. I'm sure all of us associated Detective Jenner with the same thing. He was a nice enough man, but none of us were eager to see him ever again.

Still, Denny said, "I'll go with you."

"You don't have—"

"I know I don't have to," he said. "But I will. We can go after school later this week. I'll make up an excuse for my parents."

Glitter darted toward us then, slobbery tennis ball in her mouth. She dropped it at my feet, then hopped up, putting her front paws on my knees and licking my cheek. As if to say, *And I'll come, too.*

Despite myself, I laughed.

"Okay," I said, scratching her ears. "Thank you." Then, as she departed from my lap and did another loop around the yard, I reached over and put a hand on Denny's shoulder. "Really. Thank you. You're a good friend."

"Oh, I know," he said. "I'm the best."

XXX

I'm realizing that I've said a lot about Sarah and almost nothing about the other victims. Which doesn't make me much better than the media. There was so much coverage about Sarah, but the other people who died were pretty much forgotten within a few weeks. They quickly became the unnamed dead, just part of the "nine killed."

But just like I knew Sarah, I knew these people, too. Maybe not as well. Some only by name. But they were people. Kids, most of them. And their deaths mattered just as much as hers, even if they didn't allegedly die as martyrs for their faith.

So I'm going to try and fix that as best I can, with a little bit of help from the other survivors, who knew some of these people better than I did.

I guess I should start with Ms. Taylor.

ESSIE TAYLOR

Ms. Taylor was the first person killed on March 15.

I didn't actually know her very well. I saw her in the hallway on my way to class every morning. She was young, only twenty-three, and very pretty with golden-blond hair that fell in loose waves to her shoulders. I remember that she always seemed to wear floral patterns, always in bright, warm colors—reds and oranges and pinks. I planned on taking her class the following year, since I'd need an elective and shop really wasn't my thing.

Obviously, I never got that chance.

So, since I didn't know her that well, I emailed Denny and asked if he'd write something for this.

Hey, Lee—

So you want to know more about Ms. Taylor? Let's see . . .

Well, I could start with the first day of freshman year. My first day of high school and her first day of teaching. I wasn't in her class yet, that was the next semester, but I was already a computer nerd. So during lunch, Jared and I had skipped the pizza line to go and investigate the computer lab instead.

Ms. Taylor was in there, of course. She introduced herself when we walked in and gave us permission to use one of the computers.

"Ah, man," Jared said. "They're all old. Just like the dinosaurs at the middle school. I was hoping for something better."

"That sucks," I said.

"If the school wouldn't spend so much freaking money on football, they could afford better computers."

"You're just mad you didn't make the team."

"Shut up," he huffed. "Besides, it's fine. Bomb Shelter Four comes out next month and I'll need the extra hours to play."

I mostly just sat there while Jared fiddled with the computer. None of them had screen-reader software installed yet. The school wouldn't even bother until I had a class where it was necessary. That's how they'd always been. Only accommodating when they absolutely had to.

But then Ms. Taylor was standing beside me. I knew because she said, "Denny, this is Ms. Taylor on your left."

"Hey, Teach."

"Mind if I talk to you for a minute?"

"Have I already managed to get in trouble?"

"No. Not at all." She sat down next to me, on the opposite side as Jared. "Do you think you'll be spending a lot of time in here?"

"I don't really know," I said. "It'll depend when I take my first class in here. They won't have software until—"

"Let me rephrase," she said. "Do you want to spend time in here?"

"Of course he does," Jared said. "Denny loves computers."

"That'd be correct."

"Good," she said, and I could hear the smile. "Then I need you to do me a favor and tell me exactly what you need installed. Not what they usually install for you—there's no point if you don't find it helpful. So tell me what will work best to make these computers accessible, and I'll make sure it gets done."

That's when she became my favorite teacher.

Maybe it's a small gesture, but I'm so used to people assuming they know what I need better than I do. One of the hazards of being disabled, I guess. So to have a teacher actually ask—and listen—was exciting. And she made good on her word. She got one of the computers set up with a decent screen reader and even had me help show her how it worked. None of my other teachers had cared to learn anything about my assistive tech.

And then, of course, I had her as a teacher for a while that next semester. By then I already had my extremely inappropriate schoolboy crush on her. Even though she did tell really, really awful dad jokes sometimes.

Oh God. Okay, so this was her favorite joke to tell:

"Why didn't they let the teenage pirate see the movie? Because it was rated arrrrgh!"

I swear she told the class this joke a dozen times, and every time she'd make herself laugh so hard she'd start to snort.

We can't all be perfect.

Anyway, I don't know if that's the kind of story you were looking for. I only really knew her as a teacher, so I don't know much about her life outside of school. I think her family was from northern Indiana, and she told me once she'd grown up on a farm.

But I know she was the best teacher a fourteen-year-old nerd could have asked for, and that's how I choose to remember her.

Hope this helped, Lee.

—Denny

X X X

There was one other time, before my failed attempt to confess to Sarah's parents, that I could've set the record straight.

It was toward the end of the summer. All the witnesses had been asked to come back to the high school to do a walk-through, helping the detectives working on the case to piece together exactly what happened in which order. They'd questioned us in the days that followed the shooting, but since we'd all been spread out—from the computer lab to the hallway to the girls' bathroom—it was hard to fit the puzzle together without getting a better sense of the events in real time.

It wasn't required or anything, more of a request. Mom kept reminding me of that as she drove me to the high school. If I wanted to go home, I could. "The boy's dead, anyway," Mom said, referring to the shooter, as she pulled into the parking lot behind the school. "I don't know what else there is to investigate."

But I saw this as an opportunity. By then the rumors had spread far and wide, the story of Sarah's supposed final moments eclipsing the shooting itself. But Kellie would be at the walk-through. It would be the perfect time for the two of us, together, to set the official record straight on what happened in the girls' bathroom that morning. Then people would stop talking about Sarah like she was an angel instead of my human best friend. People would leave Kellie and her family alone. And I could stop feeling guilty.

That was my plan, anyway.

Detective Jenner met us at the rear exit of the school. We'd been asked to park around back and come in through the door closest to the shop building. Probably because too many cars out front of the high school, which hadn't been reopened yet, would draw attention from the local media. Back here, though, no one from the main road would see our cars or notice us entering the building.

"Good afternoon, Ms. Bauer, Leanne," Detective Jenner said, holding open the door for us. "Follow me. We're still waiting to see if a few of the others are going to show up. Eden Martinez and Denny Lucas are already here. They're talking with Detective Weinberg about what happened in the computer lab. Once they're done, we'll be speaking with you and the others about the hallway and the bathroom. Ashley Chambers and her parents are on the way. Not sure about the others yet."

"Miles isn't coming," I told Detective Jenner. He was a young guy, maybe in his thirties, with a face that seemed even younger, though the dark circles beneath his eyes made it clear he was exhausted. "Miles lives next door to us. I asked him and he said he won't be here today."

Detective Jenner nodded and sighed. "That's disappointing, but I understand. Shame, though. I was looking forward to talking to him and Ashley at the same time about what happened in the hallway. He sounds like a real hero. But oh well. I . . ." He trailed off, his eyes flicking over my face. "You all right, Leanne?"

We'd been walking through the halls, headed toward the old computer lab. It was the first time I'd been here since the shooting, and I was trying to pretend this wasn't VCHS at all. That was easy at first. The place was empty, nearly silent aside from our voices and echoing footsteps. VCHS was never this desolate or this quiet. And I was there with my mom and a police officer, two people you almost never found yourself with in a high school.

I kept thinking this, trying to convince myself I was somewhere else, as I scanned for Kellie or one of her parents. But I didn't see anyone. I only heard other voices when we were just a few yards from the computer lab. Voices echoed through the hallway toward us—Eden was explaining something, though she spoke so quietly and quickly that I couldn't make out what she was telling Detective Weinberg.

I'm pretty sure that's when I started feeling sick. Because I could see the open door to the girls' bathroom. And I couldn't pretend we weren't here anymore.

"Lee?" Mom asked, putting her hand on my shoulder. "You're white as a ghost. Are you all right? Do you want to leave?"

I shook my head. Kellie wasn't there yet. I needed to stay. Needed to see her so we could tell the detectives what really happened. I wrapped my arms around myself and tried to breathe slowly. In through the nose, out through the mouth. That's the technique, right? I couldn't remember.

Detective Jenner left Mom and me in the hallway as he stepped into the old computer lab. Through the open door, I could see that almost nothing remained, aside from a couple of desks, one of which I could see Denny sitting beneath. His face was turned away from me as Detectives Jenner and Weinberg talked to each other, then asked a question of Eden, who was out of eyeshot.

I kept my eyes on Denny's back. I didn't dare look at anything else, especially not in the direction of the bathroom, on the other end of the hall. Denny was my friend. Denny was safe. *Just keep looking at Denny*, I told myself.

He shifted slightly, a small, uneasy movement you'd only notice after staring too hard. And I wondered what he was feeling, crouched beneath that desk, the same place he'd been just a few months ago. How hard was it to just sit there for minutes at a time while people discussed the shooting, plotted it out step-by-step, like they were solving a Rubik's Cube instead of mapping out the path of a teenage mass murderer.

A few minutes later, the two detectives emerged from the classroom, followed by Eden and Denny. He just looked a bit tired, but Eden had clearly been crying. She glanced at me, then looked away, obviously embarrassed.

"Thanks, kids," Detective Jenner said. "I think that's all we need today. We really appreciate you coming in and going over this with us." He glanced at me then. "Give us just a second, Leanne. Detective Weinberg and I need to talk through a few things, and hopefully by the time we're ready, Ashley will be here. I'd really like to go through everything in order."

I nodded, and the two detectives stepped back into the old computer lab.

"Lee?" Denny asked.

"Here," I said.

His cane tapped along the hard floor with a slight echo, until he came to stand next to me. "So," he said, leaning against the wall. "This is weird, huh?"

Despite myself, I laughed a little.

"Where are your parents, Denny?" Mom asked.

"Work," he said. "They wanted to come, but I asked them not to. It would just freak them out to walk through every step of it like that. So Eden's family drove me."

I glanced around, but I didn't see any of Eden's relatives. She must have noticed because she said, "They're outside, in the car. They came in at first, but when Detective Weinberg started going through the class seating chart . . . mentioned where Rosi had been sitting . . ." She shrugged. "Detective Weinberg was having a hard time hearing me over Abuela and my aunt crying."

"They weren't even crying loudly," Denny pointed out. "You're just really quiet. Even after they left, he had to ask you to speak up at least three times."

"Denny," Mom whispered, clearly a little horrified by his teasing.

But Eden waved a hand. "It's okay, Ms. Bauer. He's not wrong. And he knows poking at me keeps me from thinking too much about . . ." She trailed off and, after a long pause, cleared her throat. "We should go, though. My family's waiting. Good luck, Lee."

I nodded and watched as she and Denny headed down the hallway, their figures growing smaller and smaller until they'd rounded a corner and were gone. Now it was just me. And Mom. And the detectives that were about to make me walk back into that bathroom.

Relax, I told myself. *It's just a bathroom. Just a room full of sinks and toilets. Stop freaking out. You're being stupid.*

When the detectives came back out into the hallway, Ashley and Kellie still hadn't arrived. The men looked at each other, and Detective Weinberg sighed and tapped his clipboard.

"Leanne," Detective Jenner said, turning to face Mom and me. "We were really hoping to do this all in order, but we don't want to take up too much of your time. So if it's all right with you, we can go ahead and get started."

I glanced behind me, back down the empty hall. Kellie still wasn't here. How were we going to explain what had really happened if she wasn't here yet?

"Should we wait for Kellie, at least?" I asked, ashamed of the little quake in my voice. "Since we were both in the . . . in there." I gestured toward the girls' room.

"Ideally," Detective Jenner said. "But she's late, and we can't even be sure if she's coming. It's possible she changed her mind. If she does show up, we can just go over things with her separately and compare to yours."

"Um, okay. Sure."

I was just going to have to clear things up on my own. I'd tell Detective Jenner what had happened with Sarah, I'd make it clear the stories about her weren't true. And then when Kellie did show up, they'd have to believe her. Simple.

Or it should've been.

The detectives began walking toward the bathroom and gestured for Mom and me to follow. Mom put a hand on my shoulder again, but I jerked away and glared at her. I didn't want her to coddle me. I didn't want her here at all. I wished she was more like Denny's parents, wished she would stay away if I'd asked. But she wouldn't. She wanted to "be there for me." And I hated it.

The closer we got to the bathroom, the more I started to lose grip on reality. Which is the best way I can think to describe it. I kept picturing the inside, the light tiles darkened with blood. Gunshots and screams. They were like sounds, but I knew I wasn't hearing them. They were more in my mind than my ears. I could smell copper and gunpowder and the smoke from a cigarette. Every step toward that doorway pulled me further into these flashes of the past.

And then my brain began producing these fractured, terrifying thoughts. A siren of warning as Detective Weinberg stepped into the bathroom, out of sight, and I was expected to follow him.

pain fear death darkness nothing nothing the world will end we'll all be gone nothing matters nothing darkness

That's the only description I can give of how my thoughts began spiraling. I was standing in the bathroom doorway now, staring at Detective Jenner and Detective Weinberg, who were in front of the stalls, looking back at me, expecting me to step inside.

And for the tiniest, most fleeting second, I thought I saw Sarah, standing in front of the sink, examining the small mark on her neck the way she had been that morning, before the world crumbled around us.

And I ran.

I didn't even realize I'd started moving until I heard my mother shouting behind me. By then, I was rounding the corner, nearly to the entrance we'd come in through a few minutes before. Even then, I didn't stop. I shoved open the doors and ran to our car. I grabbed the handle on the passenger door, but it wouldn't open. I yanked and yanked and cursed, and my face felt so hot and wet. Tears. I wasn't even sure when I'd started crying. Was it before or after I'd bolted?

"Lee!" Mom called again. She was outside now, too, running up behind me. Her eyes were wide and terrified. "Baby."

She reached for me, tried to take me into her arms, but I shoved her—actually *shoved* her—away from me. "Get off!" I yelled. "Get off me."

"Lee," she whispered, and now she wasn't just afraid. She was hurt. She took a breath. "Let's go home."

I shook my head violently from side to side. "No! No, I just need a minute. I'll be okay. I *am* okay. I just need a second and then I can go back inside and try again. I just freaked out, but I can go back. I can do it. I *have* to."

"No, you don't," she said. "You don't have to, and we're going home."

"But the walk-through—"

"Forget it," Mom said. "It's fine. The detectives will understand. Come on."

I know I should have argued more. I should have stayed. Should've done what I'd come here to do. But when Mom unlocked the car door, I climbed inside. And when another car pulled into the parking lot next to us, I just slid down in my seat, filled with shame and regret.

Detective Jenner's office hadn't changed much over the years. Same metal desk strewn with papers. Same photo of his family sitting next to the same outdated computer. The only thing that looked different was Detective Jenner.

His hair was prematurely graying, and there were deep bags under his eyes. He looked as if he'd aged a decade in the span of just three years. Spending so much time investigating a case full of dead teenagers will do that to you, I guess.

"Leanne," he said as he walked into the office. "And Denny. Must say this is a surprise. Can I help you with something?"

I glanced at Denny. He wasn't looking at me, of course, but seeing him sitting there was still a comfort. I took a deep breath and turned back to Detective Jenner. "I need to talk to you about the shooting."

Detective Jenner's face turned slightly ashy and the lines around his eyes deepened. "All right." He walked around his desk and sat down in the metal chair. "What's going on?"

"It's, um . . . it's about Sarah McHale."

Detective Jenner was silent while I explained, telling him everything I'd told Denny before. It didn't take long. It wasn't as if there was much to tell on my end. Just that what everyone seemed to think had happened in the bathroom was wrong. When I finished, he sat back in his seat and ran a hand through his hair.

"Wow," he said. "Not what I was expecting to hear."

"I'm sorry," I said. "I was going to tell you at the walk-through, but then being there made me panic and the story got bigger after that and I didn't want to hurt anyone and . . ." Denny's hand groped along the armrest until it found mine. He squeezed and I took a breath. "I'm sorry, Detective Jenner."

"I understand," he said. "And I appreciate you telling me but . . . Leanne, the investigation has been closed for a while now. And this information doesn't really change anything. At least not on my end."

"Oh."

"We'd already ruled out any sort of hate crime or religious motivation," he explained. "The victims were clearly random, regardless of what exchange may or may not have happened with Sarah McHale."

I nodded. But the pit in my stomach had opened up. I was being honest. Finally. And it didn't matter at all.

"Can I ask why you're telling me this now?" His voice was gentle. The disappointment must have been plain on my face.

"I just . . ." The words got stuck in my throat. I swallowed and tried again. "I just . . ." But again, I couldn't get the words out. I couldn't explain what I had done and why I needed it fixed. Now.

Like always, though, Denny had the words I didn't.

"We're graduating," he explained for me. "I think Lee's worried that when we leave, anything we haven't said leaves with us. Is that right, Lee?"

I nodded and managed to mumble a quiet, "Yeah."

"I see," Detective Jenner said. "That's admirable, Leanne. I can understand why this is something you'd feel the need to come clean about. But can I give you some advice? Not as a police officer, but as an adult concerned for your safety."

"Um, sure," I said.

"Keep this story to yourself."

I blinked. "Excuse me?"

"I know it's been a while since I've been in Virgil County. And maybe things are different now. I doubt it but . . ." He sighed. "People were passionate about that Sarah McHale story. They aren't going to take it too well if anyone tries to take that away from them. I remember what happened with the Gaynor girl. Have you heard from her since she left town?"

I shook my head.

"Point is, I don't want to see anything bad happen to you, Leanne. You've been through enough. If I were you, I'd just continue to keep this to myself."

When we left the office a few minutes later, it felt like my emotions were washing over me in waves. Disappointment, then frustration, then guilt. The only thing telling Detective

Jenner had done was make me feel less certain about telling anyone else.

Denny must've known what I was thinking, because once we were in my truck and headed back to town, he asked, "So, what now?"

"I have no idea."

"Are you going to tell Sarah's parents?"

"Should I?"

Denny thought about it before answering. "I don't know. On one hand, they deserve to know the truth. Especially before they write that book. On the other . . . this is going to really upset them. Like . . . a lot."

"You're so articulate," I said.

"Compared to you? Hell yeah I am." He flashed a quick smile, then shook his head. "I don't know, Lee. It's been three years. I don't know what you do at this point. Detective Jenner might be right. Might be better just to let it go."

"What about Kellie, though?"

"She's not here. Maybe she's somewhere where people care less about this story. I hope so. Either way, it's not like you can change what happened to her."

"But if the McHales' book is published . . ."

"Yeah. That's going to suck no matter where she lives." He blew out a breath. "I don't know. I'm sorry. But whatever you decide to do, I've got your back. Not sure that means much, but it's the thought that counts, right?"

"Thanks, Denny."

RICHARD MCMULLEN

Detective Jenner was right—people in this town love their stories about Sarah. And after she died, there were a lot of other stories that popped up, too. Stories about the person she was when she was alive. How kind and generous and genuine she was.

There are dozens of stories out there. Almost everyone wants to say they knew Sarah. Everyone wants to claim a piece of her.

And yet, not a single one of those stories includes Richie. Because, as well as people think they knew her, almost no one knew she'd been in love with Richie McMullen since she was eleven. Or that they'd been "officially" dating (secretly) since the eighth grade.

If you google Richie's obituary, you'll learn that he had just turned fifteen two weeks before the shooting, that he was survived by both parents and five siblings. That his family is Catholic.

What it won't tell you is that Richie didn't own a scrap of clothing that wasn't camo. Camo pants, camo jacket, camo everything. Sarah used to tease him mercilessly about it. "You know this is a school, not the woods, right?" she'd say. "You really think you're gonna kill any turkeys in the cafeteria?"

"No," Richie replied. "Because it's deer season."

In his class photos, he had almost-white hair. But you won't find any pictures online of the time in seventh grade when he dyed it bright orange with Kool-Aid for a Halloween costume. It looked ridiculous, and it took weeks for it to completely wash out. By Thanksgiving, even the teachers were calling him "Carrot" half the time. That nickname stuck around. Sarah never called him that, but a lot of his friends did. He even signed my eighth-grade yearbook as "Carrot McMullen."

Richie and I weren't very close. He was dating Sarah, so our paths crossed constantly, but we never really went beyond friendly acquaintances. Most of the time, I was sure I got on his nerves, because I was always around, always the third wheel. Sarah never wanted to leave me behind, which meant Richie didn't get to, either.

Once, I'd even overheard him complaining to her that he wished I had more friends so that they could spend lunch alone together, seeing as how they didn't get to spend much time together outside of school. "Don't you ever want her to just like . . . go away sometimes?"

Sarah primly told him, "No," and refused to speak to him for a week.

Even so, when Valentine's Day came around, just a month before the shooting, Richie showed up at school with a teddy bear for Sarah (one she'd have to lie to her parents about) and a bag of Skittles for me.

"What's this for?" I'd asked.

He shrugged. "I didn't want you to feel left out."

Richie *hated* that first period computer science class with Ms. Taylor. He complained about it to Sarah constantly. He'd wanted to be in one of the elective Ag classes, but there'd been some sort of schedule issue, so he was stuck. Denny says he was always getting reprimanded by Ms. Taylor for playing games instead of working.

Chances are, that's what he was doing when the shooter walked into that classroom.

There was so much more to Richie McMullen. Plenty of stories I don't even know. But I hope this is enough so that, if anyone ever reads this, they won't remember him as just one of the faceless, nameless victims—one of the nine—of the VCHS massacre.

Instead, maybe you'll remember him as Carrot.

I think he'd have liked that.

I could've listened to Detective Jenner. Could've dropped Denny off at his house, gone back home, and never mentioned any of the Sarah issue ever again. For a second, I considered it. It would've been so easy.

But there was another article about the McHales' book when I got home that evening. I didn't even have to go looking on any of the VCHS message boards to find it this time, either. It was a top story on my browser's home page as soon as I logged in: "Three Years On, Parents Remember Their Daughter's Brave Sacrifice."

The headline made me squirm. Brave? Sacrifice? I hated when these kinds of words got tossed around about Sarah. It always made what had happened in that bathroom sound like something glorious, like the climax of an Oscar-winning movie rather than the blur of terror and confusion that it really was. Which I guess was deliberate, since this article mentioned that a famous actress's production company was, "according to a reliable source," seriously considering optioning the not-yet-published biography.

I logged out without reading any further. The buzz around this book was getting bigger already, and I knew what that meant. Soon there would be reporters in Virgil County again, digging up the old stories about Sarah. About all of us. And they were going to get everything wrong.

I wanted the book canceled. Wanted to stamp out the flame before it turned into a wildfire. For a fleeting moment, I contemplated what would happen if I called one of the major news outlets. If I told them what really happened with Sarah McHale—that I was holding her hand when she died. That everything they'd ever reported about her was a lie. That would get attention. That would make the publisher reconsider that book deal.

It would be so easy.

But it would also be cruel. I couldn't do that to Sarah's parents. I couldn't let them find out the truth from a newspaper article. If they had to know the truth, they deserved to hear it from me. I'd avoided telling them for three years, thinking it was better to just let them believe whatever gave them comfort. But if this was the only way to stop the book, then it had to be done.

Before I could talk myself out of it, I grabbed my keys and hurried back out to my truck.

Mom had just pulled in when I stepped out onto the porch. She waved as she got out of her car. "I bought pizza," she said.

"Save me a slice," I said as I hoisted myself into my truck. "I'll be back later."

"Where are you going?"

But I'd already started the engine and was backing out of the driveway.

The McHales live about ten minutes away from me, just past Wargin Park and down a gravel road. My hands trembled on the steering wheel, shaking harder the closer I got.

It was unsettlingly familiar, pulling into their driveway and walking up the front steps. I'd seen them around town dozens of times over the years, but this was my first visit to their home since that awkward dinner where I'd first tried to tell Ruth what had happened to Sarah.

And now I was here again. Uninvited. About to tell them something I knew they didn't want to hear.

I took a deep breath and knocked on the front door. Ruth was there within a minute, and she was, unsurprisingly, completely baffled by my presence.

"Leanne," she said, immediately replacing her confused expression with a kind smile. "What a surprise! Come in, come in." She stepped aside and gestured me into the living room.

"Who is it, honey?" I heard Chad call from down the hall.

"Leanne Bauer," Ruth said, her voice raised just enough to be heard across the house, but sounding nothing like a yell. Ruth McHale never yelled. She turned back to me then. "I just realized I left my cell phone at work. Did you call? I'm so sorry."

"Oh, no," I said. "I didn't. I just . . . I'm sorry to barge in."

"Don't apologize, sweetheart. It's always so nice to see you."

I swallowed, knowing she might not feel that way for long.

"We were just getting cleaned up for dinner," she said. "Do you want to join us? We're having tuna noodle casserole."

"Oh, thank you, but I didn't mean to intrude."

"Nonsense." Chad rounded the corner into the living room. His hair and beard were thick and almost completely gray now. He gave me a warm, genuine smile, and my chest filled with dread. "Ruth always makes too much when she cooks. We'll be eating leftover casserole for days if you don't help us out."

I glanced back at the door, wishing I'd come an hour later. Maybe two. I couldn't eat dinner with them. I couldn't sit down at their table, eat their food, then tell them everything they believed about their daughter's final moments was a lie.

But Ruth had already looped an arm around my shoulders and was steering me into the dining room while Chad went to grab the casserole. "How have you been, Leanne?" she asked as she pushed me gently into a seat—my usual seat, the seat I'd sat in a million times over the years. "How's your mom?"

"She's fine," I said. "She's one of the managers at the Dollar Market now. It keeps her pretty busy."

"Oh, that's great," Ruth said. "And what about you? Prom's around the corner, isn't it? Going with anyone?"

"Um, I'm not sure. Probably not."

"Well, that's okay. Boys are overrated, anyway."

"I heard that!" Chad called from the kitchen.

Ruth smiled. "Are you still doing theater? Chad and I were so sad we missed you in that play last year. What was it? *Arsenic and Old Lace?* It sounded like you were a real star. We read all about it in the local paper. Are you going to be in any more plays this semester?"

I chewed my lip. "No. I've been too busy."

That was a lie. The real reason I'd decided not to do any more theater in Virgil County was that newspaper article Ruth was talking about. This had just been a small drama club production. We didn't have any funding, so there weren't even real sets. Still, a reporter from the local paper showed up at the performance. Instead of writing about the show, though, the whole article became about me.

Specifically, about how wonderful it was to see one of the shooting survivors onstage, even if it was in a play about old ladies committing murder. The other cast members weren't even mentioned. Heck, the *play* was barely mentioned. The whole article was essentially a retrospective on the shooting.

I fell in love with acting because it gives me the chance to be someone else. To sink into a new persona and let Lee Bauer disappear for a while. But that was never going to happen on any stage in Virgil County.

Hopefully things will be different outside of this town. Hopefully when I'm across the country, somewhere where my name isn't so recognizable, I'll be able to do what I want: be another person for eight performances a week without people focusing on what happened to me when I was fourteen.

"Oh, I'm sure. I know how busy senior year can be. Do you have big college plans?"

I nodded. "I'm heading to California," I said. "I'm going to study acting, actually."

"So you mean we'll know a movie star?" Chad asked as he stepped into the room with the casserole dish. "Promise you'll remember us little people when you're all famous, okay?"

I forced a smile. "I'm really more of a stage person," I said. "I don't really want to be famous. Just . . . to act."

"Oh, the *theater*!" Ruth said teasingly as she squeezed my arm across the table. "That'll be wonderful. But why California? Isn't New York the place to be for stage?"

"I mean, yeah. But there's theater in LA, too. And I got into an acting program out there, so . . ." I shrugged.

It was the truth, but only half of it. I had gotten into a good acting program out west, and there were teachers there I was excited to study with. But that wasn't my only reason. New York City had been Sarah's dream. She wanted to walk the runway at Fashion Week, even though she was five foot three, and only if you rounded up. I knew it was irrational, but going to Manhattan without her would have felt like a betrayal.

"Well, movies or not, we'll still be demanding your autograph," Chad assured me. "Leanne Bauer will always be an A-list celebrity in our eyes."

Ten minutes later, I was picking at my casserole without

having taken a bite. Ruth and Chad didn't seem to notice, or if they had, they weren't going to draw attention to it. Instead, they were talking to each other, mostly about their friends and upcoming church events. And they didn't ask me any questions that required more than a yes or no. Which was good. Because I was still trying to figure out how to broach the subject of the book.

But then, they did it for me.

"Oh, before I forget," Ruth said, "I'm sure you heard our good news, right? That we're writing a book about Sarah?"

"I did," I said. My hands were shaking. I dropped my fork on the table and folded them in my lap. "About that—"

"Don't worry," Chad said. "We were going to reach out to you."

"You were?"

"Of course," he said. "You were Sarah's best friend. This book wouldn't be complete without you. We'd love to interview you for it."

"Or if you'd rather write a piece, like an essay about her," Ruth suggested. "It could be a whole chapter. We know she'd want you involved."

I cleared my throat. This was my moment. And now my legs were trembling, too. "About that," I said. "I . . . I don't think I can be a part of the book."

"Why not?" Ruth asked. "Is something wrong, Leanne?"

"There's . . . there's something you should know about what happened," I said. "During the shooting."

Chad's face went pale. Ruth reached across the table and squeezed his hand, her eyes never leaving my face.

I took a deep breath. "The thing that you think happened, with Sarah and the necklace and *him* . . . It's not exactly . . . It didn't happen."

"Excuse me?" Chad said.

"I don't know how this whole thing got started, and I should have told you years ago. It didn't happen like that. At all. She wasn't even wearing a necklace that day, and he didn't talk to her. Not a word."

"Stop." Ruth's voice was so quiet, I almost didn't hear.

But I couldn't stop. The words came out like a waterfall pouring over a cliff. "We were in the stall and she was holding my hand and he just . . . he shot her. He didn't talk to her. He didn't ask her anything."

"Stop." She was louder now, but her voice cracked. "Stop, Leanne."

"But you need to know. You can't write this book."

"Why would you say this?" Ruth asked. "Why would you lie about Sarah?"

"I'm not lying," I said. "I know this is hard to hear but—"

Chad was standing now, his hands clenched at his sides. He looked so much larger all of a sudden. I'd never considered Sarah's father to be an intimidating man, but now he seemed to tower over me. "You need to go, Leanne."

"Please. I'm just trying to—"

"You need to go," he repeated. "I won't have you lying about our daughter, trying to tarnish her memory. Not in my house. Get out."

I looked imploringly at Ruth, but she was looking at me like I was a complete stranger. Like I'd just peeled off a mask and revealed that, no, I wasn't the little girl they'd welcomed into their house for years. Instead, I was some hideous, venom-spitting beast. And, worse, there were tears in her eyes. I'd made a woman who'd never been anything but kind and loving to me cry.

It was clear they weren't going to believe me.

Maybe, I realize now, they couldn't.

"Leanne," Chad said, his voice deeper, angrier. "Leave. Now."

I stood up. "Thank you for dinner," I said. "I'm sorry."

I walked to my truck in a daze. I knew they might not take it well, but I hadn't expected to be kicked out of a house that, at one time, had been like a second home to me. To be called a liar by people who once called me family.

I thought I had been doing the right thing. But . . . I don't know. Maybe there was another way. Maybe I could have told them differently. Maybe I should've just told them three years ago.

I guess it doesn't matter now.

But, Chad, Ruth, if somehow, at some point, you end up reading this, I really am sorry. And I hope you know that nothing I've done diminishes how much I cared about Sarah. I know you think I've tarnished her memory, but her memory can never really be tarnished. Not for me. I'll always remember her as the girl who could make me laugh so hard that I couldn't breathe, who stood up for me even when it wasn't the "cool" thing to do, who loved me even when she didn't understand me.

She didn't have to die a martyr to be my hero.

Still, I wish things had gone differently. And I hope, one day, you will forgive me.

It took months before I was able to sleep at night.

In the first couple of weeks after the shooting, I'd just lie in my bed, listening to every tiny creak, noticing every little shadow, and running through a thousand possibilities of what they could be, each worse than the one before. I spent hours in the darkness, convinced I wouldn't be alive by morning. Wondering how I'd die. Terrified of the prospect of existence just *ending*.

When the sun came up, I'd finally manage to doze off, still only sleeping in bursts, woken up by nightmares or Mom, poking her head in to check on me.

I don't know what gave me the idea to climb onto the roof. It seemed logical at the time, though. From there, I could see anything coming. I would know before the danger could reach me. The roof just felt like the safest place I could be in the middle of the night.

So I grabbed a steak knife from the kitchen and headed outside. A wooden fence ran down the middle of the narrow swath of land that separated our yard from Mrs. Mason's, and once I hoisted myself onto the fence, I was able to jump onto the roof. I found a spot and sat there, cross-legged for hours, turning the knife over and over in my hands, my wide eyes watching for any signs of trouble in my dark little corner of Virgil County.

I stayed there until the sky shifted from black to an almost royal blue, with the sunlight just beginning to peer over the horizon. As the streetlights flickered out, I hopped off the roof and snuck back inside, burying myself beneath the covers on my bed before Mom could wake up.

I'd been doing this every night for a week when Miles noticed me. Or, maybe he'd noticed me before. I'm not sure. But this was the first time he'd come outside while I was up there.

Miles's grandmother, Mrs. Mason, has lived next door to Mom and me since I can remember. She's a little old lady with wispy white hair and a habit of calling everyone "sweetie." When I was eleven and my own grandmother died, she brought Mom and me dinner every night for a week, because she didn't want Mom to have to worry about cooking on top of everything else.

So when Miles came to live with her a year later, right after I started seventh grade, he took me by surprise. He wasn't at all how I'd imagined Mrs. Mason's grandson to be. I'd imagined him in khakis and a collared shirt, not a dirty hoodie and ripped jeans. I'd pictured him as having the same warm smile as his grandmother, not a face that shifted from sulky to angry and seemingly nothing else.

I wasn't sure why Miles had come to live with his grandmother, because we'd never really spoken. I know that's hard to believe—two kids, roughly the same age, living right next door to each other and never interacting. But if you knew us, especially before the shooting, you'd understand. He was a year ahead of me in school at the time. He was quiet, even back then he mumbled everything, and as far as I could tell, he didn't seem all that interested in getting to know me. Not that I tried that hard, either. I spent most of my time with Sarah, and he was definitely not the sort of guy I could see her becoming friends with.

Honestly, even now, I wonder what she'd think of him if she were still here.

But, anyway, that night was the first time I ever really spent time with him.

It must've been around one in the morning. The tiny subdivision we lived in was completely dark aside from a few streetlamps. I'd already been sitting up there for an hour or two when I heard a voice from the ground.

"Lee."

I jumped and my fingers tightened around the knife. But the voice had been quiet, almost careful. Slowly, I crawled to the edge of the roof and peered down. Miles was standing just on the other side of the fence. I almost didn't see him. He was wearing a black sweatshirt and a black beanie covered his hair. His face was pale, though, almost ghostly, and it stood in contrast to the darkness around him.

We stared at each other for a long, quiet moment before he asked, "Can I come up?"

I nodded and scurried back as he climbed the wooden fence. A second later, he appeared over the edge of the roof, pulling himself up and then crawling over to sit next to me. I saw him glance down at my hands, at the knife, but he didn't say anything.

I wasn't surprised when he'd appeared. In a way, I think I expected it.

That first night, we didn't talk at all. Not a word. It was a warm sort of silence, though. A silence that felt safe. Even though I barely knew Miles, I was glad to have him there with me. Because I didn't want to be alone, but usually, when someone else was nearby, they were staring at me, asking me questions, or trying so hard to make me feel comfortable that I felt like I was being suffocated with a pillow. But those quiet hours on the roof, that was what I'd been longing for.

I assume Miles needed the same thing. I'm sure that's why he climbed on my roof that night, but I've never actually asked him.

We spent almost every night that summer on top of my house. Some nights we sat in that same blanket of silence. Miles would bring a flashlight and a book, about the Industrial Revolution or the War of 1812. He'd read quietly, lips moving over the words, while I sat there, clutching my knife and counting streetlights. Other nights, though, we stretched out on our backs, looking up at the sky. But only when the moon was bright and there were plenty of stars. On black, cloudy nights, I couldn't stand to look up.

It was on one of those cloudy nights that Miles and I had our first conversation that consisted of more than a few words.

He was leaning back, arms crossed over his chest as he stared up. I took one glance at the sky and shuddered a little before pulling my knees to my chest and focusing on the streetlights instead. I still had the knife in my hand, and my fingers tightened around the hilt.

"You okay?" Miles asked in his quiet, almost slurred mumble.

"Fine."

He didn't say anything, but I could feel his eyes on me. He knew I wasn't fine. Neither of us had been fine in a while. And I didn't know why I was lying to him of all people.

"I don't like it when the sky is this dark," I said. "When I lie back, the darkness is all I see and I feel . . . I feel like I'm falling into nothingness. It's what I imagine death feels like."

Before the shooting, I hadn't thought much about death. Obviously, I was aware that I'd die one day, but it was an abstract concept. It felt distant and somehow irrelevant. After the shooting, though, after seeing death firsthand, realizing it wasn't necessarily a far-off threat, it felt like I was seeing the world with new eyes. Like a curtain had been pulled back and I could now see the hideous truth of mortality.

And now I saw death everywhere.

Even in the night sky.

I felt Miles shift beside me. He was sitting up now, his arm lightly grazing mine. "You don't believe in heaven?"

I shook my head. "I mean, I want to. Most people around here do, I guess. Sarah did. And I want to believe she's . . ."

I swallowed. "I want to believe there's something after, but I just can't shake this feeling that that's just this fairy tale, you know? To make humans feel better about the fact that one day we're all gonna die—that even Earth and our species won't exist forever—and most likely that just means we *stop*." I took a deep breath and tried to blink back the tears burning my eyes. "What about you? Do you believe in heaven? Or anything after we die?"

Miles shrugged. "Don't know. I don't think about it if I can help it."

"How do you manage that?" I asked, my voice already going raspy with the effort not to cry. "Feels like I can't think about anything else."

He didn't answer, because there was no answer. Nothing he could say would erase my terror at the thought—not so much of dying but of ending. My anger that I'd been brought into existence, that I was a conscious being in my body, cursed with the knowledge that one day everything I'd done, every memory I'd made, would just vanish. And that I had no control over when or how that day would come. That I could die in pain, in terror, or in peace, and what difference would it make? I'd still be gone. And one day the whole world would be gone. And nothing, not a damn thing, any human ever did would matter.

My eyes were squeezed shut and my body was shaking all over. I was spiraling. It always happened when I got on this train of thought, which was almost daily back then. It still happens sometimes, though over the years, between therapy and the right medication, I've gotten better at shutting the thoughts down before they get quite that far. But the drum of existential dread is always with me. Always beating a steady rhythm at the back of my mind.

"Lee," Miles said. His voice was close, right near my ear, but he didn't touch me. "You're still here."

"I know but—"

He shook his head. "For now, you're here."

I don't know if I would have survived those first few months without Miles. He didn't try to hold my hand or comfort me or tell me that everything was going to be all right. I had plenty of people doing that. Instead, he just sat next to me through the long, anxious nights, reminding me every so often that, at least for that moment, I was alive. I was real. I was still here.

And that I wasn't the only one who couldn't sleep.

XXX

Miles pulled himself up over the edge of the roof.

"Hey," I said as he crawled over to sit beside me. I wasn't surprised he'd come. It had been a while since I'd felt the need to climb up there in the middle of the night, but after my evening with Sarah's parents, it felt like the only place I could go. And Miles was the only person I could be with.

"Saw you through the window," he said. "You okay?"

"Not really."

He put an arm around my shoulders and I sighed, leaning against him. Normally I wouldn't have allowed this. Not because it made me uncomfortable, but because I didn't want Miles to get the wrong idea. I didn't want to lead him on. But at the same time, right then, I felt selfish. Greedy for comfort.

You're probably wondering about Miles and me. The trouble-maker and the girl next door survive a nightmare and grow close. Will they fall madly in love and end up together? Well, it's more complicated than that. At least it is for me.

I've known for a while that I'm on the asexual spectrum. I

figured it out about the time Sarah started sneaking around with Richie McMullen in the eighth grade. The way she talked about him—the way I heard older girls talk about their boyfriends and girlfriends—it never clicked for me. I've had crushes. There are boys I've had romantic feelings for, but I've never had any desire to do more than hold hands or maybe—*maybe*—kiss. It's not that I find the idea of sex repulsive. I don't, actually. In some ways, I find it intriguing. I've just never met or seen anyone I had any desire or even fleeting fantasy of doing it with. Not even any of the ridiculously attractive celebrities. I recognize that they're aesthetically pleasing, but I'm also not daydreaming about ripping their clothes off.

And that made things with Miles complicated. I knew he had feelings for me, and if I'm being honest, I had feelings for him, too. But I'd decided a while ago that I wasn't going to act on them. Not just because I was asexual, though that was definitely part of it. Sarah was the only person I'd ever come out to, and I didn't know how Miles would react to the idea of a girlfriend who wasn't sure when or if she'd ever be comfortable sleeping with him. And I cared enough about him and our friendship that I didn't want to find out. But I also tried to keep him at a distance because come August, I was leaving Virgil County. I was moving to Los Angeles, and I didn't know if I'd ever be back in this town.

Miles didn't like to talk about life after graduation. His grandma wanted him to go to vocational school, though I could tell he wasn't excited about this prospect. But he hadn't applied to any colleges yet, and he never mentioned getting out of Virgil County.

So I had promised myself that, for both of our sakes, I was going to keep Miles at a secure, friendly distance. That had proven to be very difficult, though.

"Can I ask you something?" he said.

"Hmm?"

"Do you wanna go to prom?"

I sat up, pulling away from him so I could see his face. To my surprise, he didn't appear to be joking. "Are you serious?"

He shrugged. "Could be fun."

"I just never thought you'd be interested in something like prom."

"I would be if we went together."

I bit my lip and turned away.

Miles obviously noticed my discomfort because he quickly added, "And Denny's going. Dunno. It's our last year here. I just figured the three of us would hang out."

"I didn't know Denny was going."

"Yeah. He got a date with Amber Hieber."

I let out a low whistle. "Dang. Nice job, Denny. She's really cute."

"She's just going with him because of the dog."

"Please," I said, elbowing him. "You wish you had his charm."

"Maybe," he admitted. "So . . . do you wanna go?"

"I don't know, Miles. Prom is just . . . it's expensive. And it's not really my thing, you know?"

This was a lie. I had been dreaming about prom since I was little. Sarah and I used to get dressed up in her mom's old bridesmaid dresses and hold pretend proms in her living room as kids. I used to have dreams about dancing with some sweet boy for hours while slow songs played. About staying up all night gossiping with Sarah afterward.

Then the shooting happened, and those fantasies just sort of evaporated.

I hadn't gone to my junior prom. Instead, Miles, Eden, Denny, and I had spent the evening at Ashley's house, watching John Hughes movies and playing rummy with a set of Denny's cards. They looked like any other set of playing cards, only they had Braille, too. It had been a fun night. Not romantic or fancy, but it had mostly kept my mind off of the imaginary prom nights Sarah and I had crafted all those years ago.

Part of me really wanted to go to prom with Miles. Wanted it too much. Me in a pretty dress. Him cleaned up in a tux. It would be way too easy to fall even harder than I already had.

He was staring at me now with those sad, sleepy eyes. And I couldn't stop myself from wishing.

"I'll think about it," I whispered.

He nodded. "Cool."

We fell into a comfortable silence, no longer touching as the clouds above us shifted and the stars became visible. Miles leaned back, folding his arms over his chest and looking up. With the sky now lit, it was safe for me to do the same.

After we'd been lying there for a while, Miles asked, "Gonna tell me what's going on? Why you're out here tonight?"

"I went and saw Sarah's parents."

He turned his head to look at me, two thick auburn eyebrows raised.

"You heard they're writing a book, right? About Sarah?"

"Yeah."

"Well." I took a deep breath. "The story about Sarah—with the necklace and the things she said to *him* . . . it's not true."

"Ah."

"You're not surprised?"

"Not really. I've kinda wondered. Especially with the whole Kellie thing. Dunno. The story just sounded too much like a movie to be real."

"Sarah's parents definitely disagree," I said. "They didn't take it well."

"You're just now telling them?"

I flinched, even though his voice hadn't been harsh or even judgmental. "I've tried before," I said. "Sort of. When people first started talking about it, I didn't know what to do. I didn't even know where it had started. And every time I tried to tell anyone, I'd panic. And then Kellie left town and I figured it didn't matter anymore. But now, with the book . . ." I shook my head. "I should've told them sooner, but I didn't, and now they think I'm a liar trying to take away from their daughter's memory."

"Sorry," he said. "Is that what you and Denny were talking about the other day? When you drove him home?"

"Yeah. His scholarship letter made me realize Sarah's story isn't the only myth, you know? It made me wish we could all speak up. If we could all write letters like that . . ." I paused, then sat up. "Oh."

"What?" Miles asked.

"I have an idea, I think. I don't know how it would work but . . . maybe if we all wrote letters, telling the truth about what happened that day and even afterward . . ."

"Letters to who?"

"I don't know," I said. "Anyone? If everyone did it, though, I could collect them. Put them together into something cohesive. Something people would have to listen to because it's all of us. We could set the story straight. Maybe we could, like . . . release the letters somehow so that there will be something else out there besides the McHales' book."

My thoughts were moving like a tornado through my mind, spinning violently, too fast for me to grasp. I'd have to figure out the details later, but somehow this just seemed like the answer. If Denny's letter had gotten to me like this, maybe letters from all of the survivors could make an impact. I could reach out to Ashley and Eden, and I would try to find Kellie to see if she'd do it.

"You'll write one, won't you?" I asked Miles.

"Write a letter? I'm not sure, Lee."

"What's there not to be sure about?" I asked. "Surely you wanna point out how messed up it was the way those newspaper articles talked about you, right? Like that one journalist who wrote something about how you were the kind of kid people expected to be a shooter, not a hero? That's so awful, and you could write about why."

Miles turned away, and I figured I was making him uncomfortable bringing up comments like that. I couldn't imagine how hurtful that had been, to see it in print that you were the kind of person no one expected to do something noble. That you seemed more like a villain. But that was exactly why I needed him to do this.

Miles was so much more than the troubled-boy-turned-hero. His story went beyond the fights he'd been in or his suspension record. All the reporting on the shooting had squeezed him into a box, an easily digestible line or two of text. And I wanted the world to see who he was outside of that box. I wanted people to know the intense, thoughtful, surprisingly funny Miles that I adored.

"Please, Miles?" I asked, reaching out to touch his hand. "Please?"

He turned to look back at me, and after a long moment, he sighed. "Lee . . ."

"Just think about it," I said. "That's all I'm asking."

He nodded, then turned his gaze back to the stars.

We stayed up there until dawn, when I finally snuck back inside and crawled into bed. Even then, though, I couldn't sleep. Not because of pain or guilt this time, but the opposite. For the first time in a while, I felt hopeful.

If I could make this work, then the truth would finally, finally be out there. And this weight would be off my shoulders at last.

KEVIN BRANTLEY

Here's what I know about Kevin Brantley: When the shooting happened, he was a sophomore; he kept his head shaved and always wore band T-shirts; and in elementary school, he stuck gum in Sarah's hair on the bus and tried to blame it on someone else.

I reached out to the other survivors to see if anyone else knew him better. The first person to reply was Miles. This was our text exchange.

MILES: I knew him. Hated him.

ME: Yeah? Why?

MILES: He found a picture of my dad's mug shot on the internet. Not sure how. He printed it and brought it to school. This was in eighth grade. Right after I moved here.

ME: That's awful.

MILES: I kicked his ass before he could show anyone.

ME: That's good? I guess?

MILES: We both got suspended. Not proud of it but don't really regret it either. He was a jerk.

ME: Sounds like it.

MILES: Guessing that's not the kind of story you were looking for, huh?

ME: LOL. No. Not exactly.

I decided to share it, though. Not because I have any desire to make Kevin seem like a bad guy when he's not here to defend himself. But because of another issue I've seen with how we talk about victims. They're all treated like angels after they die. Every description talks about how friendly and fun-loving and kind they were, even if that wasn't always the case.

But most of the people who died that day were kids. And sometimes kids are jerks. That doesn't make them less worthy of mourning. It just makes them people. Acting like the dead were always perfect and innocent just distances them from us even more. Maybe it's just me, but knowing these people were flawed makes them more real.

Anyway, I did get another take on Kevin Brantley. This time it was from Eden, who responded via email.

Kevin was my lab partner in chemistry. I did most of the work. But he wasn't so bad. He saw me drawing in class once and asked if I'd teach him. He said he wanted to design his own T-shirts one day. I said no because . . . well, you know how I am with people. But he offered to pay for some lessons, and I needed the money for art supplies.

We met once a week during lunch for about two months. He was kind of loud and a little lazy, but he was nice to me. Actually, he's the only guy who has ever asked me out. I don't think he really liked me. He just wanted a girlfriend. It was the last day of our drawing lessons, and I told him I was gay. Which wasn't something I told a lot of people at the time.

I kind of assumed he'd be gross about it. Make some jokes or say something homophobic. But instead he just said, "That's cool. So is my brother," and dropped it.

He sat next to me in Ms. Taylor's class. We didn't talk a lot, but sometimes he'd slide over a notebook with one of his drawings and ask what I thought. Rosi was the one who was good at things, not me, so having someone want my opinion because they thought I was good at something? It meant a lot.

I don't know if you'd call Kevin and me friends. But yeah. I definitely remember him. I wonder if he ever would have made those T-shirts he talked about.

X X X

I sent out a group text message the day after my talk with Miles, and to my surprise, Ashley and Eden responded almost immediately. They had a few questions, but they both agreed to write letters for my project. I didn't tell them what I'd told Denny and Miles. It wasn't the kind of thing I wanted to deliver over text. I just explained that, with the boys and me graduating, it felt like this was our last chance to really tell our stories.

Denny responded, too, and told me I could use his scholarship letter for whatever I decided on doing. And Miles, of course, didn't answer my text at all. I'd known he wouldn't. He was taking time to think about what he wanted to do, and I wasn't going to push him. Not just yet, at least.

Now the only thing remaining was to find Kellie Gaynor.

I'd spent hours searching for her online. She didn't seem to have any social media presence—at least not under the name Kellie Gaynor—and no phone listings anywhere. I did find her mom on Facebook, but the friend request I'd sent had been ignored. Not that I blamed her. I tried sending a message anyway, explaining that I was one of the other survivors and I wanted to get in touch with Kellie, but as far as I could tell, it hadn't even been read.

Most of the things that came up when I searched Kellie's name online were old Tumblr and forum posts from the usual VCHS true crime spots. A lot of the time, she was just listed among those who had been injured, along with Ashley and Denny, but there was some more disturbing stuff out there, too. Including an old piece of "fan fiction" in which Kellie is the girlfriend of the shooter and helped him plan the whole thing. Only then she betrays him by calling the cops from the bathroom and shooting herself in the shoulder to make herself look like a victim.

Of course, like in a lot of the weird fandom around the shooting, the mass murderer is glorified, portrayed as misunderstood and sympathetic, and the rest of us were just bullies.

The story was disturbing, but not even close to the worst I've read.

And diving that deep into the mass shooter fandom side of the internet had brought me no closer to getting in touch with Kellie Gaynor.

"Why bother looking for her, anyway?" Ashley asked.

I was at her house about a week after I'd asked her to write the letter. She'd just put her daughter down for a nap, and we were sitting at her kitchen table dyeing Easter eggs. As always, being in her house felt like being wrapped in a favorite quilt, warm and familiar. Before the shooting, I honestly hadn't liked

Ashley very much. She had always come across as self-righteous and judgmental. But now it was hard to imagine a life where I didn't have her texting me almost daily, either with a cute picture of Miriam or just checking in to make sure I was doing all right.

When I mentioned Kellie Gaynor, however, her normally sweet expression instantly turned sour.

I shrugged, then dipped one of my eggs into the pink dye. "She's one of us, too. I'm sure she has a story to tell."

Ashley scoffed. "I'm sure she does. One full of lies."

I started to tell her the truth right then. I swear I did. Ashley, if you're reading this, I'm sorry I didn't go ahead and just say it. But my eyes flitted to a photo stuck on the refrigerator door. In the picture, Ashley is wearing her wedding dress, her veil pushed back as she smiles at the camera. Her wheelchair is positioned in front of a church and Logan, wearing his tux, is kneeling beside her. A group of smiling people stand around them, looking proud. Among the crowd are Ruth and Chad McHale. And the church in the background is Virgil County Baptist.

Ashley has gone to church with Sarah's family since she was little. She'd known Sarah for most of her life. As much as I'd wanted to just tell her the truth right then, I was scared I'd have a repeat of my night with the McHales. I didn't want to be kicked out of Ashley's house. I didn't want to lose that warm-blanket feeling I had when I was with her.

Yes, I was being selfish. But I resolved that I'd tell her once all the letters were written. I could use them to explain everything. Until then, though, I'd stay silent. And safe.

"I'm sorry," Ashley said as she lifted an egg from the blue dye. "I know I'm being harsh. I just really hate her. I try not to say the *h* word often, but with Kellie Gaynor . . . who makes up the kind of lies she did? Who does that?"

"We don't have to talk about her," I said. "In fact, let's just change the subject."

"Fair enough," she said. "Oh, but I did write that letter for you."

"Already?" I asked, surprised.

"I felt inspired," she said. "I was going to email it to you, but our internet's been acting up. So I put it on a USB drive. Will that work?"

"That'd be great. Thank you."

"Hold on. I'll go grab it." She wiped her dye-smudged fingers on a clean paper towel, then wheeled back from the table, carefully maneuvering her chair through the kitchen doorway. She returned a minute later and handed me a small blue thumb drive. "I hope I did it right," she said.

"I don't really think there's a wrong way to tell your own story."

She laughed. "Hopefully you feel that way after you've read it."

We took all of the eggs out of their dye and laid them on paper towels. "Is this how you're supposed to let them dry?" Ashley asked me. "I actually have no idea what I'm doing. I don't think I've dyed Easter eggs in fifteen years."

"I'm not sure, either, but it seems right?"

Ashley laughed. "Having a kid makes you realize how very little you know about being an adult."

"I think you're doing a pretty great job."

She beamed at me. "Thank you. I know this sounds weird considering our very minor age gap, but I feel like I got a little bit of practice with you and Miles and Denny. Eden a little, too. Not that I'm comparing you to my six-month-old, but . . . I don't know. I felt very protective of you guys. I still do sometimes."

"You have kind of been our mother hen," I said. "But I think we all appreciate it. Especially in that first year. We were all such a mess."

And I still am, I added mentally. That was part of why I spent so many Saturday afternoons at Ashley's house. When my world felt like it was spinning too fast, I knew Ashley would be there to hold me still. She didn't get as emotional as my own mother. Instead, she was just this calm, nurturing presence that never seemed too shaken.

"Well, speaking of being a mother hen," she said. "I have to ask. Do you want anything to eat or drink?"

I shook my head. "I'm fine. Thanks." It was the third time she'd asked me that afternoon.

"You sure? We have lemonade and chocolate milk and sweet tea."

"I'm okay."

"And water, of course."

"Really. I'm fine."

Ashley shook her head. "Sorry. I can't help it. My mother always told me that if your guests don't have a cup in their hands, you're being a bad hostess."

"Does this tiny cup of Easter egg dye count?" I asked, pointing at the pink.

"Hmm. For now? Sure. But if you're here much longer, I'm forcing some chocolate milk on you."

I left before she could make good on that promise. I wanted to get home and read the letter she'd written. I was eager to see if it would hold the kind of revelations Denny's had. If it would make me see the shooting or our lives afterward in a new light.

And it definitely did that.

Dear Friend,

Almost every day for the past three years, someone has asked me, "Ashley, how do you cope with the things you've seen?" or "Ashley, how do you stay so positive after everything that has happened to you?" I always give the same answer, and I am sure there are people who won't believe me but . . .

Forgiveness.

I think most people see me as unlucky. I wasn't even supposed to be in that hallway when ▓▓▓▓ walked out of the computer lab with a gun. I was in the wrong place at the wrong time and it changed my life forever. It would be so easy to be angry about that, to spend the rest of my life asking, "Why me?" I think that's what people expect me to do. Or maybe it's just what people think they would do.

But I'm not angry.

I'm not going to say I'm grateful. That might be taking it a little too far. But I will say that, three years on, I like who I am. I like where my life is and where it's going. And the truth is, I don't know what the alternate version of me, the version that wasn't in that hallway, would look like. She might not need a wheelchair, sure, but she also might not have the beautiful family that I have now. She might not have the faith I do. She might not have found her purpose the way I have.

So I forgive.

I wasn't in a good place during my senior year of high school. Logan and I had broken up over winter break. He was a year older and had moved to the next county over for a job. We'd been together since my freshman year, and not seeing him every day like I was used to had taken a toll. I was selfish and frustrated and whenever we were together, I found myself picking fights for no reason. Eventually we both got tired of it and broke up two days before Christmas.

On top of that, graduation was approaching, and I had no idea what I wanted to do after. All my friends had plans—college, vocational school, working on their parents' farm—but I didn't feel excited about anything. I was leaning toward cosmetology school, but only because nothing else interested me. I felt completely lost, and for the first time ever, I didn't feel like my faith was guiding me.

I went to church with my parents and sister each Sunday. I was the president of the Fellowship of Christian Students at VCHS. I went to youth group with my friends on Wednesday nights, and I prayed. I prayed so much, but nothing seemed to be changing. It felt like God wasn't listening to me. And, I have to admit, my desperation turned me into someone who wasn't a very good Christian.

The way I saw it, I was doing everything right, and God still wasn't guiding me to what I wanted. Meanwhile, I saw my friends and classmates and even my own family not being as "good" as I was, not being the kind of Christians I thought they ought to be, but that didn't seem to matter. They seemed happy, and I wasn't. They seemed to have purpose, and I didn't. And the only way I could make myself feel better about that was to judge them. To remind them—and myself—that they weren't as "good" as I was. I pointed out every little sin I could find because it made me feel better about myself. I'm not proud of that.

In fact, the last time I saw Sarah McHale, I was pretty terrible to her.

I'd gotten a hall pass during Senior English to use the bathroom. Mrs. Keebler, our usual teacher, wasn't the type to allow students out of class, even to use the bathroom, so normally I never left until the bell rang. But Mrs. Keebler was out that day, and we had a more lenient substitute, Mr. Shockley. He was one of those young guy teachers who told us we could call him Keith and let students cuss in class. He was on the usual rotation of substitute teachers, so we all knew him pretty well, and none of us were surprised when he suggested we pull out our phones and discuss the poetry of our favorite bands.

That March, my playlist was full of Christian rock and breakup songs, and I really wasn't in the mood to discuss either with my classmates. So when it was almost my turn to pick a song, I decided it was a good time to go pee, and Mr. Shockley handed over the hall pass.

The girls' bathroom was around the corner and down the hall, past the computer lab. I remember the door was open when I walked by. I even remember glancing inside and everything looking completely normal. Ms. Taylor was at her desk, a handful of students were on their computers, talking and laughing with the kids around them. It was just so ordinary that it's hard to imagine what happened only a few minutes later.

Anyway, when I got to the bathroom, it was empty. But almost as soon as I entered the stall, I heard Sarah and Lee walk in. I didn't know Lee very well at the time—just that she was Sarah's best friend. Sarah and I had gone to the same church since we were kids, though. Our families often shared a pew at Virgil County Baptist. I liked Sarah, she was a sweet girl, but she hadn't been coming to the Fellowship of Christian Students meetings lately.

I found out why when she and Lee started talking.

"How bad is it?" Sarah asked.

"Not that bad. Your shirt mostly hides it."

"Maybe I can cover it with foundation?" I could hear her purse unzipping. "It's a good thing you noticed. If my parents saw this, they'd lose it."

"It's ridiculous that you can't have a boyfriend until you're sixteen."

"I know. I'm trying to get them to change the rule, but if they find out I got a hickey behind the shop building when I was sup-posed to be at an FCS meeting . . . I'd probably be locked in my room until I'm thirty."

Sarah was in the middle of rubbing foundation over a tiny bruise, just above the collar of her shirt, when she saw me. Her dark eyes went wide. Lee glanced at me, too, and she moved protec-tively in front of Sarah, as if she could hide what her friend was doing. It was too late, though.

"I was going to ask you where you've been the last few Tuesdays," I said, "but I guess I have my answer."

"Oh my gosh, Ash. I'm sorry. I just—"

"Hey, I get it. Who needs Jesus when you have boys that'll suck on your neck?"

I knew I was being mean, but I couldn't stop myself. She was breaking her parents' rules and lying and skipping out on FCS meetings—things I never did—but she didn't seem to feel lost at all. On top of that, this little freshman had a boyfriend, someone she liked enough to sneak around with, and I'd just been through a breakup. I was lonely and she wasn't. I was struggling and she wasn't. And it was so easy to tear her down a little.

Sarah's round face turned tomato red. "You aren't going to . . ."

"Tell your parents? No," I said. "If you feel comfortable telling lies, why should I stop you? Just remember, though. They might not know what you're doing, but God does."

Both Sarah and Lee watched me as I walked to the sink and washed my hands. When I looked up into the mirror, I realized there was one other person in the bathroom with us. Kellie Gaynor, in all of her black-clad glory, was standing in the corner, smoking a cigarette while she glared at me. I rolled my eyes at her.

I feel no regret about how I judged Kellie Gaynor back then. If anything, she ended up being worse than I thought.

When I finished, I grabbed a paper towel and dried my hands. "You'd better get back to class," I told Sarah and Lee. "Or else you'll have another lie to tell."

Neither of them said a word to me as I walked out of the bathroom. I knew the bell would be ringing in a few minutes, and I hoped that if I walked back slowly enough, Mr. Shockley wouldn't have time to make me pick a song from my phone to analyze.

At first I didn't think twice about the silhouette of the boy standing in the computer lab doorway. Until I heard the popping.

I froze, right in the middle of the hallway. I'd been hunting with my dad enough times to know what that sound was.

Gunshots.

Gunshots a few feet from me.

Gunshots in my high school.

It didn't make sense at first, which is why I just stood there, watching as ▮▮▮▮▮, his back to me, fired into the computer lab. I couldn't stop staring at his back, blankly wondering why he would shoot at *computers* of all things. Because the idea of him shooting people didn't quite register.

Not until I looked down, at the sliver of classroom visible between his feet, and saw blood spreading across the carpet.

That's when I ran. But it was like the way you run in a dream, when you feel like you are running as hard and fast as you can but you aren't getting anywhere. The bathroom wasn't actually that far from the computer lab, but it felt like it took forever to get there. Up ahead, coming from the other end of the hall, I saw two more people, Coach Nolan and Miles Mason, and I opened my mouth to shout to them.

But before the words left my mouth, I felt something hit me—hard—in the middle of my lower back. I tumbled forward in what felt like slow motion. I don't remember if I tried to stand up after I hit the ground. I just know that I closed my eyes and started to pray as more gunshots fired in the hallway. There was shouting and running and then something heavy fell on top of me and I gasped.

"Shh," a harsh voice hissed in my ear. "Don't. Move."

It was Miles Mason. A kid I'd never given the time of day. He was a couple years younger than me and, by all accounts, a bad seed. He was one of VCHS's most notorious troublemakers—certain to be held back a year because he'd missed so much school while being suspended. He spent more time in detention than in class. Miles Mason was the kind of kid I warned younger students to stay clear of.

And there he was, throwing himself on top of me. Protecting me.

I lay as still as I could, playing dead beneath Miles and trying not to think about why I couldn't feel my legs. I opened my eyes just a little, peering through my lashes, and realized we were right near the girls' bathroom. I saw a pair of shoes, ██████ shoes, walk inside.

Where I'd left Sarah and Lee a few minutes ago.

I held my breath and tried not to sob as I heard more gunshots. And then a pause.

And then I heard a conversation that changed my life.

"What's this?" It was his voice. "A cross necklace? Who the hell wears this ugly-ass cross necklace?"

"Me."

The voice was strong. Not quavering or scared. And I knew it was Sarah's voice. It had to be. It could only have been Sarah.

"Yours?" he asked.

"Yes. It's mine. Can I have it back?"

"You think Jesus is looking out for you now?"

"I do."

Pop. Pop.

The next few minutes are still a blur. There was yelling and crashing and footsteps and Miles whispering for me to not move, don't move. But I couldn't even if I'd wanted to. And then he climbed off me and there were sirens and police officers and blood and an EMT asking me my name.

The next clear memory is hours later, after I woke up from surgery. My parents and my little sister, Tara, were all there, hugging me and crying, and a doctor told me I'd been shot in the spine and I might not be able to walk again.

I'd have to deal with my feelings about all of that later. First, I had to tell everyone what I'd heard. I had to know what happened to Sarah, because I needed to apologize to her.

"Sarah McHale?" the detective who had come to ask me questions in my hospital room said. "Unfortunately . . ."

He didn't have to finish the sentence.

I'd heard Sarah's last words, though. They were brave and defiant as she declared her devotion to the Lord. Just a few minutes before, I'd been shaming her for not being the kind of Christian I was, but then she was the one to stand up to this monster, to use her last moments refusing to deny her faith. I don't think I would have been strong enough to do that.

I told everyone who would listen about what Sarah had done. The police, her parents, our preacher. I also told them about Miles, being the hero I never would have expected. And I vowed from that day on to never be the judgmental person I'd been before. That wasn't what being a Christian was supposed to be about. That wasn't what God wanted from me.

And for the first time in months, I felt like I had some clarity. Yes, my life was upside down and I was going to have to learn how to fit into this new reality, but I felt like God was guiding me again. I knew what He wanted from me. And I knew the first step was to forgive. Forgive myself for the person I had been, for the way I'd treated Sarah the last time I'd seen her, and to forgive the boy who shot me, because being angry at him would solve nothing.

The only person I've had a hard time forgiving is Kellie Gaynor.

Shortly after the shooting, she started telling people that the cross necklace police had found in the girls' bathroom was hers. That she was the one who had spoken to ███████. I don't know why she lied. It's not like anyone would believe her, anyway. Kellie was an angry, rude person who'd never stepped into a church in Virgil County as far as I knew. So for her to try and take that away from Sarah, to take her last moments of bravery from her . . .

I don't wish Kellie Gaynor ill. But I want nothing to do with her. And I hope she thinks about her lies every day and regrets them.

It's not super logical, I know, that I could forgive a boy who put a bullet in my back but not Kellie. Maybe it's that I already had bad feelings about her and she just proved me right. Maybe it's that her lies made a mockery of my faith and tried to damage a moment that meant so much to me. Maybe it's that she could suffer the way I had, the way the other survivors had, and still bring herself to fabricate stories and take something away from the dead.

Or it could just be that by the time I found out what she was doing, I was all out of forgiveness.

When that boy shot me, it was random. He didn't know me. He was younger than me, and I don't think we'd had a single class together. He was just messed up and angry, and I was there. But something about what Kellie did feels personal. She tried to take something away from Sarah. And, because what Sarah did had resolidified my own faith, had been my light in the darkness after the shooting, it felt as if she was taking it from me, too.

I'm sure God would want me to forgive her. I'm sure that's what I'm supposed to do. But it's not something I've been able to just yet.

I stayed in the hospital for several weeks. I finished my classes there while doing physical therapy and trying to get used to my new life on wheels. Honestly, I think that transition was harder on my parents than it was on me. I'm not going to say it was easy or that I didn't get frustrated quite a bit, especially in those first months, but I was alive. God had watched out for me, and I knew I shouldn't take that for granted. I finally understood that He had a plan, and this was part of it.

And alongside all of the struggle, there were also good things that happened to me after the shooting. First, Logan and I got back together. He visited me in the hospital every night, driving an hour each way just to see me after work. By the end of the summer, we were engaged. On Valentine's Day of the next year, a month before the one-year anniversary of the shooting, we got married. And six months ago, I gave birth to a beautiful little girl, Miriam.

The other thing that happened was that I finally figured out what I wanted out of my life. And two years ago, I started applying to nursing school. The nurses I knew when I was in the hospital kept me comfortable and sane and held my hand when things got really tough. I want to be that person. In a strange way, getting shot was the light I needed toward my path.

I don't want to romanticize what happened to me or the other victims that day. I feel like I need to emphasize again that it wasn't easy. Sometimes it's still not. Some days I still get upset, thinking about the things I used to be able to do. Some days, especially in the spring, memories of the shooting keep me awake at night. I've had to forbid my dad and sister from ever talking about hunting in my presence, because it instantly makes me think of the sound of those gunshots.

But, at the same time, I have a good life. I hear so often from people that if they went through what I have, if they were disabled or in a wheelchair, they don't think they could go on. But if I let myself feel that way, I would have missed so much good. My family and my future and my friends—Lee and Eden and Miles and Denny, the other survivors who have come to mean so much to me— there are so many wonderful things in my life that I am eternally grateful for.

There were a lot of tragedies the day of the shooting, but I am not one of them. I have found peace and beauty and a renewed sense of faith. I am not someone to be pitied or mourned, because I survived, and I found my place in the world. I am able to wake up every morning, smile at my husband, hold our little girl, and feel certain that I am on the path God intended for me.

Miles Mason and a group of surgeons may have been the ones to save my life, but forgiveness—that's what kept it worth living.

With love,
Ashley Chambers-Osborne

XXX

Ashley was the one who started the story about Sarah. How had I not known that?

I'd never been sure exactly how the myth began. I'd just assumed that it started and ended with that cross necklace the police had found in the bathroom. That they assumed it was Sarah's, given her family and church connections, but I'd thought the rest of the story had just been spun out of a real-life game of telephone, passed around town, getting bigger and bigger until Sarah became a saintlike figure.

But Ashley had started it all. She'd overheard something and, in all of the chaos, thought it was Sarah. But I knew it hadn't been. Because I'd been with Sarah, squeezed into a stall, looking her right in the eye. I'd been so focused on her, on the sound of my heartbeat, that I hadn't remembered hearing anything else around us.

Now I knew that, for Kellie, it hadn't just been about some necklace. It had been about her words. *Her* words given to someone else. She'd been branded a liar not just about that piece of jewelry but about the way she'd used her voice. She'd been made an outcast and her words had been used to make Sarah a hero.

Don't judge me for saying this, but while Ashley's letter made me feel worse for Kellie, it also made me feel a little relieved. Because it meant this whole thing wasn't entirely my fault for not speaking up. I still felt guilty, of course. I'll probably always feel guilty. But Ashley's assumptions about what she'd overheard were to blame, too.

But the main thing Ashley's letter did was reaffirm my decision to try and get the truth out there.

Not everyone was on board for that, though.

Miles spotted the note tucked beneath my windshield wiper before I did. We were leaving school on a Tuesday afternoon in early April. I'd stayed after class to get help from my English teacher. We were reading *Othello*, and despite my love of theater, Shakespeare was still kind of out of my depth. I was hoping to get some clarity on a few passages I'd highlighted.

Miles had waited for me in the cafeteria, and once I was done, we headed out to the student parking lot together. It was nearly empty.

"You've got a note," Miles said, pointing to the folded piece of paper on my windshield.

"Weird." I unfolded it. The handwriting was large and the letters were round. Miles shifted next to me, coming to read over my shoulder.

Leanne,

I'm sorry I missed you. I was hoping we could have a chat. Come by the church sometime or give me a call.

Brother Lloyd

"Why was he at the school?" Miles asked.

I folded up the note and shoved it into my pocket. "No idea. Maybe he's doing something with the Fellowship of Christian Students."

"Don't they meet in the mornings?"

I shrugged.

"It sounds like he was waiting for you," Miles said. "That's creepy."

"I'm sure it's fine," I said. Honestly, I was far less freaked out about the idea of Brother Lloyd waiting in the school parking lot than I was about *why* he was waiting. If he wanted to talk to me, that meant Sarah's parents had probably told him what had happened at their house a couple weeks earlier.

Brother Lloyd was the preacher at Virgil County Baptist. Even though I didn't go to church there, I'd met him several times. He'd officiated Ashley's wedding and spoken at the funerals of several of the shooting victims. Including Sarah's.

He'd seemed like a nice enough guy, if a little pushy. Growing up, anytime he'd seen Sarah and me together, he'd tried very hard to convince me to join their congregation, something I know embarrassed Sarah, who'd made a point to never pressure me about church stuff. And even though I never did join their church, he was still very friendly whenever we crossed paths.

Somehow I didn't think this was just a social call, though. He wanted to talk about Sarah, and I doubted we'd be in agreement during that conversation.

"You gonna call him?" Miles asked as we climbed into my truck.

"No. I think he just wants to talk about what I told the McHales."

"Mm."

"Speaking of," I said as I turned the truck out of the parking lot. "Have you thought any more about that favor I asked you? About writing the letter?"

He sighed. "I dunno, Lee."

"Come on," I said. "Denny and Ashley have already done it. And Eden's going to. Please."

"No one wants to hear what I've got to say."

"I do."

He frowned and looked away, the conversation clearly over, whether I liked it or not. For the most part, Miles had gotten his anger under control. But I knew that old fury was still inside of him. If he was pushed too far, it might awaken. I wasn't in the mood for an argument, so I let it go for the moment. We could come back to it later.

We *would* come back to it later.

Once we were parked in my driveway, I slid out of the truck and was halfway up the steps when Miles said my name. I turned back and saw him, still standing by my truck.

"Be careful," he said.

"What do you mean?"

He shrugged. "I dunno. This Brother Lloyd dude and the McHales . . . just be careful, okay? Don't get chased out of town or anything."

"That's not going to happen, Miles."

And I was right. It didn't happen. Not exactly. But still. Maybe I should've listened to him.

XXX

I didn't find out what people were saying about Kellie Gaynor until the start of the summer, about a month and a half after the shooting.

I'd had Mom take me to visit Ashley in the hospital. She'd gotten my number from Sarah's parents, and even though we hadn't known each other well at the time, she'd sent me a message to see how I was doing. She was the one in the hospital, the one going through physical therapy and adjusting to her new wheel-chair, but she was checking on me.

We'd texted back and forth for a few weeks. That's when the text chain between the five of us had gotten started. Ashley was the one to bring us together. She'd been the one to reach out to all of us, to create a network for all of the survivors, so that we had a safe space to yell or vent or cry when no one else could handle what was going on in our heads.

All of the survivors but Kellie, of course.

I didn't know why she'd been left out of the group at the time. I'd assumed it was because Ashley hadn't found a way to get ahold of her number yet. Or maybe that's just what I wanted to believe. I'd known people in town were angry with Kellie about something. I'd seen some of the harassment firsthand. But I was still very much in the dark about so many things that had happened during the shooting.

Or things people *said* had happened.

It had been weeks before I'd even heard about the rumors regarding Sarah. Mom had worked hard to keep most of the gossip and news away from me. At the time I hated her for it, but I think I understand why now. It was just so much. It was everywhere and constant, and I was barely getting by as it was. I felt like I was always either sobbing or screaming, and the only times I felt any sense of calm were when I was with the others.

Which was why I wanted to visit Ashley. I'd had to beg Mom to take me. She hadn't wanted to at first. She thought the hospital might be too much for me, and as much as I resented her for coddling me, she wasn't wrong. Walking through those sterile halls, hearing coughing patients, crying families, it all just reminded me of inevitable death.

But, hey, what didn't?

Mom dropped me off and went to run errands, promising she'd be back in exactly an hour. I found Ashley's room with the help of a nurse. She was sitting in her wheelchair, dressed in some comfy-looking purple pajamas, and she'd just turned on the TV when I walked in. She turned and grinned at me when I tapped on the open door.

"Lee!" she said. "Come in, come in! Oh my gosh, you cut your hair!"

I reached up and touched the soft fluff at the top of my head, barely long enough to call a pixie cut. The hairdresser had had no choice but to buzz most of it off after I'd attacked it with the kitchen scissors a few weeks earlier. "Yeah. I, um, didn't like it long anymore."

"It looks nice. Very edgy," she said. "Guess what I'm doing right now."

"Watching TV?"

"Well, yeah," she said. "But not just any TV. Saturday morning cartoons. Do you have any idea how long it's been since I've watched Saturday morning cartoons? Because I don't even think I remember the last time."

"Me either," I said, glancing up at the television screen. It was some show I didn't recognize. "I don't think I even know what airs on Saturday mornings anymore."

"Let's find out," she said.

You'd think it would've been weirder, seeing her for the first time since the shooting. Especially since we weren't friends before. I expected things to be awkward or depressing. She was still in the hospital, after all. And maybe there was a little bit of unease at first, on my part, but that faded fast. We watched cartoons for a while, Ashley occasionally asking me about the other survivors: how Denny's physical therapy was going, if I'd talked to Miles recently. She told me about one of the cute male nurses and how she was finishing out her senior year with a tutor.

I think one reason it felt so difficult to be around people back then—and even now sometimes—is that they only had two responses to the shooting. They either wanted to talk about it constantly, ask questions, hear the details, or they wanted to pretend it hadn't happened at all. Like maybe if no one mentioned it, I'd forget. Ashley didn't do either of those things. We didn't talk much about the shooting, but when it came up, we didn't try to ignore it, either.

And when it did come up, toward the end of our visit, it gave me my answer about why Ashley had only connected five of the six survivors.

"It's crazy about Sarah, huh?"

The question seemed to come out of nowhere. I turned away from the television and focused on Ashley, but she wasn't looking at me. Her eyes were still on the cartoons, but I noticed that she was twisting locks of her dirty-blond hair around her fingers.

"Yeah," I said. "It's . . . it's something."

"She was so brave," Ashley said.

I shifted uncomfortably in my chair. Brave. It had only been six weeks, and I already hated that word. At the time, I was convinced the only one of us who had really been brave was Miles, and even he changed the subject any time someone mentioned how he'd thrown himself on Ashley.

Sarah hadn't been brave. Sarah had been terrified.

But before I could even think about how to bring that up to Ashley, she continued. "It's disgusting what Kellie Gaynor is trying to do."

I blinked at her, confused. "Kellie?"

Ashley turned her head to face me then. "I figured, of all people, you'd be the most angry. Well, you and Sarah's parents."

"What are you talking about?"

"You haven't heard?" Ashley asked. "Oh. I assumed you . . . Well, prepare to be furious, I guess. Kellie has been going around telling everyone that necklace—the one the police found in the bathroom—was hers."

Her words settled slowly, bringing with them a sinking realization. I'd known the necklace wasn't Sarah's as soon as I heard the rumors, but I'd never considered who it might have actually belonged to. We lived in a rural, religious community, and that was a highly trafficked girls' bathroom. That cross necklace could have been lost earlier in the day. It could have belonged to any girl at VCHS.

I'm ashamed to admit this, but I'd never even considered that it might have been Kellie's, even though she was the only other person in the bathroom with Sarah and me when the shooting happened. She didn't strike me as the kind of girl who'd wear a cross around her neck, so I'd never put those puzzle pieces together.

But she was saying it was hers.

And I knew it wasn't Sarah's.

That was why she was being harassed. That was why Ashley had excluded her from our survivors' network.

Why we were five instead of six.

"I know," Ashley said, clearly misinterpreting the look on my face. "It's ridiculous. I can't believe anyone would be awful enough to try and take this away from Sarah. But at least no one believes her. I mean, who would believe *her* of all people . . . ? Lee?"

I was on my feet, though I didn't remember standing up. I cleared my throat. Then did it again. But the tightness there didn't want to go away. I was surprised and confused. I should've corrected her then, but it would've meant explaining the whole truth about Sarah, and I wasn't sure how to even begin with that yet.

"It's been an hour," I managed to say. "Mom is probably waiting for me. I should go."

"Oh, okay," Ashley said. "Perfect timing, actually. My parents should be here soon. They promised to bring me Long John Silver's for lunch."

I raised an eyebrow at her.

"What?" she asked. "My sister doesn't get it, either, but I swear their fish is really good. Especially if you put some vinegar on it. Oof." She shook her head. "Crap, now I'm starving. I hope they get here soon."

I walked over to her and leaned down to give her a hug. Her arms wrapped tightly around my shoulders. In the years that followed, I'd come to regard Ashley's hugs as the best in the world. But that day, her embrace didn't warm me the way it eventually would. I felt cold. Numb.

Looking back, it feels like I should've been more upset. Or angry. Or guilty. This realization about Kellie should have impacted me more than it did. But I think my body and mind were so exhausted by that point that this bit of news just pushed me over the edge into emptiness.

"Hey," Ashley said as I pulled away and moved to leave the room. "Take care of yourself, okay? If you need anything, call me."

I nodded. A lot of people said things like that, but Ashley actually meant it. She was there for all of us.

Most of us.

I don't know how she feels about me right now, after everything that's happened. I don't know if we'll ever get back to being the kind of friends we were before I started writing this letter. And God, if she ever reads this . . .

Anyway, there is one thing I do know. And that's that, despite the issues with Sarah and Kellie, I'm grateful to Ashley. I'll always appreciate how much she cared, how genuine and giving she was. Even if, these days, there's a good chance she hates me.

After leaving two separate notes on my truck's windshield and sending one (ignored) friend request on Facebook, Brother Lloyd finally managed to catch up with me. I knew it would happen eventually. Our town was small, and if you really wanted to corner someone, you could track them down pretty easily.

I was running errands for my mom on a Saturday afternoon. I'd popped into the drugstore, which was right down the street from Virgil County Baptist. My guess is that Brother Lloyd saw me drive by from one of the church's windows and hurried down the street to wait for me. Or maybe I'm being paranoid. Maybe he really did just happen to be right outside the drugstore when I walked out with a plastic bag full of tampons and Mom's favorite cheap makeup products.

"Leanne," he said, beaming brightly at me. Brother Lloyd is a short, slim man with blond hair and a receding hairline. What he lacks in hair, though, he makes up for in attire. Or at least he did that day. He was wearing a nice baby-blue button-down with a striped tie and black slacks. In a town where putting on a clean pair of unripped jeans is considered dressing up, this was verging on too fancy. "It's so nice to run into you."

"Hi, Brother Lloyd," I said, moving past him toward my truck.

He followed me, of course. "I've been trying to get ahold of you. I wanted to see how you were doing."

"Yeah. I got the notes you left." My keys were in my hand now, and I was trying to figure out how difficult it would be to extract myself without coming across as rude.

"Good, good. Glad you saw them. I was beginning to wonder when I hadn't heard from you, but I'm sure you're busy with school and all that." His smile slipped into something more determined then, and he cleared his throat. "Listen, Leanne, the McHales came and spoke to me."

I unlocked the driver-side door and pulled it open, not making eye contact with Brother Lloyd as I tossed the plastic shopping bag onto the other seat. "That's kind of what I figured."

"They're worried about you," he said. "And I must say, I am, too. Some of the things you've been saying lately . . . well, they have me concerned."

"Concerned," I repeated as I hoisted myself into the truck.

The preacher moved quickly, positioning himself in front of the door so that I couldn't shut it. He was smiling, though, an expression of forced kindness. As if that was somehow going to make me feel less uneasy about this situation.

"Yes, concerned," he said. "It just doesn't seem like you've been yourself lately."

"With all due respect, sir," I said, "you barely know me."

"You're right," he admitted. "But I knew Sarah very well."

I gritted my teeth. I hated when other people tried to tell me how well they knew Sarah. They didn't. No one knew her like I did. They knew an idea they'd built up in their heads. A caricature of a pious girl devoid of flaws. Brother Lloyd may have seen Sarah's face every Sunday at church. He may have been the one to baptize her. But she didn't share the things with him that she shared with me. I remember the eulogy he gave at her funeral, the way he'd described her. He didn't know her *very well*.

I wasn't even sure he truly believed he had.

"The stories you've been telling about her lately," he continued, "I know you wouldn't be making up these kinds of things about her if something wasn't going on with you. So instead of lying about Sarah, why don't you talk to me about what's really wrong?"

"I'm not lying about Sarah," I said. "I told her parents the truth."

"Come on, Leanne," he said, crossing his arms over his chest. "We both know better than that."

"Brother Lloyd, I should be going."

He acted as if he hadn't heard me. "Sarah McHale is a hero to a lot of people, you know. Not just around here, but all over the country. She's inspired a lot of teenagers to recommit to their faith. There's even a Christian rock song about her. I think it's called 'Her Cross Necklace.' Have you heard it?"

My fists were clenched around the steering wheel. "Yes."

"Nice song, huh? Not really my genre. I still mostly listen to gospel because I'm not as cool as you young folks but . . ." He shrugged. "Anyway. Her story means a lot to people. You know that. Why would you try to take that away from them? From Sarah?"

"Because it wasn't her necklace," I said. "And she didn't say anything to—"

Brother Lloyd waved a hand to silence me. "Calm down. Calm down. I know you've been through a lot, Leanne, but that's no reason to lash out at others. And especially no reason to say these things about Sarah, who isn't here to defend herself."

"I need to go," I said, more firmly this time.

"All right," he said. "But before you do, please hear me out. I'm not trying to bother you. I mean it when I say I'm just concerned. If word gets out that you're saying these things . . . people aren't going to take too kindly to it."

"You mean if you and the McHales tell anyone I'm saying these things."

"Well, I don't see why we ever have to speak of it again if I have your word it won't be going any further. If you don't plan on telling these lies to anyone else, then—"

"They aren't lies. And I won't promise that. I want people to know the truth."

Brother Lloyd sighed and bowed his head. "I'm sorry to hear you feel that way. I hope you change your mind, but in the meantime, my congregation will be praying for you."

And as I drove away a minute later, headed back down the street and past his church, I couldn't help but think about how much that last sentence had sounded like a threat.

SARAH MCHALE

So I know I said I was focusing more on Sarah than the other victims, but I'm starting to realize that I've told you a lot about who she wasn't and almost nothing about who she was.

Sarah was always an extrovert. She loved people, loved attention, loved to be the girl making everyone either laugh or fall in love with her. For about a month in sixth grade she was obsessed with astrology, and she took great pride in being a Leo. I, on the other hand, was a Cancer. "That's why you're such a hermit," she'd tease. "You'd never leave the house if it wasn't for me."

She wasn't wrong. I had the best time when we stayed in, usually holed up in her bedroom, and watched movies or played board games. I liked it most when it was just us. But Sarah always wanted to go places, do things, be seen. And I was always dragged along.

Maybe *dragged* is a harsh word. I chose to go wherever she did, because the alternative of spending time without her was too painful. Her parents always joked that we were "joined at the hip," and there were times when I wished that were literal. Sarah was my only close friend, the only person I felt totally at ease with, and there were times—especially in middle school—where I lived in constant fear that she'd find another friend, a more out-going, enthusiastic girl that she liked more than me.

So wherever she went, I followed.

Looking back, maybe our friendship wasn't always the healthiest. Sarah could have a bit of a domineering personality. Like the time when we were nine and she insisted on cutting my bangs.

"I'm not sure," I told her. "My mom might get mad."

"She won't when she sees how good it looks," Sarah insisted. "You'd look so much better with bangs. And I know what I'm doing. I saw how to do it on the internet."

"I don't know, Sarah."

"Trust me," she said, already wielding a pair of scissors.

I did not look better with straight bangs and, yes, my mom was mad. I wore butterfly clips in my hair for months, waiting for it to grow out. Sarah, however, maintained that it was a worthwhile adventure for us both.

"At least we both learned something," she said. "You learned that bangs aren't for you, and I learned that cutting hair isn't as easy as it looks."

Sometimes her overwhelming personality got us both in trouble, but other times, I was grateful for it. Like when we were in seventh grade and some boys started picking on me.

I was an awkward-looking kid. Too tall. All knees and elbows. Angles and no curves. Actually, I guess not much has changed now, other than my hair. Back then it was long and stick straight with not even a hint of volume. Sarah, on the other hand, was already beautiful, even without the makeup stash she started keeping in her locker that year. There were a lot of jokes about Sarah only being nice to the "ugly girl" because she felt bad.

"Lee's lucky Sarah is a good Christian," we overheard Evan Samuels saying during lunch. "Because clearly that's just charity." That, being our friendship.

It was a stupid insult made by a twelve-year-old boy, but it still stung.

Sarah, never one to shy away from conflict, marched right over to the boy and said, loud enough for all his friends to hear, "Maybe you're the one who's lucky I'm a good Christian. Because it's the only thing keeping me from kicking your ass."

Evan was so stunned (I doubt a girl had ever threatened to kick his ass before) that he didn't say a word as Sarah walked back over to me, looped her arm through mine, and said, "Come with me to get an extra slice of pizza." Like nothing had just happened.

Even though she was always trying to push me into doing more with my appearance—from failed attempts to curl my hair to raiding my closet and telling me that nothing I owned was "flattering to my body type"—if anyone else talked about my looks in even a slightly negative way, Sarah was there to shut it down.

I still don't really care about clothes or makeup. Most days I forget to even run a comb through my hair. But every so often, when I'm getting ready for school, I'll pull out the only lip gloss I own. It's this sheer, rosy color, and even though I think it looks a little silly on me, I know Sarah would've loved it.

I can almost hear her now.

"See, Lee! You look so pretty! Now, if you'll just let me do something with those eyebrows . . ."

God, I miss her.

It's always a relief to get out of Virgil County, even just for a day or so. And after my uncomfortable encounter with Brother Lloyd, the weekend—and my brief escape—couldn't come soon enough. Back in December, I'd promised to visit Eden at college before her finals began.

It was a few hours' drive, but I'd packed my truck with a change of clothes, some snacks for the road, and a console full of Mom's old CDs.

Mom wasn't home from work yet by the time I left on Friday afternoon, but she texted me. Be safe. And you'd better not be reading this while you're driving! I replied that I wasn't on the road yet and promised I'd call when I got to Eden's dorm. Normally she would have been far more anxious about letting me make this kind of trip on my own, but I think she was not-so-secretly hoping I'd fall in love with Eden's campus and change my mind about heading to Los Angeles after graduation.

I parked my truck in the parking lot Eden had directed me to in her email a few days earlier, then I headed toward a large brick building with a sign over the door declaring the name of the dormitory.

I pulled out my phone and texted Eden, letting her know I was downstairs. It was a little after eight and already dark out. I could see other college students walking across the quads, wearing hoodies with the school's logo on the front. Boys laughed and girls called to one another as they journeyed off in different directions, moving toward one Friday night destination or another.

I stood awkwardly outside of Eden's building, worried someone might pass by and think I looked suspicious, just standing there by the locked door. Even though I was dressed just like everyone else in my oversized gray sweatshirt and distressed jeans, I felt like someone should have noticed the uneasy, lingering stranger. No one even looked twice at me, but I couldn't help thinking they should have.

Maybe I looked normal, but so had the guy who brought a gun into my school.

I hadn't gone too far down this spiral, at least, when a short girl with shoulder-length hot-pink hair stepped out of the building. She glanced around for a minute before her dark brown eyes rested on me. "Lee?" she asked.

I looked her over for a second. This wasn't Eden, obviously, but I had a pretty good idea of who she was, and I was excited to meet her.

"Are you Jenny?" I asked.

"Yes!" She shoved the door the rest of the way open and bolted toward me, arms outstretched for a welcoming hug.

But between her too-fast movements and the slam of the door behind her, I couldn't help but let out a yelp and flinch away.

Jenny stopped, frozen in her tracks, a look of regret passing over her round face. "Oh crap. I'm sorry. I should've known better. Eden also doesn't like it when people . . . You know what? Let me start over and introduce myself like a normal person." She straightened, smiled, and extended her hand. "Hi. I'm Eden's girlfriend, Jenny."

"Jenny Stewart-Goo," I said, taking her hand.

"Just Jenny is fine," she said. "I take it that means Eden talks about me."

"All good things," I assured her.

"Same for you," she said. "Come on. Eden sent me down to grab you. She's upstairs working on a presentation. She should be finishing up soon, though."

Jenny pulled what looked like an ID from the back pocket of her jeans. She waved it in front of a square sensor next to the door, which beeped to let us know it was unlocked. As she put the ID away, I caught a quick glance at the photo, which had Eden's face on it.

"This way," she said, leading me to the stairs. "Unfortunately, she's on the top floor and there's no elevator."

I wasn't bothered by this, as it gave me extra time to talk to Jenny.

"So David Goo is your dad?"

She looked over her shoulder at me as we hit the first landing. Her dark eyebrows raised with surprise. "You know who my dad is?"

"I'm actually a fan of his," I admitted. "I've read like four of his plays."

David Goo is a Korean American playwright based in Los Angeles. I'd stumbled across one of his plays on the syllabus of a drama school I'd been researching last year, and I'd been blown away. He writes the kind of characters you could lose yourself in. The kind of characters with layers you can peel back, with motivations and backstories and relationships an actor can wrap around themselves, to become someone completely new but equally real. Plays like his are the reason I want to do theater.

I was also a little bit obsessed with Jenny's mom, Irina Stewart, who's an acting coach in Los Angeles. But I decided not to mention that, in case she thought I was a stalker or something.

"Wow," she said. "You're the first person I've met in Indiana who's had any idea who he is. But Eden did tell me you're moving to LA this fall, right?"

I nodded.

"I'll be heading back there after graduation. So if you need anything or just want a buddy to complain about traffic with, hit me up. Maybe I can introduce you to my dad."

I smiled at her, pressing my lips tight together to keep from shrieking with excitement at the prospect.

A minute later, we were on the top floor, and Jenny led us

down a short hallway, stopping at a door near the very end. She drummed her fingers lightly against the wood instead of knocking, then turned the knob.

I'd heard people say college dorm rooms were small, but I still wasn't prepared. Mom and I didn't live in a big house by any means, but my bedroom, for just me, was the size of the room Eden and her roommate shared. There was hardly an inch of wall left uncovered. The decor was a mix of posters featuring different country music artists, anime wall scrolls, what looked like a few old protest signs, and drawings that I recognized as being done by Eden.

There were two beds—both neatly made—two dressers, and two desks. Sitting at one of them, her eyes transfixed on a laptop screen, was a tall girl with dark blond hair. Eden stood behind her, chewing her nails.

Neither of them looked up when we entered. I remembered Jenny saying Eden was working on something, so I didn't interrupt. Instead, I just stood by the door, unsure of where I should go. While I could guess which of these roommates had chosen what decor (Eden had talked about Misty, the country music–loving activist, several times in our emails), it was spread pretty evenly around the square box of a room, making it impossible to know which side belonged to which.

I'd initially planned to follow Jenny's cue, but she was no help. She'd moved to stand next to Eden, clearly reading the laptop screen over the other girl's shoulder.

After a second, the blond girl, who I could only guess was Misty, sat back in her chair. "It's good."

"Yeah?" Eden asked. "I don't know . . ."

"Well, I do," Misty said. "It's a solid presentation. I have a few tweaks—mostly just what order you go over everything in. And there's some new research that was just published about gun violence that I think you could work in. But I can make those edits tonight, if you want. Overall, I think this is even better than your usual presentation. It's really powerful."

Eden didn't sound like she was excited about this, though. "Thanks, Misty."

"I'm sure it's great," I said. "Your presentations always are."

She glanced over at me and gave a small smile.

For the past few months, Eden's been giving speeches at colleges around Indiana and Illinois. Her focus is usually on campus safety and gun control, though of course she weaves in discussion of the shooting, too. A couple of her speeches have been filmed and are online, so you might have seen them.

I stumbled on a recording of one of her speeches one night when I was googling the massacre. It was strange to watch her stand on a stage and speak so calmly, so directly, about the shooting. Eden had always been quiet and uncomfortable with too much attention on her. But with an audience in front of her and a PowerPoint presentation projected behind her, she became a different Eden.

It seemed like she'd come such a long way in the last three years. Like she had it all together.

"Come on," Jenny said. "You can worry about the presentation another time. Lee is here."

"She's right," Misty said. "I'm staying in to work on some homework tonight. I'll make the edits and you can take a look later." She turned to me then and gave a quick wave. "Sorry. We're being rude. I'm—"

"Misty," I said. "I figured. I'm Lee."

"Nice to meet you," she said. "So what do y'all have planned for tonight?"

"Antonio—that friend I told you about from my freshman seminar—he's having a party at his house. Just off campus," Eden said, walking over to one of the dressers and sliding open the second drawer.

I noticed Misty and Jenny exchange a quick glance.

"Really?" Jenny asked. "I was thinking maybe we could stay on campus. Give Lee a taste of college life. There's a two-dollar movie playing in one of the auditoriums. And I think one of the independent theater groups is doing a show. I know you like theater, Lee."

"The campus newspaper gave it bad reviews," Eden said. She was still rummaging through the dresser drawer. "And the movie . . . it's one of those midnight movie things, right? We can go to the party first, then go to the movie after. I promised Antonio I'd at least stop by. We don't have to stay long." She pulled a cute dark green shirt from the drawer. "Is that okay, Lee?"

"I'm fine with whatever," I said, even though I really would have preferred to stay in this dorm room and just spend the evening catching up with my friend. We hadn't seen each other since

Christmas. But I also didn't want to be the one to say no. "I don't really have any cute clothes with me."

"It's okay," Eden said. "Most people will be dressed like you. I'm only changing because I have ink stains on this shirt."

Jenny grinned at her. "Like any true artist," she said.

Eden ducked her head, looking embarrassed but pleased. She pulled off her T-shirt and replaced it with the green top. Then she adjusted her glasses and shook out her wavy black hair. "Okay," she said. "Thanks for helping with the presentation, Misty."

"Anytime. You guys have fun," Misty said, and I noticed she looked meaningfully at Jenny when she added, "And call me if you need anything."

An hour later we were in a large house just off campus, sitting on a couch that smelled like sweat and beer as at least fifty other people moved around us, laughing and chatting while hip-hop music played from a speaker nearby.

As much as I wanted to relax, to have fun at my first college party, I couldn't help feeling a bit on edge. My eyes kept darting to the nearest exits, and the panicky part of my mind, that little voice that the anxiety meds never quite silenced, wondered how easy it would be to escape a space this crowded. If any of these people pulled out a weapon, how many of us would be lost?

If Eden was feeling similarly anxious, she didn't show it. She was sitting between Jenny and me, already on her second cup of vodka and Sprite. She'd offered to get me a drink, but I'd said no. The idea of having my reflexes slowed in an unfamiliar place, especially one so loud and crowded and with so few easily accessed escape routes—that is literally the stuff of nightmares for me.

I tried to distract myself by looking over at Jenny, who I noticed hadn't gotten a drink, either. "So is your dad working on anything new?" I asked her.

"Huh? Oh. I actually don't know. He's pretty private about his writing. I didn't know about his last play until he had a cast and a director."

"Are you like that, too?" I asked. "I know you write the scripts for *Calliope*, right?"

Jenny's face lit up. "You read our webcomic?"

"Of course I do," I said. "All of Eden's friends back home do. Well, except Denny. He can't see the illustrations. But I think Eden sends him the scripts, right?"

Eden nodded and took another sip of her drink.

"Wow," she said. "I hope you like it. I'm not nearly the writer my dad is but—"

"Are so," Eden said. "You're great."

"And you're biased." Jenny kissed her on the cheek, then looked back at me. "But, to answer your question, no. I'm the total opposite. I make about a million people read my scripts for *Calliope* before it's final. Including my dad, actually."

"I bet he gives great feedback."

She laughed. "Not really. He mostly just tells me it's great and how proud he is. My mom is the critical one."

Eden let out a breath. "No kidding." She turned to me. "Two

months ago, her mom sent us a two-thousand-word email breaking down all of the world-building problems in our series."

"Apparently we are very inconsistent in how magic is used." Jenny laughed. "I had no idea my mom was such a nerd, but it turns out she grew up playing Dungeons and Dragons and is a bit of a snob about fantasy."

"I've always wanted to play D and D," Eden admitted. "I've just . . . been too shy to find people I could play with, I guess."

"Aw," Jenny said. "Well, when you come visit me, I'll make Mom teach us. I'm sure you'd play a very sexy half-elf druid."

Eden snorted. "I was thinking more like a gnome. A girl gnome with a sword."

"Hey, that could be sexy, too."

They smiled at each other in that way that couples do, and I had to look away. Suddenly I was overwhelmed with this feeling of missing Miles. I'd seen him just a few hours ago, on our ride home from school, but the way Eden and Jenny looked at each other, the way they talked to each other, made me wish he was here.

I forced that feeling away as hard as I could. Miles and I were not a couple, and we weren't going to be.

After a minute, Eden and Jenny seemed to remember that I was there with them. I heard Eden clear her throat, and then Jenny said, "You'd like Dungeons and Dragons, Lee. It . . . involves acting. Sort of."

"Yeah," I said. "But it also involves math, right? With dice and stuff? That's not really my thing."

"Also any kind of acting in D and D would be improvised," Eden pointed out. "Which Lee hates."

"I don't hate improv," I said. "I'm just not good at it. I'm the kind of person who likes a script."

"I'm sure you'll get better at it when you start taking acting classes," Jenny said. She turned to Eden. "And since both Lee and I are going to be in LA come this fall, you had better come visit."

"I know, I know," Eden said.

"So you guys are going to do the long-distance thing?" I asked.

"We're . . . going to try," Eden said, taking a swig from her cup.

"We know it's not ideal," Jenny admitted. "But I don't have a job lined up—thank you, English major—and I can't afford to stay in Indiana without one, so I've got to move back in with my parents until I find something or opt for grad school."

"You're not quitting the webcomic, though, right?"

"Of course not," Jenny said. "*Calliope* is our baby. Our weird witch baby."

"With inconsistent magic use," Eden said. She said it like a joke, but something in her face seemed to tense as the words came out. It was a flicker of stress I'd seen there before, and it made me uneasy.

Jenny noticed, too. "Hey," she said, her voice a little softer. "I'm the one who does the writing, remember? If the story has faults, it's because of me. Not you. My mom had nothing but nice things to say about your illustrations."

"I know. I'm fine." She took another drink.

I was about to ask another question, try and change the subject, when a shadow passed over us. A large figure had stepped in front of the couch, specifically in front of Eden. I was so startled that I pushed back, pressing into the cushions. But Eden just looked up at him slowly; her eyes had a weary look to them that no one her age should ever have.

"You're that chick, right?" the guy standing in front of her said. "The anti-gun chick."

Jenny cut in before Eden could answer. "Back up, dude."

The guy ignored her. He was tall, dressed in a red T-shirt and jeans, with a baseball cap perched on his head. He had the wispy beginnings of a goatee, though it did nothing to mask the fact that he had a baby face. "So what? You just don't give a damn about the Constitution? The Second Amendment?" he asked.

"Oh my God," Jenny said, rolling her eyes. "Seriously, leave us alone. Go home and write some angry tweets or something."

"Stay out of it," the guy told Jenny. "We're talking here." He gestured to Eden, though she clearly wasn't doing any talking at all.

I wrapped my arms around myself and huddled as far into the corner of the couch as I could, already picking out the exits in my head. This guy was standing too close, his voice was too harsh. My brain was screaming, *Threat! Threat!*

I started imagining what it would be like to die right here. Would the whole world just be swallowed in black? Would it feel like sleeping? What would happen to my mom when she found out? Or Miles? Did it really matter since they were going to die one day, too?

Chill, I told myself. *It's fine. You're fine. You're not going to die at a house party. You can be an anxious nihilist later.*

I made myself look over at Eden, but I immediately regretted it. I'd expected her to snap back at this guy. To retort with all the facts and statistics I'd seen her use in her presentations. To be the stronger Eden, the girl she was onstage. But that's not what I saw.

She was curled in on herself much the same way I was, her head bent, her hands shaking. Shriveled. Scared. Sad.

"Do you have any clue how ignorant you sound when you give those speeches? You think taking away our guns is the answer?"

"She never said anything about taking away your guns," Jenny growled. "She advocates for harsher restrictions and for campus safety measures."

"Except her version of keeping campuses safe is no guns at all, even for those of us with permits," the guy said, giving in to the fact that Jenny wasn't going to stay out of this. "Which is stupid. I know what she went through at her high school. And if one teacher had had a gun in their desk, they could've stopped that kid."

"Are you kidding me?"

Eden stood up then. It was so abrupt that I jumped and the guy in front of us stumbled back a step in surprise.

"Yeah. You know what I went through." Her voice was so quiet I almost didn't hear it over the music and party chatter around us. "You know," she said, the words cracking in a way that told me she was on the verge of tears, "what it's like to open your eyes and see that everyone in your classroom is dead."

"They wouldn't be, though," the guy insisted, "if that teacher had been armed."

"Sure." Eden stepped past him and began walking toward the kitchen.

"Eden," Jenny called.

Eden glanced over her shoulder. "I'm just going to find Antonio. Tell him I showed up. I'll . . . I'll be back."

Jenny watched her go, and I could see that there was more than a hint of worry in her eyes.

Meanwhile, the gun guy turned to me. "So who are you?" he asked. "You anti-Constitution, too?"

Jenny responded before I could answer. "She's my cousin, and she's not involved in any of this, so leave her alone."

He looked at me, then at Jenny. "She's . . . your cousin?" he said, a note of obvious disbelief in his voice.

"My mom's white, dumb-ass," Jenny said. "And this conversation is over."

It took a few more minutes of Jenny shutting him down before the guy finally walked away. Eden still hadn't returned.

"Sorry for speaking for you," Jenny said once he was gone. "I'm sure you could handle yourself. I just . . . didn't want to keep arguing with him."

"No, I appreciate it," I said. "Eden's really strong to stand on a stage and relive what happened and argue for what she believes in. But I'm not quite there yet."

"Yeah," Jenny said, looking off toward the kitchen. "She's . . . she's strong."

We made awkward small talk for a while longer. I tried to ask more questions about her parents, about Los Angeles, but I could tell she was distracted, constantly casting an eye around the room in search of Eden, who'd never emerged from the kitchen.

Eventually we both left the couch and began moving around the living room, navigating through the crowd. "If we're going to make that midnight movie," Jenny said, "we'd better get going."

But we both knew the movie wasn't going to happen. There was just this feeling that the night had shifted into something darker. I don't know if it happened when the guy came over to us or in the moments before, when Eden's face had tensed as she talked about Jenny's mother's critique of their comic. But the whole mood of the evening had changed.

Eden wasn't in the kitchen. We found her twenty minutes later in one of the house's bedrooms, sitting in a corner with a bottle of vodka in hand while she watched two girls play video games on the TV. In the hour since we'd seen her, she'd clearly been drinking quite a bit.

"Eden," I said, moving toward her. "You okay? We were looking for you."

She looked up at me with glazed eyes. "Lee," she said. "I'm sorry. I'm ruining your visit." She tried to stand up, but her legs shook and she splashed some of her vodka onto the carpet. "We should go to the movie."

"We don't have to," I said. "Are you okay?"

But I knew the answer. I realized it when I looked over at Jenny, when I saw the sadness and exhaustion in her eyes. I could hear it in the way she sighed as she stepped forward and gently pulled her drunk girlfriend to her feet. Jenny knew, and now I did, too.

Eden was not okay.

X X X

I didn't know Eden before the shooting. Her cousin, Rosi, was in my grade and we were friendly, if not friends.

Rosi and Sarah had sat next to each other in several classes throughout the years, a side effect of alphabetically arranged seating charts, and they'd always gotten along. So once every couple of weeks, Rosi would sit at our little table during lunch. I'm not sure she ever sat at the same lunch table two days in a row, honestly. Rosi had friends from every clique, which meant there was always an empty seat for her, no matter what side of the cafeteria she was in the mood for.

Rosi was the first one who suggested I cut my hair short. We were sitting at the tiny round table near the vending machines, and she just looked at me, very seriously, and asked, "Have you ever thought about a pixie cut?"

"No way," I said. "I'd just end up looking like a boy."

"I don't think so." She leaned in, almost uncomfortably close to my face as she tilted her head from one side to the other, examining me. "Your face is very . . . angular. And you've got amazing cheekbones. I think you'd rock some super-short hair."

I can't say I didn't think of her that spring, the day I took a rusty pair of scissors and began hacking away at my hair. When Mom saw what I'd done, she rushed me over to her friend Gretchen, who worked at the local salon in town. We ended up buzzing all of my hair off, and as it began to grow in, I thought of Rosi.

In some ways, keeping it short now feels like a tiny memorial to her.

But this was supposed to be about Eden.

Eden came to Sarah's funeral, and I'd gone to Rosi's. We'd gravitated toward each other at both, as everyone around us tried to say how sorry they were and how glad they were that we, at least, were okay, and how God had a plan and so on and so forth. Eden was the only person there who I knew understood. Ashley and Denny were both still in the hospital, and this was before Miles had started climbing onto my roof at night.

We didn't even say anything as we exchanged numbers after the service for Rosi. She'd just handed me her phone and watched as I typed in my number. Mom had pulled me away almost as soon as I'd handed it back to her. But later that night, she texted me. It's Eden.

We started spending time together after that, particularly as the spring began to warm into that lovely space before summer when the air is still dry and the breeze is still cool and it feels nice to just lie in the grass. She'd pick me up in her van and we'd drive down to Wargin Park, where we'd sit by the pond all afternoon. She'd draw and I'd read plays—that was the summer I decided I wanted to be an actress—and no one bothered us there.

Most of those days by the lake have blended together in my mind now. Like a collage of pictures with no real chronology. We were there to escape, after all. To try and not feel or think for a little while. To fade into the background and leave this version of ourselves behind.

I could tell Eden was struggling with that, though. And in my collage of memories there's this one that stands out, in the center of the other pictures, larger and clearer, while the rest have tattered and faded with time.

We were sitting by the lake, under a large willow tree. I was on my stomach, eyes focused on the flimsy paperback copy of *The Crucible* I'd purchased at a thrift store a few days earlier. I could hear Eden's pencil scratching against her sketch pad a few feet away. I was trying to disappear. To lose myself in the text so that Lee didn't exist in that moment. But the sound of her vigorously erasing pulled me back to reality.

I could tell something was wrong, though I didn't want to ask. It was in the way she gripped the pencil, just a little too tight, and in the speed of her eraser scrubbing the page. When she was finished, she blew off the eraser dust and began sketching again. I went back to my book without a word.

But a few minutes later, she was erasing again, harder this time. And when I looked up at her, the pencil in her hand looked like it might break.

"Eden?" I asked tentatively.

"It's not perfect," she said, less to me and more to the page she was furiously scrubbing against. "I keep trying but it's not perfect."

"I'm sure it's great," I said. "You're a great artist."

But she wasn't listening to me. Her entire focus was on that paper, and it seemed like she was trying to erase everything she'd done, not just a messy line or two. I didn't understand. Why not just start on a new page if the drawing wasn't working?

"I don't . . . know . . . why . . . I *bother*!" She screamed the last word and dragged her eraser so hard against the drawing that the page tore beneath it.

I could sense the eruption before it came. I sat up and scrambled backward, toward the base of the tree. As Eden's eyes darkened and her lips pressed into a tight line, I fought my own urge to flee. Nearly everything set off my flight instinct back then. But I was trying to stay calm, stay logical and rational. Eden was just upset about her drawing. Eden wasn't a threat.

One of those things was correct. Eden wouldn't hurt me—I don't think she could hurt anyone, not physically—but this wasn't just about an imperfect drawing.

With a sharp tearing sound, Eden ripped the page out of her sketchbook. Then she was on her feet, running toward the water just a few yards away. I jumped up, not sure what she was planning to do.

"Eden!" I shouted.

But she stopped at the edge of the water. Then she unleashed this deep, pained yell that sent the ducks on the lake scattering and made me recoil, pressing my palms into my ears to black out the sound and the panic that came with it. I could see Eden's arms moving, tearing at the sheet of paper with large, violent motions. Then she hurled them all into the water, the tiny white slips floating across the dark surface of the lake. Like flower petals.

Eden kept screaming and her hands raised to her hair, grasping fistfuls of long, dark waves and pulling. It was the middle of a weekday and there was no one else around, thank God, but I knew I couldn't let her go on like this.

With my hands still covering my ears, I approached her. "Eden," I said. Then yelled. "Eden!"

When her screams quieted to heavy pants and her hands slowly unclenched from her hair, she turned to look at me. And it was like she was seeing me for the first time that day. Like she'd completely forgotten that I'd been there, right next to her, all morning. She stared at me for a long, silent moment, then, gingerly, stepped around me, moved past me, and headed back to the willow tree. She picked up her sketch pad and the backpack she used in place of a purse, and walked away. Leaving me alone at the park with no ride home.

I called and texted her, but Eden didn't respond. Eventually I had to call my mom and ask her to come get me after work.

Mom was angry. "What kind of friend just leaves you there?" she demanded. "Anything could have happened to you."

"I've already lived through a school shooting, Mom," I said, not hiding the annoyance in my voice. "What worse could happen in the middle of the day at Wargin Park?"

"Plenty," she said.

I shrugged. I didn't want to talk to her about Eden. She didn't get it. Didn't understand what it was like to live in our heads.

I saw Eden a few days later, but neither of us mentioned what had happened at the park. We went on like that day had been wiped off the calendar. A missing moment in time.

To this day, despite all the conversations we've had, all the hours spent together, all the emails and text messages exchanged, it's never come up.

✕ ✕ ✕

Jenny and I had to practically carry Eden back to her dorm. Her legs wobbled as she walked between us, one arm slung around my waist, the other around Jenny's shoulders. Her head rested on my shoulder, her long, wavy hair sticking to her face.

"I'm so glad you came to visit," she slurred near my ear. "It's so good to see you, Lee."

"You too, Eden," I said, stumbling as she leaned into me with a little more weight than before.

"Where's your student ID, Eden?"

"Back pocket." She removed her arm from Jenny, almost losing her balance before I could steady her, and reached into her jeans. She held out the ID and Jenny took it. Eden's dorm building was just up ahead.

By this point we were half dragging Eden up to the door. Once we got there, Jenny waved the ID in front of the small sensor and there was a buzz that told us the door had unlocked. I pushed the door open with my shoulder, and we pulled Eden inside.

"Please don't let the RA be here," Jenny said with a quiet moan. "Please, please."

But the RA wasn't there. We managed to get Eden up the stairs and to her dorm room without encountering anyone, thank God. Rather than digging through Eden's purse for the key, Jenny tapped lightly on the door. A second later, Misty appeared. She was still in her clothes from earlier that day, her dark blond hair pulled off her neck and twisted up with an alligator clip. She glanced at Eden, then turned her eyes to Jenny.

The look that passed between them said everything I needed to know.

This wasn't the first time.

Misty stepped aside to let us into the room, then shut the door behind us with a quiet click. Jenny and I eased Eden down into a sitting position on her tiny twin bed. The minute we moved out from under her arms, though, she flopped back onto the baby-blue comforter with a drunken giggle.

"On your side," Jenny said, using both hands to roll Eden.

"I'm not gonna puke," Eden said.

"We'll see about that."

Misty picked up an empty wastebasket and put it next to Eden's bed. It felt like I was watching a routine. Something practiced and choreographed.

"Lee," Jenny said, "where are you sleeping?"

"Oh. I have a sleeping bag."

"Do you need a pillow?" Misty asked.

"That would be great. Thank you."

By the time we got my sleeping bag unrolled, Eden had passed out. Misty excused herself to take a shower, leaving me and Jenny to take off Eden's shoes and glasses.

"So . . . how long has this been going on?" I asked.

Jenny sighed and ran a hand through her hot-pink hair. "A while? I didn't think much about it at first. She's a freshman. She's on her own for the first time, and I don't know. Freshmen party. Except . . . she doesn't really party. She just drinks. Too much."

"Have you talked to her about it?"

"I've tried. So has Misty. But neither of us really knows what to say. I mean, we can't even begin to imagine what she's been through. And every time we bring it up or tell her she should see a counselor, she just shuts down. Says she's got too much to do. And it's not like it's affecting her grades or anything. She's doing fine in class. She gives these presentations every other week. Everyone else thinks she's doing great. But then every weekend it's . . . *this*." She gestured to Eden's unconscious form on the bed. "I was hoping maybe when you were here she'd try to keep it together, but clearly I was wrong." She crossed her arms over her chest. "I'm sorry. I shouldn't be unloading this on you."

"No, it's fine," I said. "I'm glad I know."

"Misty thinks we should tell her parents, but I'm scared she'd hate me if I did. She works so hard to make her family proud." Her voice dropped to a whisper. "I'm scared for her, Lee. I'm graduating and Misty is transferring to be closer to home. What if something happens to her? I keep having this recurring nightmare that she calls me and asks me to come help her, but I'm already back home in California and I can't get to her. I just . . . I don't know what to do."

I couldn't give her an answer. I'd had no idea things were this bad with Eden. Jenny was right. From the outside, she seemed fine. Great, even. The model of what a survivor could and should be. Ashley and I had talked a dozen times about how proud we were of her. How far she'd come since high school, where hardly anyone had even heard the sound of her voice. Between the activism and her webcomic, I'd assumed that moment by the lake three years ago was far behind her.

But maybe she was still screaming. Just in a different way.

"I should go," Jenny said. "I've got a test on Monday, which means I'm going to have to spend the weekend studying. If she wakes up, will you make sure she drinks some water?"

"Yeah. Of course."

"Thank you." Jenny leaned down and kissed Eden's forehead before turning to leave the room.

I sat on my sleeping bag and pulled out my cell phone. I had a text from Ashley, instructing me to tell Eden hello for her and asking how my visit had been so far. I hadn't spoken to her since reading her essay, and I'd let her last few texts go unanswered. I wasn't angry with her. Not exactly. She hadn't meant to lie. As far as she knew, she'd told the truth about Sarah and the necklace. But I still wasn't sure how to talk to her about that.

How do you tell someone that something they were so sure of, something that was profound and meaningful to them, wasn't real?

I wasn't ready to tell her, but I also knew that if I kept ignoring her texts, she'd get worried. So I typed back a quick reply. Eden says hi back. I didn't answer her question about how the visit had been so far. I didn't want to lie, but the truth couldn't have been conveyed in a text message.

I'd just hit "send" when Eden sat up, turned, and began vomiting into the wastebasket next to her bed. Selfishly I was relieved that we'd rolled out my sleeping bag closer to Misty's bed, out of range of the splash zone. I dropped my phone and jumped up, walking over to Eden and pulling her hair back while her body expelled as much vodka from her system as it could.

A few minutes later, she finished and wiped her hand across her mouth. Slowly she lay back down on the bed. I went to the minifridge in the corner and found an unopened bottle of water. After unscrewing the cap, I handed it to her. She tried to sip without sitting up but sloshed a bit of water onto her face and shirt, though she didn't seem bothered.

"Where's Jenny?" she asked in a croaky voice as she handed the bottle back to me.

"She just left."

"Is she mad at me?"

"No."

"Are you?"

"No."

"I ruined your visit."

"You didn't."

She groaned, and a faint shine of wetness began to form

around the edges of her eyes. "I'm a mess, Lee. You wanted us to write about the truth. This is my truth."

"Eden . . ."

"Do you think the others are as messed up as me? I know Ashley's not. Maybe Denny is. Or Kellie. I should ask her . . ." Her eyes had slid shut and her voice was fading, but I hadn't missed those last words.

"You know how to get in touch with Kellie?" I asked.

"Mm-hmm." She was nearly asleep now, her thoughts fading in and out mid-sentence. "Spoke at her college . . . saw her . . ."

The door opened then and the sudden noise made me jump. But it was just Misty, dressed in gray sweatpants and an oversized white T-shirt with a towel wrapped around her head and a shower caddy tucked under her arm.

When I looked back at Eden, she was sound asleep again. I screwed the cap back onto the water bottle and left it next to her on the bedside table. The smell from the wastebasket was becoming overwhelming. I bent down and pulled up the edges of the bag and tied it up as tight as I could.

"Is there a garbage chute or something?" I asked Misty.

Misty glanced over at me and sighed. "I'll take it."

"No. I can do it." I had the feeling Misty had been tasked with dealing with vomit more than once recently. "I just need to know where—"

But Misty had walked over and taken the bag from my hands. "The closest trash can is in the bathroom, and I need to go back in there anyway. I forgot my toothbrush, so . . ." She glanced over at Eden, sprawled on her bed, and I didn't miss the look of exasperation on her face before she walked back out of the door.

I was on my way to my sleeping bag again when I noticed Eden's cell phone. It was lying on the edge of her desk. It was hard *not* to notice with its bright green case. Before I could talk myself out of it, I grabbed her phone and opened the home screen. She didn't have a passcode set up, so I was able to go to her contacts without any trouble.

I scrolled through, hoping but not believing I'd find what I was looking for. When I got to the *G*s and found "Gaynor, Kellie," I was so surprised and thrilled that I actually laughed.

There were footsteps in the hallway. I forwarded the contact to myself, dropped Eden's phone back onto the desk, and ran across the tiny room. I was trying to convince myself that, even if she were sober, Eden would have shared the contact with me.

Except she hadn't. She'd seen Kellie, been at her college, and she hadn't told me. Maybe I wasn't supposed to know. I definitely wasn't supposed to have her contact info.

But I was doing something good. Trying to make things better. That made this all right. Kellie would be glad to hear from me when I told her about the letters.

Yes, I know. It felt flimsy even to me. But it was just enough to keep me from feeling sick with guilt.

The door opened just as I reached the other side of the room. I bent down and made to unzip my backpack as Misty stepped inside.

"Got my toothbrush," she said, and I heard the lock click behind her. "And I'm heading to bed in a few minutes. I hope that's okay?"

"Of course," I said. "I was just changing into my pajamas."

Once the lights were out and I was curled up inside my sleeping bag, I pulled out my phone and checked the contact I'd forwarded myself. I now had Kellie Gaynor's phone number and email address. Finally.

But before I could even try to contact Kellie, I received the next letter.

Eden emailed me late Saturday night. I'd only gotten home from visiting her a couple hours earlier. We'd spent the morning just relaxing in her dorm. She worked on *Calliope* while I read *Equus*. We didn't talk about the night before despite her obvious hangover.

So I was more than a little surprised when I received her email that night, and that was nothing compared to how I felt after reading it.

Dear Whoever,

I'm not the best with words. People have always called me shy, but that's not really it. I just never really know what to say. I spend so long searching for the right word that by the time I have what I want to say worked out in my head, the conversation has moved on. Pictures have always made more sense to me.

Maybe that's why I've written seven drafts of this letter. That, or maybe it's because Lee asked me to write the truth. I've been giving people the truth they want to hear, showing them the pictures they want to see, for so long that I don't know which way is up anymore.

All I know is I try *so hard*. And everyone thinks I'm doing so well, but I'm scared and I'm angry and I'm tired all the time, and I can't tell anyone that because they don't want to hear it and because I don't know how to say it.

And also because of Rosi.

I didn't really like my cousin. I'm not supposed to say that, but if I'm telling the truth, there it is. We didn't get along at all. I'm sure she was nice to other people, but not to me. She was my younger cousin. She set the bar, though. And I could never reach it.

Rosi was the better Martinez. She never missed a single Mass. Her Spanish was perfect. At school she was popular and had good grades. And I was the quiet, geeky lesbian who spent all her time reading manga and drawing instead of studying. I barely managed a C in my high school Spanish class. Rosi was better than me at almost everything, and she loved to remind me of that.

Every time we were at Abuela's house, Rosi would wait until I walked into the room to start asking our grandmother questions about growing up in Mexico or about Abuelo, who had passed away before we were born. Within seconds, they'd both fall into rapid Spanish that I couldn't follow, full of laughter and smiles. If our parents were around, they'd join in, too. And I'd be stuck sitting there, left out. Abuela was always the first to notice me, but whenever she'd try to pull me into the chatter, even switching back to English, I just didn't have words. Not in any language. So I'd shrug and Abuela's face would fall, and over her shoulder Rosi would give me this look of pity, like she hadn't done it on purpose.

She mostly ignored me at school. We were a year apart, so it wasn't that hard. She had a big group of friends, who all seemed to really like her. I mostly just had my sketchbook. We only had one class together, and we sat on opposite sides of the room. Outside of school we may have been cousins in a close-knit family, but within those four walls, we might as well have lived in different universes.

But as much as I resented Rosi—hated her, sometimes—the moment I realized she was dead was the worst of my life.

I'm not going to go into too many details about the shooting. Whoever's reading this has heard it all. I can't really add anything.

But Lee asked me to write about the "truth." About things people don't know. And for me what people don't know is after. It's when I opened my eyes, curled up in a ball under a table in the computer lab, and realized that no one in my class was moving. When I crawled over to Denny and realized that only some of the blood on the carpet was coming from his arm. When I realized that Rosi, my baby cousin, wasn't breathing.

Rosi was a brat, but she was my family. And I never imagined I'd have to see her with a bullet hole in her . . . No. Sorry. I can't even write it. That's not the point, anyway. The point is that seeing her like that, it screwed me up. Bad.

But I didn't want to be screwed up. My family needed me. Before, I was allowed to stay in the shadows. I was allowed to be quiet while Rosi was the star. I didn't realize what a gift that was when Rosi was around. I was jealous of her. But once she was gone, I had to be the one to shine.

I couldn't be Rosi. I figured that out quick. I couldn't make Abuela laugh so hard she got the hiccups. I couldn't bring home the kind of grades that made my family brag about me to anyone who would listen. I couldn't make them happy the way she did.

I tried. All through my junior and senior year I tried. But I couldn't be her.

I had to find a way to be *something*, though. A new way to make them proud. Because I didn't want them to think that it should've been me who died that day.

They've never said that. No one in my family would *ever* say that. Not even Rosi's parents. And if they thought it, I know they'd feel awful. They'd be running to confession right away. But I didn't want them to have to feel the guilt of thinking it. And I didn't want to think it about myself.

I started college about two years after the shooting. One night, my roommate, Misty, asked if I wanted to go to a protest with her.

Like I said, I'm a quiet person. And since the shooting, loud noises and sudden movements stress me out, so a protest is probably the last place I should've been. But the only other option was to stay in my dorm room, alone, on a Saturday, and as much as the other things freak me out, being alone is worse. When I'm alone, every little sound makes me panic. I start imagining all the horrible things that could happen.

I don't even think I registered that the protest was about gun control, though I'm sure that's why Misty invited me. She had made us signs and stuff—she went to a lot of protests and knew the drill—and I just sort of expected to stand there, holding one of her cardboard signs, moving my lips to the chants other people came up with. It's embarrassing to admit, but back then, I actually didn't care that much.

But then a local reporter took our picture. He asked for mine and Misty's names and where we were from, and when the paper came out the next day, there I was, holding up my sign, Eden Martinez, VCHS survivor, fighting for gun control. I hadn't told the reporter I was a survivor, but it wouldn't have been hard to put together.

I don't know how the paper got to Abuela. My college is a few hours away from Virgil County, but somehow, she saw it. She called me, crying, and told me how proud she was. Told me the family was so proud. Because I was making a difference. I was fighting for Rosi. My parents shared the article on Facebook, and my aunt and uncle wrote me kind emails. For the first time, I was the star. I was the Martinez they wanted me to be.

That's how I got into activism.

It's also how I started drinking.

It wasn't a lot at first. One of the other protesters had offered me a shot, said it would help dull my anxiety. And it had. I'd never had a drink before that day, but I liked it. Liked how it lowered the volume on that panicked voice always screeching in my head. So when Misty took me to another protest the next weekend, I made a point to get my hands on another shot.

But I wanted the feeling more often than just at protests. So I started drinking regularly. Just a little on weeknights, just enough to slow my rapid thoughts so I could sleep easily. On weekends, though, I let myself drink more. Enough to not just dull the edge but to break off the knife at the hilt. Enough so I couldn't feel any of it.

I kept going to protests. Misty was so excited to have a buddy that she offered to get involved with other organizations. She helped me write editorials about campus safety for the college newspaper. She educated me with statistics and facts, and I told her as much as I could about what it was like to be in a real active shooter situation. And when I got invited to give my first presentation, in an auditorium full of people, and I started freaking out, Misty decided to combine her statistics and my experience. While I panicked, she and my girlfriend, Jenny, wrote a script I could follow.

Because of their help, the first presentation went well, and I got asked to do it again. And again. And again. At high schools and colleges all over Indiana. Over the past few months, I've been on TV and in a couple of national publications. I even had the chance to sit down with some state lawmakers. And it's not just my family watching me now. I get messages from strangers on social media. From teenagers and adults and other activists.

"You're a warrior," one girl wrote to me on Twitter. "Keep up the fight."

Warrior. That's the version of me everyone wants to see. I'm a fighter. A girl who's willing to shout to be heard. A girl who's willing to relive the worst day of her life in presentations to get her point across. They see me as powerful and determined and someone to admire and—

And I'm so scared of letting them know I'm not that.

I don't want it to sound like I don't care about the things I fight for. I do. Now more than ever. I do want to fight. I want to keep people safe. I want to make sure no one ever sees what I saw and is haunted by it the way I am. I want to be the activist who makes my family proud, not just for them but because that's the version of Eden I want to be.

But behind my sword and my shield, I am crumbling. As I write this, there is a bottle of vodka sitting on my desk, next to me. Drinking was the only way I could bring myself to write this. Drinking is the only way I can bring myself to do a lot of things. I drink almost every night just so I can make everything in my head fuzzy. Because when it's sharp, it hurts too much. And I keep telling myself that I'm fine and that I have it under control. That I'm a college student and college students drink sometimes and it's not impacting my grades or anything so I'm fine.

But if I'm fine, then why am I hiding a bottle of vodka in my desk drawer, only to take it out and drink when nobody's around?

Jenny and Misty only know about the drinking at parties, which is when I tend to drink so much it makes me sick. I know they're tired of it. I know they're getting angry with me. And they'd be furious—and worried—if they knew I was drinking on week-nights, too. Not enough to be hungover the next day. Just enough to get by.

I don't think I'm fine.

And I'm scared.

Misty's mom is having health problems, so she's transferring to a school closer to home, back in Tennessee. I'm going to have to live with someone new. As frustrated as I know Misty must be with me lately, she's been the best friend I could imagine. She's helped me through panic attacks, rewritten speeches and sent emails when I couldn't handle it, and made me laugh when I needed it most.

And Jenny is graduating this year. God, just the thought of that makes me feel sick. If Misty leaving scares me, Jenny leaving has me terrified.

Jenny Stewart-Goo is my first girlfriend. We met a few weeks into my first semester, at an Anime Club meeting, of all things. The club was actually terrible. It was mostly just a bunch of white guys who tossed out random Japanese words for no reason other than to impress each other. They insisted on watching illegally down-loaded anime with subtitles, because it was "just better that way," even though one of the other girls who had shown up was legally blind and couldn't see the screen well enough to read subtitles. She didn't come back after the first meeting. I almost didn't, either. The only reason I did was because Misty was on a date that night and I didn't want to be alone in my dorm.

So while the boys in the club tried to out-Japanophile each other, I sat in a corner and sketched. I didn't think anyone even noticed I was there until a voice next to me said, "You're really good."

I jumped and let out a little yelp. Jenny was nice enough to act like this wasn't weird, though.

"Sorry," she said. "But your drawings are really good. Can I see more?"

I showed her the rest of the stuff in my sketchbook. Turns out, she was into comics and had always wished she could draw, but she was more of a writer. She loved fantasy, especially stories with witches and magical creatures. By the end of the movie we were supposed to be watching, we'd already brainstormed out an idea for our first webcomic. That's where *Calliope* was born.

We stopped going to Anime Club gatherings and started meeting in the library instead. She'd write and I'd draw, and by midterms, I had both a beautiful, talented girlfriend and my first webcomic.

Calliope isn't very well known, and when we published it, I chose to alter my name a little—to E. B. Martinez—so that I had one thing in my life that wasn't connected to activism or the shooting. Working with Jenny means getting to escape into this fantasy world where guns aren't even a thing, where we can just play and explore. It's the only thing *fun* in my life. And I don't know what's going to happen with *Calliope* or with my relationship when Jenny leaves.

"We'll make it work," she told me a few days ago when I brought up her moving back to California. "We can take turns visiting each other over the summer. I'll come back to see you in the autumn or maybe over your winter break. And you can come visit me during spring break."

"What about between visits, though?" I asked. We were sitting on the quad with our textbooks in our laps. "You'll be in Los Angeles. I feel like everyone there is so . . . pretty."

"You're pretty," she said.

I shrugged. "Maybe. But I'm pretty and here. And they'll be pretty and *there*. With you."

"Do you really think pretty is enough to make me cheat on you?"

"No," I said. "I know you wouldn't do that. But . . ."

"But nothing." She raised to her knees, knocking the books off her lap, and reached across the space between us to put a hand on either side of my face. "I love you, you stupid freshman. That's not changing, even if my time zone does."

She kissed me then, and I wanted to believe her.

But I remember the look on her face the other night, while she and Lee dragged me, drunk and stumbling, back to my room. She looked worried, but also exhausted. Like taking care of her mess of a girlfriend is weighing on her.

And if I'm a mess now, where will I be in a year? When she and Misty are gone and there's no one to bother hiding the vodka bottle from?

I know I need to ask for help, but I don't feel like I'm allowed to. I feel like I'll be letting everyone down. I don't *want* to be weak. I want to spite all of those jerks who send me death threats on social media because they think I'm here to take their guns away. I want to show those arrogant white guys on my campus who try to argue Second Amendment rights with me that I am just as smart and powerful and loud as they are. I want to keep making my family proud so that they never have to think that the wrong girl died.

I want to be a warrior.

But that version of me is a lie. I can get on a stage and deliver a presentation I've rehearsed a dozen times. But the minute someone gets in my face and asks me to go off book, I crumble. That's my truth.

I'm not a warrior. I'm a fraud. And trying to keep up the charade is killing me.

I'm going to regret sending this email to Lee tomorrow. I know it. I'm going to wish I hadn't shared all of this, but if I don't, I might never say it. I might never get help. So here it is. The truth. The real Eden Martinez.

I'm sorry.

—E

I called Eden as soon as I finished reading her letter. She was sniffling when she answered, and I could tell she'd been crying.

"I just got off the phone with my parents," she told me. "I . . . told them how I've been feeling. And that something has to change."

"How did they react?"

"Confused. Which is fair, I guess. And now they're really worried."

"So what are you going to do?" I asked.

"I'm thinking of taking a semester off," she said. "Maybe more. I don't know. But I'm taking a break from school, from public speaking. I think I need to spend some time with my family to figure things out. Maybe Alcoholics Anonymous. Probably therapy."

"I'm sorry," I said. Because what else was there to say?

"Don't be. If I hadn't made myself write the letter, I . . . I don't know." She took a deep breath. "I'm going to call Jenny. I'll talk to you soon, Lee."

I hung up the phone and started composing a new email. I now had three letters, and I only needed two more. And, thanks to Eden, I knew how to get in touch with Kellie.

I decided to start with an email. I sent along links about the McHales' book and explained that I knew the truth, and that I wanted to create some sort of counternarrative.

It was a short, to-the-point message, but I ended it with this:

I'm sorry I didn't say anything sooner. I was scared. But now is our chance to set the record straight.

I hit the "send" button before I could second-guess myself. For some reason, I was sure she'd want to help with this project. She must've wanted the truth out there more than any of us. In my head, it wasn't complicated at all.

Though I was aware that not everyone thought my efforts to bring out the truth were a good idea. It became pretty clear within a couple days of returning home that Brother Lloyd and Sarah's parents hadn't kept quiet about the "lies" I'd been telling.

At first it was just a few dirty looks in the hallway and a quiet mutter of the word *bitch* under someone's breath as I walked by. But no one actually approached me or said anything about Sarah, so while I suspected the hostility toward me was related, I couldn't be sure. Not until lunch on Wednesday, at least.

I was sitting with Denny and Miles at our usual table when Amber Hieber, Denny's soon-to-be prom date, came over to join us.

"Mind if I sit?" she asked, putting down her tray and smiling at us with full, painted pink lips.

Miles lifted his gaze from the book he was reading, something about the Cuban missile crisis, and we exchanged a wary look. It's not that we're unfriendly. We smiled and casually chatted with our classmates like anyone else. (Well, I did. Miles, maybe not so much.) But at lunch, we tended to keep to ourselves. There was an invisible barrier around our table that no one had tried to cross in years. And while Amber seemed nice enough, I don't think either Miles or I knew what to do with a new person in this space.

The same could not be said for Denny.

"Of course we don't mind," he said. "Glitter might, though. She's used to being the prettiest girl at the table."

"Hey," I said.

"Are you going to argue that you're prettier than Glitter?" he asked.

"I might be," I said. "How would you know?"

"Touché."

Amber's eyes darted back and forth between us, clearly not sure if I was making fun of Denny's disability or if this was just friendly banter. After a minute, she tossed her white-blond hair over her shoulder and said, "So, Denny, I was thinking we could make prom plans? I've been talking to some of my friends, and Jordan Mabry's dad works for a car company and says we could get a pretty good discount on a limo."

"A limo, huh?" Denny said, a big grin spreading across his round face. "Is it one of those hot-tub limos?"

"I don't think so." Amber giggled, and I couldn't tell if she actually thought Denny was funny or if she was flirting with him. "Just a regular limo."

"Too bad," he said. "But I'm in."

"Oh, and obviously you guys are invited, too," Amber said, looking over at Miles and me. "If you're going to prom, I mean. Are you?"

Miles peered at me over the top of his book, a bushy eyebrow raised. "Are we?" he asked.

"I . . . uh . . ."

I was still trying to formulate the words for some sort of answer when I felt something hit me in the back of the head. It didn't hurt. Just a light tap. I reached up and touched my hair, but I felt nothing there. When I turned around, I noticed a group of juniors at another table. They had their heads together, conversing in low voices, and occasionally one would look up and glare at me.

Ashley's younger sister, Tara Chambers, was one of them.

I shook it off and turned back to Miles. "About prom. I still don't—"

It happened again. Another small, but annoying, tap on the back of my head. This time, when I turned around, I noticed one of the juniors, a boy with red hair and glasses, was holding a tiny object in his hand, his arm pulled back like he was about to pitch a baseball in my direction. He dropped his arm when he saw me looking, and I noticed the small tray of Tater Tots on the table in front of him.

"Is that kid . . . throwing Tater Tots at me?" I asked Miles, feeling kind of baffled.

It's not that bullying isn't a problem at VCHS. It definitely is. Most people even seem to think that was the motive behind the massacre, though I always hate that narrative. In part because, even if the shooter was bullied, it certainly wasn't by me or Sarah or several of the other victims. And I'd argue that the minute he opened fire, he became the ultimate school bully, so hearing people assume that he was tormented as some sort of excuse for what he did just infuriates me.

My point is that VCHS has the same sort of bullying issues any other high school does, but Tater Tot throwing still seemed so bizarrely juvenile.

Miles slammed his book shut and turned to look at the table behind me. "What the hell?" he asked, raising his voice a bit above his usual mumble so they could hear him.

"Hell is exactly where she's going," the redheaded kid said, tossing another Tater Tot at me. This one bounced off my shoulder. Next to him, I saw Tara nod.

There was a flicker of a shadow in Miles's eyes, and he started to stand up. I grabbed his arm and held it tight. "Leave it," I whispered, my words almost pleading. "It's not worth your getting in trouble."

VCHS had a zero-tolerance policy for violence since the shooting. And as much as part of me wanted to see Miles punch Tater Tot kid in the face, a much larger part of me couldn't stand the idea of my friend being expelled so close to graduation.

Miles stayed tense, like a cat ready to pounce, but he didn't leave his seat. Instead, he just glared at the kid behind me. Which,

I guess, was enough to scare the redhead off from throwing any more food in my direction.

"What's their problem?" Denny asked.

"They go to my church," Amber said, her voice low as she gestured to Tara and the redheaded boy. "And, um . . . our preacher may have mentioned Lee this past Sunday."

"Virgil County Baptist?" I guessed.

She nodded. "Yeah. He . . . he said you've been telling stories about Sarah McHale. Said something about how it's the devil working through you, and how we need to remember Sarah's devotion to her faith."

"Did he instruct you all to throw food at me?" I asked.

"Of course not," she said. "He did say we should pray for you, though."

"How nice of him," Miles muttered.

"You don't sound like you believed him," Denny noted.

"Well." Amber tugged on a lock of her shiny hair and turned big hazel eyes on me. "Honestly? I always believed the Sarah story. I didn't really know Sarah, but . . . she was so nice. And always at church. And it seemed more likely than what that Kellie girl said. But you were Sarah's best friend and you were there with her when it happened. And, I don't know, you just don't seem like a liar to me."

"Thank you," I said, surprised by just how much I appreciated Amber in that moment. "But I'm guessing you're in the minority if Brother Lloyd is telling everyone his side of things."

Amber shrugged. "I think my parents are in the same place as me, if it helps. I'm not sure they ever actually believed the Sarah story to begin with. But even if most people do think you're lying, I'd like to think the rest of my congregation is mature enough not to throw things."

I would've liked to believe that, too. But I remembered what the Gaynor family had gone through. The vandalism, the threats, the way grown adults attacked a teenage girl still recovering from a gunshot wound. If people were half as mad at me as they were at Kellie Gaynor three years ago, then Tater Tots were the least of my worries.

I didn't want anyone to think I could be shaken, but honestly, I was scared.

I found out my best friend was a martyr from a bulletin board at the drugstore.

It was in April, almost a month after the shooting. Mom and I were on our way home from my therapy appointment, and we'd stopped by the pharmacy to pick up my medication. I stayed near the front of the store while Mom went back to pick up my prescription. It was one of those days where I needed space from her. Where every word she said, every move she made, irritated me.

It was also a Death Drum day. Most days were back then, but I distinctly remember that day being worse. Every fleeting thought, no matter how mundane or innocuous, somehow led me on a nihilistic brain spiral. This was most evidenced by my reactions to the various flyers and posters tacked and taped to the community bulletin board near the front of the store.

A flyer encouraging people to recycle? *What's the point? Eventually the sun is going to explode anyway, and then the planet and all of humanity will be gone and nothing we did will have mattered.*

A missing cat poster? *Do animals have any concept of death?*

That each day we creep closer to nothingness and there's nothing we can do about it? I bet they don't. I bet it's nice to be a cat.

An advertisement for the upcoming Little Miss Virgil County contest? *Why do people even bother having kids? They're going to die one day, too. Why doesn't anyone else seem to realize that everything is pointless and death is unavoidable and all of this is just a distraction?*

You get the point. It was a Bad Day. And it only got worse when I saw the picture of Sarah.

It was *the* picture—the school photo with the braids and the cross necklace she wore just that one time. It was the first time I'd seen it since the photos had been handed out at school months ago, when Sarah had taken one look and grimaced, swearing she'd never wear her hair in braided pigtails again because it made her look like a toddler.

But there it was, smiling down at me from this community bulletin board, with big, capital letters announcing:

YOUTH RALLY IN HONOR OF SARAH MCHALE, THE GIRL WITH THE CROSS NECKLACE.

Then in smaller letters, just below her image:

Come, Worship, Remember.

I stared at the flyer for a while, reading it over and over, sure I was missing something. The rally was being held at Hillcreek Christian, a church all the way across town. If it was at Virgil County Baptist, Sarah's church, I might not have thought twice about it, aside from that weird label. I had no idea why anyone would call her "the girl with the cross necklace."

But why would there be a rally for Sarah at a church she'd never even attended? Nine people, not including the shooter, had died. It wasn't just Sarah. In fact, I was pretty sure two of the other victims, Brenna DuVal and Aiden Stroud, had gone to that church. Why wasn't this for them?

And didn't a youth rally seem kind of inappropriate?

Keep in mind, this came shortly after my first internet spiral breakdown, when Mom was still trying to do what she could to keep the news away from me. I'd only left the house a handful of times since the shooting. I hadn't even seen Denny or Ashley yet. Miles hadn't climbed onto my roof. And I'd only run into Eden at Sarah's and Rosi's funerals.

I'd been largely isolated, and nothing about this post-shooting world, especially that flyer, made sense to me.

"Prescription filled," Mom said, joining me at the bulletin board near the door. "Let's go home, Lee baby."

I pointed to the flyer, to Sarah's face. "What's this?"

She glanced at it, then looked away quickly. She knew something. I knew she knew something by the slight downturn of her lips, by the darkening of her brown eyes. We had the same eyes, and I remembered Sarah telling me how the color of my irises seemed to shift when I was lying.

"Don't worry about that," Mom said. "Let's just go home."

She tried to put a hand on my shoulder, but I pulled away. "What is it about, Mom? Why is some random church having a youth rally for Sarah?"

"We can talk about it in the car."

"No!" I stomped my foot, like a child. I was so mad. So mad that she kept trying to coddle me. I didn't want her to hide things from me. I wanted to know everything. Even if it hurt. Even if it was bad for me.

"Leanne."

"Tell me!"

I screamed it so loud that people nearby stopped and turned to look at us. The cashier, standing behind the counter a few yards away, raised an eyebrow, clearly wondering if he should say something.

Mom waved a hand at him, then took me by the elbow and steered me out the glass doors, the cheery bell jingling obnoxiously overhead. As soon as we were outside, I smacked her hand off me and curled in on myself, refusing to move any farther until she explained why my best friend's school photo, the photo she hated, was on that bulletin board, and why people gave a damn about her necklace.

Mom sighed and ran a hand through her hair. "There have been a few rallies around the state in Sarah's memory," she said, her voice resigned. "That's all."

"But why?"

Mom shrugged. "Why do churches do anything? You're asking the wrong person."

My lack of religious inclination comes from my mom. She was raised Baptist, but after the way her congregation treated her when she got pregnant with me at sixteen, she lost interest in organized religion. To this day, I'm honestly not sure if she lost faith in a higher power or just in the church. She doesn't like to talk about it. She always says that whatever relationship she does or doesn't have with God is her business, and no one else's.

"But why Sarah?" I demanded. "Why *just* Sarah? And what was that stuff about a necklace?"

"I . . . I think it's about what happened in the bathroom, baby."

"The bathroom?"

She chewed on her bottom lip. Another expression we had in common. "A lot of people are talking about what Sarah . . . what she said to *him*." My mother has never, not once, said the name of the shooter aloud. "The police found her cross necklace at the crime scene. And with *him* asking her about what she believed before she died and her standing up to him . . ."

She trailed off, tears springing into her eyes as she looked at my face. I'm sure I looked startled. Or maybe even sick. I *felt* sick. And confused. Sarah hadn't had a necklace on that day. She hadn't said a word to anyone but me in that bathroom once the shooting started.

But Mom must've thought my expression meant something else. She tried to rush forward, to hug me, but I dodged her.

"I'm sorry," she said, wiping the wetness from her eyes before wrapping her arms around herself. "Talking about this must be . . . I can't imagine. I'm sorry. We don't have to . . . Lee?"

I had already started storming off, away from the store and to the parking lot. I didn't want her hugs or her tears or her explanations about Sarah. I didn't want to turn everything into death in my mind. I didn't want, didn't want, didn't *want*.

That day, I wasn't thinking about how the story must've gotten started. Or where it had come from. Kellie Gaynor didn't even cross my mind. All I could think was that I hated everything about this world I was living in. This post-shooting reality. My brain was making me miserable. My mom was driving me nuts.

And now, not even my memory of my best friend felt safe or real.

BRENNA DUVAL

Brenna was eighteen, a senior, when she was killed. At six foot one, she was the star of the girls' basketball team. She'd already scored an athletic scholarship. The previous fall, when VCHS had released its School Pride Calendar, a way of raising funds for the various sports teams, Brenna and her boyfriend, Aiden Stroud (the captain of the football team), were featured on the cover.

She'd been the student assistant to Coach Nolan during my first semester, when I was taking his World Civics class. Mostly that meant she sat at his desk and played games on his computer until he needed her to go make copies.

But I remember this one day, toward the end of the semester, when we were all sitting around, waiting for Coach to arrive. The bell had already rung, but he wasn't there yet. Then Brenna came running into the classroom, a grin spread so wide that it seemed to split her face in half. She shut the door behind her and said:

"Listen up. Coach is busy with something at the front office. He'll be here in, like, two minutes. So we don't have much time."

She then instructed us to turn all of the desks around. None of the freshmen hesitated. We were all on our feet, and the room began to fill with the sounds of metal scraping against tile. Brenna kept watch by the door while we worked, occasionally glancing over her shoulder and urging us to hurry as we moved on to turning the unoccupied desks.

"Keep the rows straight," she said. "Like they're supposed to be this way."

Sarah was in that class with me, and she couldn't stop giggling as we flipped around the last two desks in our row.

"Here he comes!" Brenna announced, turning away from the door. "Sit down, sit down."

She bolted across the room, her long legs carrying her from the door to Coach Nolan's chair in just two strides.

A split second later, the door opened, and Coach Nolan was greeted by a class full of freshmen staring him down. Our desks were no longer facing the whiteboard but, instead, the door at the back of the room. His eyes widened in surprise, and he just stood there, blinking, for a second.

"You're late, Coach," Richie McMullen said, his voice mock-stern.

Coach Nolan looked at him, then at Brenna. "You did this, didn't you, Ms. DuVal?"

"No idea what you're talking about, Coach. Isn't this how the classroom is always arranged? Doesn't look any different to me."

"Funny you say that, because I didn't say anything about how the classroom was arranged." He shook his head, but a smile was obvious beneath his mustache. "All right. You guys want to have class facing this way? We'll have class facing this way."

It didn't end up being as fun as it sounds, though. We had a pop quiz that day. And facing the back of the room instead of the front didn't make much of a difference.

It had barely even been a prank, but it was enough to cement Brenna as being "cool" in the eyes of a classroom full of freshmen.

She would always smile and say hello to us in the hallways when none of the other seniors even bothered. She'd exchange high fives with the underclassmen jock boys while leaning against her locker in that casual-but-clearly-posed way you see in teen movies.

I was always surprised when she acknowledged me. I assumed she forgot who I was the instant she walked out of Coach Nolan's classroom every day. I was quiet, not the girl who raised her hand and volunteered answers. My grades in that class weren't the highest or the lowest. I was solidly average. A brunette with an unmemorable face.

But one day early in the next semester, after my World Civics class had ended, I found myself spending a lunch period in the gym. Sarah had a dentist appointment, and rather than sitting alone in the cafeteria, I had decided to take a bag lunch into the gym and sit in the bleachers while I got a head start on some of that night's homework. Brenna was there, along with a few other girls from the basketball team.

They were taking turns shooting free throws. I'd look up between math problems and watch them for a minute before going back to my work. The other two girls, whose names I didn't know, did pretty well, only missing a couple of shots. But Brenna didn't miss a single one.

"Bell's about to ring," Brenna told them, catching the ball and dribbling it for a minute. "Nice job, ladies. We're going to destroy Wright County next week."

The girls whooped, high-fived Brenna, then headed for the gym doors. She stayed behind, though, and shot one last free throw.

I was gathering up my stuff when I heard her say, "They suck, don't they, Bauer?"

I looked around, half sure she must be talking to someone else, even though that was irrational. I was the only Bauer in our school, let alone in that gym. "Um," I said when I realized she'd been speaking to me. "No. I thought they were good. They made most of the shots."

"Most isn't *all*," she said. "They shouldn't be missing free throws."

"Are you worried about beating Wright County?" I asked.

She snorted. "No. We'll definitely beat the Wright County girls. They're on a whole different level of terrible."

"That's good, at least."

"Not good enough, though." She looked me over, blue eyes narrowing. "How tall are you, Bauer? Five eight? Five nine?"

"Somewhere in the middle there."

"You're tall compared to some of our girls. You should try out for the team next year," she said.

I laughed. I couldn't help it. "I don't really do sports," I said. "At all. Even jogging more than half a mile makes me feel nauseous, so . . ." I trailed off, horrified to realize I was telling this cool senior girl how out of shape I was.

"Too bad," she said. "Because right now it's looking like this team is going to *suck* when I'm gone."

I don't know if Brenna was being arrogant or honest. Maybe both.

I do know that she was right, though. Since she died, our girls' basketball team *has* kind of sucked.

"So . . . about what Amber said . . ."

Miles and I were in my truck, headed home from school only a few hours after the Tater Tot incident.

"I know," I said as I shifted gears. "But it's not going to keep me from getting the truth out there. I'm still collecting the letters. I've emailed Kellie again. And texted her, too. She hasn't responded yet, but I know she will. And you'll write yours and then—"

"I was talking about prom," he said.

"Oh." I bit my lip and kept my eyes glued to the road. "Sorry. I thought . . . Prom just hasn't been on my mind."

"I get it," he said. "But it's coming up in just a couple weeks."

"Are they even selling tickets anymore?" I asked.

"No," he said. "But . . . I kind of already bought two."

"You did what?" I cut my eyes at him before refocusing on the road. "Miles, those aren't cheap. And I haven't said I was going yet."

"I know," he said. "Grandma insisted, though. She was upset I didn't go last year. I told her I might this year but that I didn't have a date yet, and she gave me money and told me to buy tickets just in case. I wasn't gonna tell you. I didn't want you to feel like you had to go with me because of the money or something. But . . . yeah. I have tickets."

"That was sweet of your grandmother."

"She asked if I was taking you," he said. "She likes you."

"She barely knows me."

"She knows I like you."

I felt the blush beginning to creep up my neck, the heat of mingled guilt and happiness.

"So," he said. "Am I? Taking you?"

"Miles . . . I . . ."

"Lee," he said, his voice sounding clearer and less sleepy than usual. "If it's about me . . . if you don't like me, I get it. But we can go as friends. Whatever you want."

"It's not that I don't like you," I said. "But I'm . . ."

"What?"

I sighed and turned the truck onto my driveway. I turned off the engine and pulled the keys from the ignition. "Miles," I said, looking down at the purple, crescent moon–shaped key chain Denny had gotten me for Christmas two years earlier. I ran my thumb over the raised dots on its surface, the Braille that spelled out my name. I knew that, right then, in his pocket, Miles had a blue star embossed with his name. We were a set. "Miles, I'm asexual."

There was silence in the truck at first. Which I guess was to be expected. When I finally worked up the courage to look at him, he was staring at me. He didn't look disgusted or annoyed. I hadn't expected him to—that wasn't Miles at all—but deep down, I think I'd still feared it. Instead, he just looked confused.

"Asexual?"

I lifted a shoulder and let it drop. "Somewhere on that spectrum. It's not that I'm repulsed by sex. I'm not. Ideally, I'd love to find someone I want to sleep with one day but . . ." I pick at my nails, thinking of the best way to explain. "Okay. Think of it like when you open the fridge because you're hungry, but nothing is appealing. You don't have anything against eating—you'd like to eat at some point—but you can't imagine eating anything you see in that fridge."

"So . . . sex is eating."

"This might be a terrible metaphor."

"No," he said. "I think I get it. So you've never been attracted to . . . anyone."

"Not in that way, no," I said. "I've had crushes. But they've all been emotional. Not physical. I've never felt that kind of sexual attraction. Not even to any of the hot famous guys on TV."

"Not to me either, then."

I bit my lip and looked down at my hands again. "No," I said. "Not even to you."

"Oh . . . Okay."

"I'm sorry, Miles."

"Don't," he said. "That's . . . that's not something you have to apologize for. It's cool."

But when I looked up again and found Miles looking out the window, away from me, I knew that I'd hurt him. I hadn't been apologizing for who I was. If anything, I was sorry that I'd waited this long to tell him. I felt like a jerk, like I'd let him believe something more could happen between us when I'd known for a while that it couldn't. At least, not the way I thought he'd want. But I liked him *so* much, and even though my feelings for him weren't sexual, they were romantic.

Maybe, selfishly, I'd kept this from him for so long because I wanted him to keep liking me. I kept him at a distance, trying to keep my own feelings safe, but I'd failed us both in that way.

"So . . ." He turned back to me. "What about prom?"

I blinked. "You still want to go with me?"

"Yeah."

"I just figured . . ."

He raised an eyebrow. "Did you think I wanted to have sex on prom night?"

"No," I said. "I mean . . . I don't know."

"Where would we even do it?" he asked, his slow words vibrating with a hint of laughter. "We could never afford a motel. And I'm not giving it up in the bed of your dirty old truck."

"Hey," I said. "Don't put down my truck just because you're sad about not getting laid."

We both smiled at each other, and I was relieved to still be able to do this, to joke like this, even after being honest with him. But eventually, both our smiles slipped, and we were left staring across the cab of my truck at each other.

"Do you . . . like me?" he asked. "You can be honest. I just . . . You said you still have crushes. Am I one of them?"

"Of course you are," I whispered, because the idea of saying that any louder felt too overwhelming. "But that doesn't matter."

He stared at me, downturned eyes unblinking, challenging me to answer unasked questions.

"Do you really want a girlfriend who might never want to sleep with you?" I asked.

He shrugged. "Hadn't really thought about it before."

"Well, I have," I said. "Because I've lost one best friend already. I couldn't take it if I lost you, too. Besides, I'm leaving in a few months. It's a bad idea. We're a bad idea."

"Okay," he said.

"I'm sorry," I said. "For not telling you sooner, I mean. I talk so much about the truth being important, but I hid this and—"

"It's fine," he said quickly. Which, considering Miles never spoke quickly, did seem a little strange. He just shook his head, dark curls flopping around his pale face. "Don't worry about it."

"If you were serious before," I said, "about it being okay to just go to prom as friends . . . I think I could do that."

"I was serious," he said. "So you'll go?"

"Sure," I said. "Just as friends. Everything else is off the table."

He nodded. "Just friends. Like we've been for the past three years. Nothing changes."

"Okay," I said, though I still felt nervous. Even if Miles was okay with going to prom in a completely platonic way, I wasn't sure if I could keep my own emotions in check. It wasn't that spending an evening with him, dancing, wearing a nice dress, didn't sound wonderful. It did. Too wonderful. Too easy to get caught up in the moment and let myself forget that our friendship needed to come first.

But I pushed that fear aside and sat back. We were going to prom together. That was settled, and if I just kept an eye on the boundaries, we might even have a great time.

"I guess this means I need a dress," I said. "And you need a tux. That'll be interesting. I don't think I've ever seen you in anything but T-shirts and hoodies."

"Me either," he admitted.

"I promise that if you look ridiculous, I won't tell Denny."

Miles chuckled. "Thanks."

"It must be weird for him," I said after a minute. "All this prom stuff. It's hard for me without Sarah, but he lost *two* best friends. And now all these big end-of-high-school things are happening without them."

Miles nodded. "Yeah. I think I forget that sometimes. About Jared and Rosi."

"Same. I mean, it's not that I forget them so much as just, like . . . I don't know. He's always cracking jokes, making me smile when I get upset about missing Sarah. Maybe I'm just selfish, but it's easy to forget he might miss his friends, too."

"He doesn't talk about them as much as you talk about Sarah," Miles said. "We all gotta deal with this stuff differently."

"Yeah, I know." I reached for the door handle. "I'm just glad the three of us have each other at least. It will be tough going to things like prom and graduation without Sarah—and Jared and Rosi, I'm sure, for Denny—but at least we don't have to deal with it alone, you know?"

He nodded, then opened his door.

Once we were out of my truck, I pulled out my cell phone and checked to see if I had any messages. But all I had was one from Mom, telling me she'd be home late. She'd picked up a second shift because the other manager was out sick. I sighed and put the phone back in my pocket.

Miles looked over the hood of the truck at me. He raised a single, questioning eyebrow.

"I was hoping to hear from Kellie," I said. "I've texted and emailed, but she hasn't responded."

Miles shoved his hands into his pockets. "Sounds like she doesn't wanna talk."

"She will if she gives me a chance to explain my plan," I said. "I'm worried she's not even opening my emails because she sees my name and thinks I'm just harassing her like everyone else here did. She might hate me for not speaking up sooner. I just . . . I want to make it up to her. I want all of us to have our stories out there so it's not just the McHales' book about Sarah."

"Maybe . . . she doesn't want the truth out there."

"That doesn't make sense," I said. "She tried to tell people the truth years ago. Why wouldn't she want them to know now?"

He just shrugged.

"Speaking of which," I said. "Have you—"

"No," he said, scratching the back of his head as he looked away from me. "I really don't wanna write anything, Lee."

"Why not?" I asked.

He shrugged again.

I stared at him, wishing I had the same power to read him that he had over me. Sometimes I can. Sometimes I am painfully familiar with every little jerk of his head or slump of his shoulders. Sometimes I can read a novel's worth of thoughts just by looking at his eyes. But other times, it's like there's a wall between us, and I question how well I really know Miles Mason.

"Are you embarrassed?" I asked. "About your writing? I know you've failed English before, but I'm sure it won't be that bad. I can help you edit if you want."

"You . . . think I'm saying no because . . . I'm not smart."

"What? No," I said. "I do think you're smart. But if you're worried about not being a great writer or something . . . if that's not why you don't want to do this, please stop me from making this worse."

"That's not why," he said.

"Then what's the problem? Why don't you want to write the letter?"

"Just don't, okay?" He turned and started walking toward his house. "I'll see you tomorrow."

"Miles," I called after him.

"I got homework," he said. "Don't wanna fail English again."

"Miles." I sighed. "You know I didn't mean it like that."

"I know," he said, giving me one last look over his shoulder. "See you later, Lee."

I gave a little wave and let him disappear into his grandmother's yard before I headed up the front walk onto my porch. I didn't know what reason he could possibly have for not wanting to write his story. Denny, Ashley, and Eden had jumped at the chance to get their voices out there, even if I wasn't sure what "out there" was yet in terms of sharing the letters. And I was sure that, once Kellie heard me out, she'd want this, too. So why was Miles so resistant?

I decided to leave it alone for a couple of days. But I wasn't going to let it go. I couldn't. Not at that point. The idea of collecting the letters and sharing them with the world, shoving them right under Brother Lloyd's nose, had taken hold of me. I woke up thinking about the letters. I fell asleep thinking about them. I dreamed of them. The claws of this idea, this new goal, had sunken in deep, and almost every thought seemed to swirl around how and where and when I'd show them to the world.

And if you're reading this, then I guess I succeeded. The letters are out there. Just not in the way I initially imagined.

JARED GRAYSON

From Denny:

Whenever people talk about Jared, they always seem to remember him as a farmer's son. I can't tell you the number of times I've heard, "That Grayson boy. Such a shame. He was from a real good family. Good hardworking people."

No shade to Jared's parents, they are good people, but comments like this don't really speak to who Jared was. They don't mention that he spent every summer mowing lawns or working on his family's farm just so he could save up money for the newest generation of gaming console. Or that his room was so messy, you couldn't sit on the bed without hearing the dreaded crunch of a video game case cracking beneath your butt. Or that he was a ridiculous flirt. He even flirted with my sister, who he had less than zero chance with, and he knew it. But with girls he actually liked, like Rosi, he seemed to forget all the cheesy pickup lines he'd learned from the internet.

The first time I hung out at his house was in seventh grade. We'd barely been in his room for two minutes when I heard the telltale sound of a computer booting up. "Do you like RPGs?" he asked. "Like Age of Dragons or Bomb Shelter?"

"Um . . . no?" I said, and gestured to my sunglasses.

"Oh, right."

Then there was a long pause. At twelve, I'm not sure Jared knew how to interact with people outside of video game talk.

"Well," he said eventually, "do you want to play one?"

"I'm not sure you're getting this whole blind thing."

"No, hear me out," he said. "I can play the visual parts and tell you what's going on. And then when, like, important choices come up, I'll let you pick. These games are all about the story, anyway. At least they are for me. It'll be fun."

It was fun. Maybe more fun for him—he got really into the ESPN-like play-by-play of all the combat—but it ended up being a cool way to spend time with a friend and feel like I was a part of something, gaming, that had previously been off-limits for me. It would never be my passion the way it was his, but I did end up playing a few of those audio-only video games.

I sometimes listen to live streams of people playing the newest games that I know Jared would have liked. I want to stay on top of what's happening in his favorite franchises. I like to think about how he would have reacted to big plot twists or the way he would have gushed about new badass DLC. (Lee, that's short for downloadable content. I know you don't have your nerd card yet.)

So yeah. When I think of Jared, I think of games. I don't think he'd have it any other way.

X X X

It didn't take long for Mom to find out about the harassment I was getting from Brother Lloyd and his congregation.

She started getting suspicious when my truck was keyed in the school parking lot. I'd lied and told her that my driver-side door wasn't the only victim, and that some asshole must have been vandalizing classmates' cars for the fun of it. It was obvious she didn't completely buy it. I may be an actress—or an aspiring actress, more accurately—but like I've said, I'm not the best at improv. Still, she let it slide.

But then someone egged our house in the middle of the night.

I woke up on a Saturday and found Mom on the porch, scrubbing away at our front window. Until that moment, I didn't even know egging houses was still something people did. But I guess things become classic for a reason.

"I just don't know why anyone would do this," Mom said as I stepped out onto the porch. "I've heard of kids doing this kind of thing on Halloween, but it's the middle of April."

"Can I help?" I asked, the guilt twisting in my stomach like an agitated snake.

"No. Thank you, though, Lee baby. I think I've got it." She shook her head and pushed dark brown bangs off of her face. "But . . . do you have any ideas? Why anyone might target our house? I took a look around and it doesn't look like any of the neighbors got hit."

She looked at me. It was the look mothers give when they know something, but they want you to be the one to say it. Denial wasn't an option this time. And even if it had been, I'm not sure I would've taken it. I had a sudden flash of Kellie Gaynor and all the ways people had found to torment her and her parents. Someone had broken Mrs. Gaynor's windshield. And a week later the word *liar* was spray-painted in red on their front door. And that's not even taking into account the harassment they faced in person.

If people were mad at me for speaking up, they wouldn't hesitate to take it out on our property. Or on my mom. Which was something, I realized then, that I probably should have considered sooner.

"Mom," I said. "Can we talk?"

She lowered the rag she was using to clean the window. "What's going on, baby?"

"Maybe we should talk inside."

A minute later, we were seated across from each other at the kitchen table. I folded my hands together and focused on my ragged, bitten fingernails as I explained to Mom what had really happened in the bathroom three years ago. I tried to skip all of the more painful details, knowing there was a good chance she'd end up crying as I went through the events, and I wasn't prepared to deal with that this morning.

It had taken a while, but my relationship with Mom had improved since those first few months after the massacre. There were still rough patches, when I was overcome with irrational anger about what had happened, and she felt like the only safe target, the only one I knew wouldn't leave me, no matter how I treated her. Or when her attention felt like suffocation. But over the last three years, thanks to a combo of therapy and time, we'd slowly learned to work through those moments, learned what buttons not to push and when to step away.

Still, I'm not sure I'll ever stop feeling shame for how I treated her back then.

"So then I heard about Sarah's parents writing a book," I said. "And I . . . I couldn't let the story get bigger. I couldn't let it blow up again when it's not true. It's just going to make things worse for Kellie Gaynor. And Sarah would hate this, too, and I . . . I didn't think about how this was going to affect you. I'm sorry, Mom."

"Lee baby." She reached across the table, pulling my hands apart so she could take them in both of hers. When I looked up, I was surprised to see that she wasn't crying. Her eyes were gentle, sad even, but dry. "You don't have to apologize to me."

"But it's going to get worse," I told her. "You remember what happened to the Gaynors. They practically got chased out of town with pitchforks."

"And that might happen to us, too," she said. "But I'm not going to be the one to tell you to keep quiet. I'm going to support you, no matter what you decide to do." Her eyes went dark and her mouth twisted into a grimace. "And I'll wring the necks of anyone who threatens you about it. Have you been okay? I'm guessing that's why your truck got keyed. Has anything else happened? Do I need to talk to the police?"

I shook my head. "No. Just the truck and the egg . . . and a few Tater Tots to the back of the head. Besides, do you really think the cops in this town are going to do anything? Half of them go to church with Sarah's parents."

Mom sighed, but she didn't argue. Detective Jenner had been right. People in this town, including the local authorities, loved the Sarah story. And they weren't going to protect me if I was the one trying to take it away from them. They hadn't protected Kellie's family, either.

"Maybe I should talk to Chad and Ruth myself," Mom said. "They've always been such nice, reasonable people."

"I wouldn't," I told her. "They were pretty upset when I tried to tell them the truth. I don't think they'd encourage people to do this . . ." I gestured toward the living room and the front window. "They aren't like that. But I think we should probably leave them out of it."

Mom squeezed my hands. "Then is there anything I *can* do? Anything to help make this easier?"

"Besides inventing a time machine so I can go back and never let this rumor get so big? I don't think so."

"If I had a time machine, I'd stop the shooting from happening altogether," she said, and the tears I'd been expecting (and dreading) finally appeared in the corners of her eyes.

I removed my hands from hers and stood up, heading over to the cabinet where we kept the bowls. "I'm just going to have to deal with it," I said. "I've already got a few of the letters. I don't know what I'll do with them, but once I have them all . . . I'll come up with something." I grabbed a box of Froot Loops and began to pour myself a bowl. "It'll be something I can put out there. Something to show people that Kellie wasn't lying."

Mom waited until I'd poured the milk into my bowl and joined her at the table again before asking, "How does Kellie feel about you doing this?"

"I haven't gotten ahold of her yet," I said. "I've been emailing and texting."

"So you don't know if she actually wants this?"

I frowned at her. "Why wouldn't she?" I asked. "She tried to tell everyone the truth three years ago. I should've helped her then, but I didn't, so I am now. I'm sure she'll be glad."

"A lot can change in three years, though."

"What do you mean?" I asked.

Mom opened her mouth, then shut it and shook her head. "I don't know," she said. "Like I said, I'll support you no matter how you decide to handle this. But you should make sure Kellie is okay with it. If you try to make these letters you're collecting public, that's going to bring a lot of attention on her again. She might not be prepared for that."

"The McHales' book will do the same thing," I said. "She's going to get attention no matter what. I'm sure she wants to set the record straight more than any of us."

"Maybe you're right," Mom said. She stood up and wiped the stray tears from her eyes. "I'd better go get ready for work. I'm taking over Nancy's shift at the store for today. You going to be okay here alone? With everything that's happening?"

I rolled my eyes. "Yes, Mom. No one's going to show up with the pitchforks yet. Give it a week or two."

She swatted at my shoulder. "Don't be a smart mouth. And don't forget to take your medication."

"I won't," I said. She was halfway down the hallway to her bedroom when I called after her again. "Mom?"

"Hm?"

"Thank you."

"For what?"

There were so many answers I could have given. So many things that I'd never thanked her for. That she'd never ask me to thank her for.

For not talking me out of telling the truth, even if it meant life was going to get harder for her. For putting up with me for the past three years, even when I took all of my anger and frustration out on her. For being my biggest ally and champion and protector, even when I didn't want her to be there at all.

"For everything."

When I think of Kellie Gaynor, two memories flash in my mind. The first is a quick snapshot, her ashen face and wide, dark eyes when she turned around in the bathroom door and told Sarah and me to hide. It was the first word she'd ever said to me.

Hide.

The second memory plays more like a short film. It happened weeks later, at the local grocery store. It was the first time I'd left my house since the shooting. I'd told Mom I wanted to go to the store with her. I didn't want to be left alone in our house. Not yet. But five minutes in and I already felt panicked. The store wasn't even that crowded. There were maybe a dozen people with shopping carts. But it was enough that anytime someone came around the corner, my heart started to pound. When someone in the aisle next to mine dropped a can on the ground with a loud thud, I started crying.

"Lee baby," Mom said, her own voice shaking. She reached out to touch me, but I jerked away. I didn't want to be crying in the middle of the cereal aisle and I definitely didn't want her to cry, either. That would just get more people staring at us. And besides, this wasn't about her. She lowered her hand slowly and said, "You can go wait in the car if you want. I won't take long."

"I'm fine," I snapped. "I can take care of myself."

But thirty seconds later, I turned around and headed back toward the front of the store, leaving Mom to do the rest of the shopping herself. I wasn't sure if I was going to wait in the car or just stand near the front of the store, by the exit, so I could see down each of the aisles and make a quick escape at any sign of danger.

But before I could decide, I saw her.

Kellie.

She was emerging from the freezer section, a curtain of dyed-black hair obscuring part of her face, her wounded arm still in a sling. She was staring at her boots and she hadn't noticed me yet, which was just as well. I wanted to say something to her, but I wasn't sure what just yet. "Hi" didn't really seem sufficient given what had happened the last time we saw each other.

I was running through a few possibilities in my head as she got closer and closer to me, when a middle-aged woman in a pink floral dress stepped out from the canned goods aisle and bumped right into Kellie.

Kellie stumbled but caught herself. She turned to look at the woman, and if I'd assumed the collision was an accident, that thought went out the door almost immediately.

"You ought to be ashamed of yourself," the pink-floral woman yelled.

I recoiled and wrapped my arms around myself. Even from this distance, I could see Kellie start to shake. Though she didn't move. She stared back at the woman and turned her chin upward, letting her hair fall back, out of her face. She didn't say anything, but she didn't run, either.

"You're nothing but trash." The woman's voice was so loud that everyone in the store seemed to have heard, stopping and staring, but no one doing a thing to intervene. "A lying piece of trash."

I should be clear: This was before I'd seen those flyers at the pharmacy. Before I'd learned about the Sarah rumors. I had no idea why this woman was screaming at an injured teenager in the middle of the grocery store. And it wasn't just the one woman in the floral dress, either. There were others gathering around, most glaring, a few hurling curse words at her.

It wasn't something I'd ever seen before—a group of grown adults surrounding a teenage girl, talking to her like she was a cockroach, a vile thing to be squished by whatever means necessary.

"Kellie." A sharp voice came from the front of the store. A tall woman with strawberry-blond hair and thick-rimmed glasses was looking back at the scene from the checkout line. Even through her lenses, I could tell she had an expression of anger and shock on her face. "Kellie, honey, let's go."

The woman, I realized, was her mother.

Kellie took a few steps, breaking free from the small crowd, but as she moved toward the checkout counter, one of the bystanders spat at her.

"Go to hell," the man, who must've been in his forties, hissed.

"Kellie," her mother said again, her voice now tinged with a touch of fear.

Kellie kept her head down as she hurried over to her mother, who was grabbing the freshly bagged groceries as fast as she could. She shoved one of the bags into Kellie's good arm and began steering her toward the exit.

But it's the moment after that that sticks with me. The moment just before Mrs. Gaynor pushed open the glass door. In that split second, Kellie looked back, and our eyes met. I don't think she knew I was there until that moment. And as she recognized me, her eyes narrowed and her lips twisted into a sneer.

No one had ever looked at me with the same sort of fury that Kellie Gaynor did in that moment. It was so powerful, so visceral, that I flinched. She could have slapped me and it would have been less startling.

When I think of Kellie, I will always remember that look on her face as she left the grocery store.

And I'll remember that I stayed quiet, even when I had plenty of chances to speak up.

XXX

I hadn't heard from Ashley since the text messages we'd exchanged during my visit with Eden. I'd thought about calling her, but I wasn't sure what I would say. Especially once I knew that Brother Lloyd had talked about me to his congregation. And if her little sister was part of the crowd that had decided to hate me, I worried she had, too.

I found out soon enough.

Miles and I had driven to the next town over after school one day. If we were going to prom, we both needed something to wear. So we'd made our way to one of the strip malls that had, on one end, a place where Miles could rent a tux with the money his grandmother had excitedly given him when she found out he was taking "such a nice girl" to prom. On the other end, there was a consignment shop where I hoped I'd find an affordable dress that I could sell back in a couple of weeks.

Mom didn't have the money to buy me a new dress, not even from one of the department stores, and I was trying to save every penny I could for my move to Los Angeles. But buying used clothing isn't really the shameful thing in Virgil County that it is elsewhere. A lot of girls at VCHS would be getting their dresses secondhand. Being poor—or at least on the very bottom of lower middle class—was kind of the norm. In fact, you were more likely to be teased if it appeared as though you'd spent *too much* money.

Anyway, I chose a spot in the middle of the parking lot so we could each go to our separate destinations and reconvene once we'd finished shopping.

"Meet at the pizza place in two hours?" I asked, pointing at the restaurant roughly in the middle of the strip.

He raised one thick eyebrow. "Two *hours?*"

"Listen," I said. "You're going to walk in, probably get measured, and try on a couple of tuxes that will all look the same and be done with it. I have way more options to deal with. And since I'm shopping secondhand, the sizing is a little less straightforward. You've got it easy. I need two hours. Which, really, all things considered, isn't that much. Oh my God, if Sarah was here . . ." I trailed off as that old, familiar pain seized my chest.

Sarah would have loved shopping for prom. Not just for her dress but mine, too. She would have dragged me to every store within an hour's drive. She would have taken pictures and notes on her phone so we could compare and make the perfect choice. It would've involved weeks of shopping.

But instead, it was just going to be me, shopping in one store, without her.

Miles covered my hand with his own and squeezed,

anchoring me the way he always did. "Okay. Two hours." He paused. "I have a question, though."

"Yeah?"

"Should we . . . Are we going to coordinate?" he asked, his words slipping out in a quiet slur. "You know. Colors."

"You mean, like . . . match? Your tie or whatever matching my dress?"

He shrugged. "I guess."

"Do we have to?"

"I don't care if you don't."

"Hmm. Well, I say we pick what we like, and if we end up clashing, we'll revel in it."

Miles gave a lazy smile. "Let's both pick ridiculously bright colors."

"Oh yes," I said. "We can blind all of our classmates."

"Well, Denny has always said he needed more blind friends."

We both laughed before sliding out of my truck. I'd worried that, now that he knew about my asexuality, things would be awkward between us. But, if anything, it was the opposite. I felt more at ease with Miles than ever. The last secret I kept from him had been revealed and, while I still didn't know where that left us in terms of our feelings for each other, things were comfortable. Easy.

Unless I brought up the letters, of course.

I didn't, though. Not that day.

He gave me a quick wave before slumping off to the other end of the parking lot. I turned and started toward the consignment shop, but I'd only gone past two rows of cars when I saw Ashley's van parked in a handicapped spot. And there was Ashley, with her husband, loading shopping bags into the back.

I ducked my head and tried to walk past as quickly as I could, but of course it couldn't be that easy.

"Hey, Ash," I heard Logan say before I'd managed to slip by. "I think that's Lee over there."

Ashley looked over her shoulder, her eyes meeting directly with mine. She was in her power chair with Miriam on her lap. She looked away from me and passed Miriam to Logan. "Will you put her in the car seat for me, babe? I'll only be a minute."

Once he'd taken Miriam, Ashley turned and began moving toward me. I stopped a few feet away, lingering on the sidewalk just across from the spot where Ashley had parked. I couldn't move, even though all I wanted at that moment was to run to the consignment shop and hide behind clothing racks. Ashley's stare had pinned me in place.

She maneuvered her chair up the small curb and stopped when we were only a few feet apart. At first, she said nothing. I guess she must've been waiting for me to speak. We both knew I owed her an explanation. But my mouth felt dry and my tongue was heavy. After nearly a minute, all I could manage was a quiet, "Hey."

"Hi," she replied, her tone terse. After another pause, she said, "What's wrong with you, Lee?"

"Ashley—"

"I know what you've been saying . . . about Sarah," she said.

"Brother Lloyd told us. It's all anyone in my church can talk about. They keep asking me why my friend would tell these kind of lies. And I don't know what to tell them because I have no idea."

"It's not a lie," I said. "I'm sorry, Ashley. I should've told you, I know, but the necklace wasn't—"

"Stop." She held out her hand, palm facing me. "Just stop. I can't believe you, Lee. I thought you wanted to tell the truth. I thought that was why you had me write that letter."

"That is why," I said. "I want to tell the truth and this—about Sarah. It's the truth. It's the whole reason I decided to do this."

"It is not the truth," she argued. "It can't be. I heard her. I was outside the bathroom and I *heard* her."

I shook my head, but Ashley kept going.

"If it really wasn't her necklace—if she really didn't talk to him—you would have told everyone sooner. You would have told *me* sooner. I thought we were friends, Lee. I thought of you like my family."

"We are friends, Ashley."

"We're not." And I could see tears in her eyes then. She wasn't just mad. She was hurt. Really hurt. Ashley wasn't the one of us who cried. Me, sure. Eden too, sometimes. Even Miles and Denny had shed a few tears since the shooting. But never Ashley. She was the one who held us when we cried. Who comforted us when we were hurt. Who protected us from those who might hurt us in the first place.

But I was the one making her cry now. Just one more thing to feel guilty about, I guess.

She ran a hand across her face, pushing the small salty drops off her cheeks. "If we were friends, you wouldn't have made me out to be a liar."

"I wasn't trying to make you a liar," I said. "Until I read your letter, I had no idea you were the one who started the rumor. If I had, I would have said something to you first. But by then, I'd already told Sarah's parents. I'm sorry, Ashley. I never meant to put you in the middle of this, but . . . but you're the one who told everyone. I didn't say anything sooner, so it's my fault, too. But—"

"I *heard her*," she said again. "I heard what she said. It was Sarah's necklace and she stood up to him and hearing that . . . hearing her changed my life. It gave me faith and strength that I needed. And I told everyone because it was so . . . it meant so much to me. And if it didn't happen—if it wasn't her—then I don't know what's real and I . . ." She trailed off as she tried to wipe her face again, but there were far too many tears now. They refused to be pushed aside and continued pouring down her cheeks.

I stepped forward, instinctively going to hug her, but she moved her chair back before I could get any closer.

"I know what I heard was real," she said. "It has to be. Because if it's not, then I'm a liar. And I'm *not* a liar. I'm not a bad person."

"Of course you're not. I never said you were."

"In your version of the story I am," she said. "According to you, I told everyone a lie about Sarah."

"Technically, you did," I said. "I know you didn't mean to, but, Ashley, I was with her. I was the one holding her hand when she died. It didn't happen. Not the way you remember. I'm sorry."

I'd never wanted her to feel guilty, even though I did. It had been a mistake. A big one, yes, but a mistake made by a traumatized seventeen-year-old girl. "I should've talked to you as soon as I read your letter. I'm sorry. Let's just . . . let's talk about this. I—"

But she turned her chair and moved back toward the curb without a good-bye. Or even, as maybe would have been more appropriate, a "go to hell."

I let her go without calling after her. I knew it wouldn't have done any good. But I stood there, in the same spot, until long after I saw her van leave the parking lot.

By the time I was able to move again, I really wasn't in the mood to shop for a dress. I only tried on a couple and took the first one that fit, barely even taking note of what it looked like. I ended up waiting for Miles at the pizza place a good while before we were supposed to meet, and when he showed up, having stopped by the bookstore after getting his tux fitted, he was disappointed to find that I hadn't followed through with our plans to wear the brightest colors we could find.

"It's black," he said, peeking into my bag. "Your dress."

"Oh . . . yeah. Sorry. I forgot."

"It's cool," he said. "I'm sure you'll look great."

"What color tie or vest or whatever did you get?"

The right corner of his mouth quirked upward. "It'll be a surprise," he said. After a second, though, his half smile faded away. "What's wrong?"

"Nothing." I chewed my bottom lip. "I'm fine."

He just tilted his head and narrowed his eyes at me. He wasn't buying it. I don't think I'd expected him to.

"It's just . . ." I dipped a breadstick into the small container of marinara sauce we were sharing. I'd ordered us food while I was waiting for him to get to the pizza place. "I ran into Ashley. In the parking lot."

"Oh."

I didn't have to say anything else. He knew exactly what seeing her would have meant. And based on my demeanor in that moment, he could probably have guessed how the conversation had gone. I appreciated that he didn't push for details. Instead, he just gave me some cash for his half of the dinner bill and offered to carry the bag with my prom dress out to the truck for me.

We drove back to Virgil County in silence, but at some point along the way, his hand had moved to cover mine as it rested on the stick shift. And I didn't pull away.

AIDEN STROUD

Aiden Stroud was eighteen, captain of the football team, senior class president, a shoo-in for prom king, and a friend of the boy who killed him.

No one likes to talk about that last bit. It muddies the waters, makes people uncomfortable. How could the good boy, the victim we insist on raising to a pedestal of perfection, have been friends with the troubled young man who killed nine people? I don't have the answer to that, but by all accounts, they'd been friends since preschool. Maybe not inseparable, the way Sarah and I were, but close enough that, if you dig back far enough into the archives of social media, you find photos from a party a few months before, where Aiden, dressed in a football jersey, has his arm slung around the shoulders of his eventual killer.

I've seen that photo dozens of times during my internet spirals. I've stared at it for hours, wondering what happened. Had something changed, had they fought? Had he even known Aiden would be in that classroom? According to Denny, Aiden had only come in the room at the end of class to bring Brenna a book she'd left in his locker. He wasn't supposed to be there.

I have to stop myself from wondering, because it never gets me anywhere.

But this isn't about him. Or, it's not supposed to be. It's about Aiden. But I don't think it's possible to really talk about who

Aiden was, outside of his bland, generic obituary in the local paper, without mentioning that connection.

I knew Aiden the way everyone did. As one of the most popular, outgoing guys in school. To me, he was mostly just Brenna DuVal's jock boyfriend. But he was in Ashley's grade, so I wanted her perspective. Obviously things are complicated between us, so I had Miles text her and ask about him.

MILES: You knew Aiden, right?

ASHLEY: Aiden Stroud? Yeah. Of course. Why?

MILES: Lee's thing.

ASHLEY: Oh.

MILES: So anything you wanna say about him?

ASHLEY: I guess. Let me think.

MILES: Okay.

ASHLEY: We made out at church camp once.

MILES: Ha.

ASHLEY: Seriously. Before I started seeing Logan. He and Brenna were on one of their breaks. He used way too much tongue for church camp.

MILES: I didn't know he went to your church.

ASHLEY: Only for a year, I think. When his parents split up, he and his mom moved across town. He started going to Hillcreek Christian. I'm sure he made out with some girls there, too, though. He and Brenna broke up a lot. And Aiden always found someone to kiss.

MILES: That's definitely not the story I was expecting.

ASHLEY: I'm making him sound awful. LOL. He wasn't gross or anything. Just flirty. He was also super sweet. He was the guy anyone could call if they needed a ride home from a party. Even if he wasn't there, he'd come pick you up just so you didn't drive drunk. I never had to call him, but a few of my friends did.

MILES: So he never drank?

ASHLEY: Not that I know of. He told me once he lost a cousin in a drunk driving accident, which was why he always volunteered to drive people home.

MILES: Makes sense.

ASHLEY: Actually, the last time I hung out with Aiden was at a party. Right before Christmas. I never drank either because I was too scared of getting in trouble. So we were just sitting on the couch, and he let me blubber to him for an hour about all of my relationship drama with Logan at the time. I'm sure he was annoyed and bored, but he didn't act like it. He told me he was sure Logan and I would work things out. That he knew, somehow, we'd end up together. He was right, I guess.

MILES: Seems like he was a good guy.

ASHLEY: He was. Aside from the too-much-tongue at church camp.

MILES: We all have flaws.

ASHLEY: The weird thing to think about is the end of that memory. After we talked about Logan, ▮▮▮▮▮ came over to us. He was drunk, and Aiden drove him home. Ironic, huh? Aiden cared about keeping him safe but . . .

MILES: Yeah.

"Oh, Lee baby, you look beautiful."

There were tears in Mom's eyes when she looked at me, standing in the center of the living room in my prom attire. But for once, these weren't tears of sadness or pain. She was happy, and that lifted at least a fraction of the anxiety from my chest.

"Thanks, Mom," I said.

The dress was actually quite nice, if simple. It was jet black with thin straps that supported a heart-shaped neckline, giving the allusion that I actually had curves. The skirt flared out a bit at my hips so that it swirled around my ankles as I walked. It wasn't dramatic or glamorous, but I was okay with that.

"Here," Mom said. "I found some things for your hair."

My hair was too short to do much with besides comb. But Mom walked over to me with a handful of small clips, each with little crystals attached. They were cheap, but once she shoved a couple into my hair, on either side of my face, they did add an element of polish.

"Oh," she said, "and I picked up the lipstick you asked for."

She reached into a shopping bag by the couch and pulled out a small tube and passed it to me.

I smiled down at the familiar plastic casing. Carefully I pulled off the cap and rolled up the lipstick. It was a pretty shade of berry red that I knew would apply like a sheer wash of color across my lips. I handed the tube back to Mom and gestured for her to apply it, knowing I'd make a mess of it if I tried myself.

This had been Sarah's favorite drugstore lipstick. On a whim, I'd asked Mom to pick it up from the store, and I was glad I did. It was silly. Sarah had been gone for more than three years, and I didn't believe in ghosts or spirits or an afterlife at all. But wearing that lipstick still felt like carrying a little piece of her with me that night.

"Done," Mom said, capping the lipstick and dropping it into the little black handbag she'd lent me for the evening. "Oh, my little girl is all grown up and going to prom. Where did the time go? It feels like yesterday that the nurse was handing you to me in the hospital. You were so tiny. And beautiful."

"Mom."

I was relieved to hear a light tapping on the front door, saving me from more of her sentimental gushing.

"Oh. There he is." Mom went to the door and pulled it open. "Hi, Miles."

Miles mumbled a greeting, and I stepped up next to Mom so I could see him. I figured he would look handsome in his tux—and he did, for the record—but the minute I saw him I burst into fits of laughter so painful that I almost doubled over.

Miles just grinned.

Even though I'd forgotten the deal we'd made the night we went shopping, he really had taken it seriously. The suit was black, as expected, but beneath the jacket, his vest and tie were a bright shade of neon orange.

It took a minute for me to get my laughter under control, and by then I had noticed Mrs. Mason standing in our yard, clutching her digital camera.

"My grandma wants to take pictures," he said sheepishly.

"Oh my God, I almost forgot!" Mom grabbed her cell phone and shooed us out into the yard. "Hi, Mrs. Mason," she said as she followed us down the steps and onto the grass. "Aren't they adorable?"

We spent a solid twenty minutes posing in different spots around our two yards, with Mom and Mrs. Mason trying to find the best place to take photos. They positioned us like dolls, telling us where to look and how to stand. Occasionally, they'd jump into the pictures themselves. I was sure they'd taken over a hundred shots before they were interrupted by the buzz of my phone.

I pulled it from my purse and saw that Eden was trying to video chat with me.

I clicked to answer immediately. "Hey," I said.

Eden's face appeared on the screen. She was sitting on her bed, and I could see the bottom half of one of her anime wall scrolls on the wall behind her. Her hair was pulled back into a messy ponytail, and beneath her glasses, I could see dark circles. But she smiled back at me.

"Is Miles already there? Did you see the orange monstrosity?"

"You knew?" I asked.

"He texted me a picture earlier," she said. "Isn't it hideous?"

"And perfect," I said, smiling over at Miles, who had moved so that he could see Eden over my shoulder.

"Well, let me see you guys," she said. "You know that's what I'm here for."

I passed the phone to my mom, who greeted Eden warmly as she backed up away from us and positioned the phone so that Eden could see Miles and me in our prom clothes.

"You two look great," Eden said once I'd taken the phone back from Mom. "Even with the orange."

"Thank you. We're meeting Denny and his date at the school. Wish you were here with us. We miss you."

"I miss you guys, too." She smiled and shook her head. "I should let you go. You don't want to be late."

"Hold on," I said. I looked over at Miles. "I'll be right back. I forgot something in the house."

He nodded and went to join my mom and his grandmother, who were already examining the pictures on Mom's phone.

I took my phone inside and shut the door behind me. I hadn't actually forgotten anything, but I didn't want to talk to Eden in front of everyone. I hadn't told Miles yet about what had happened when I visited Eden or what she'd admitted in her letter. I figured she would tell him when she was ready.

"So, how are you?" I asked, sinking down onto my couch.

"Uh . . . well, Misty and Jenny raided the room. Poured out all the alcohol. So it's been kind of tough. But for the best, I guess."

"Are you going to be okay?"

"I hope so," she said. "I never thought I'd say this, but I'm looking forward to coming back to Virgil County in a couple weeks. It'll be great to have you guys around again. Even if it's just for the summer before you and Denny leave."

"We'll keep in touch," I promised her.

"I know," she said. "And Jenny's already planned her first trip. My parents said she can stay with us over Fourth of July weekend. I've warned her that she'll have to deal with an interrogation from Abuela. I think Jenny's got an advantage, though. Abuela told me she likes her pink hair."

"Your family will love her," I said. "I bet it'll be a lot of fun. And you know we'll want to hang out with you guys, too. I have a feeling she and Denny will get along well."

"Oh crap," she said. "I hadn't thought about that. I don't know if I can handle two extroverts at the same time."

I laughed, and a minute later we said our good-byes.

Miles was waiting by my truck when I stepped back outside.

"You two have fun," Mom said, kissing me on the cheek. "Be safe. Call me if you need anything."

Mrs. Mason gave me a hug, too, before embracing her grandson. "You grew up to be such a good boy. I'm so proud of you," I heard her say.

But Miles didn't seem happy to hear this. His face reddened

and he ducked his head as she pulled away from him. "Thanks, Grandma."

"You ready to go?" I asked.

He nodded.

We'd opted out of the group limo to save a little bit of money. Besides, being trapped in a confined space with half a dozen people, several of which weren't people I knew well, felt like a panic attack waiting to happen on a night that was already bound to be anxiety ridden.

So we climbed into my truck and headed toward the school.

VCHS didn't have a big prom budget, so the dance was being held in our gym. Despite this, it was actually pretty beautiful. A lot of effort had gone into making it look less like a basketball court and more like a ballroom. Banners in our school colors hung from the ceiling. The lights had been dimmed and a spotlight roamed around the floor as a DJ played an old Tim McGraw song. There were balloons and streamers and tables filled with snack foods.

And, yeah, it was a little cliché, but honestly, it was pretty much exactly how I'd imagined as a kid. The only difference was that Sarah wasn't with me.

I swallowed. I knew that wasn't going to be the last time I thought of her tonight. But I was determined to have fun, despite the longing ache her absence left me.

"Lee! Miles!"

We turned and saw Denny and Amber coming toward us. Amber looked beautiful in a baby-pink dress, but Denny was the one who got all of the attention. He was wearing a completely white tux with a matching white top hat. On anyone else it would have looked ridiculous—and, okay, maybe if you didn't know Denny personally, it still would have looked ridiculous—but it just seemed to make perfect sense.

"You look amazing," I said.

"I know," Denny replied.

"I was talking to Glitter."

For the record, the dog was wearing a black bow tie and was, in fact, quite precious.

"You always gotta outdo me, don't you?" Miles asked.

Denny grinned, the apples of his cheeks pushing up his dark sunglasses. "It gives me purpose."

"Why are we still standing here?" Amber asked. "Come on. Let's dance."

"The lady's right," Denny said.

Miles looked at me, that eyebrow raised, and I nodded, following him to the center of the room.

As we weaved through our peers, I realized just how crowded this gym was and couldn't help but make a mental tally of where all the exits were, and I decided that there weren't nearly enough ways out. If there was any kind of threat, there would be a stampede for the doors. It would be a nightmare to get out of there. And a lot of people wouldn't make it.

A list began to form in my mind of all the ways I might die at prom. A fire. A bomb. Another shooting. There were too many possibilities. Too many paths that led to oblivion.

I focused on steadying my breathing and kept my eyes on Miles's back as I followed him through the crowd.

"How do you dance with a guide dog?" I heard him ask Denny, who laughed. But before I got the answer, a hand closed like a vise around my wrist.

I yelped and spun around, my chest seizing up with panic. This was it, I thought. This was the end. The last thing I was going to see before I died was . . .

Tara Chambers.

She was standing too close, her face a twisted, hateful version of her sister's as her fingernails dug into my arm. I tried to pull free, but the terror had made me shaky, and her grip was tight.

"You should leave," she spat. "No one wants you here, you filthy liar."

"Hey." Miles was pushing his way through the crowd, back toward me. "Back off."

"She's the one who needs to back off," Tara shot back. "She's the one causing trouble."

"Uh, maybe I'm missing something, because I'm blind and all." Denny was suddenly at my other shoulder. "But that's really not how this seems."

"I can't believe you all would defend her," Tara said. "After everything my sister has done for you? For her? How can you let her get away with this?"

"Get away with what?" Amber demanded. Now she'd joined us, too. "Talking about Sarah? You weren't there, Tara. Neither of us were. You don't know what happened, either."

"You too, Amber? What about Sarah?"

"What about you let go of Lee," Miles said, his voice low and more menacing than I'd heard it in years.

Tara growled and tossed my arm away from her. I stumbled back, still startled and trembling as Miles caught me, placing a hand on my shoulder to keep me steady. To keep me grounded.

"It should've been you that died in the bathroom that day, Lee," Tara said, before storming off, red dress whipping around her like flames.

"I can't believe she just said that," Amber gasped. "That's awful."

"You okay?" Miles murmured.

I nodded. "I'll be fine. Just startled. Thanks, you guys."

"Don't let her ruin your night," Denny said. "Come on. I've got to prove to Miles that I'm the better dance partner."

"Why's it gotta be a competition with you?"

"You're only asking me that because you know I'm the obvious winner."

One of the teachers chaperoning the dance volunteered to hold on to Glitter while Denny and Amber danced. After a few minutes, my nerves had mostly settled, but my heart was still racing for a completely different reason.

Miles had his hands on my waist, and my arms were around his neck. Neither of us are dancers, so we mostly just stood in one place and swayed along to the music. The DJ (also known as Mrs. Keebler, our English teacher) seemed to have a soft spot for country love songs. I wished she'd play something faster. Something that wouldn't make it so easy to lean into Miles and rest my head on his shoulder.

"Dunno if I said it earlier, but you look beautiful," Miles said.

"Thanks," I said, hating the blush I felt crawling up my neck. "You don't clean up bad yourself. Though, the orange . . ."

"Worth it for the way it made you laugh."

"I regret not following through on our clashing colors idea," I said. "Can you imagine if I showed up in, like . . . lime green?"

He smiled. "That would have been great. But nah. I like this one." He hesitated a moment. "Lee, I gotta ask something."

"Okay," I said, feeling wary.

"I was thinking . . . how'd you feel about some company on your drive to California?"

"You want to go with me?"

"Just for the drive. Maybe stay a weekend and fly back." His shoulders shrugged beneath my hands. "Not like I got plans after graduation. Honestly never thought I'd make it this far. But I got a little money saved and . . . I don't know. Grandma thinks I should look into vocational school—like for welding or something—but I've been thinking of maybe going to community college for a couple years, maybe transferring, majoring in history . . . if any bigger school will have me. Anyway, thought maybe a road trip would be a good chance to figure some stuff out. If you'd be up for the company."

"I'd love that," I said, unable and unwilling to fight the grin that—almost painfully—stretched my cheeks.

"Yeah?"

"Yeah! It's a long drive, and Mom probably can't afford to take that much time off work. And I'd . . . I'd love for you to come with me."

"Good."

"Good."

We danced in silence for a few minutes after that. I hadn't realized that we'd been drawing closer to one another until there was almost no space between us. It just felt right, being near him like this. It felt like all those nights on my roof, the calm that came with his arm around my shoulder or his fingers laced through mine. The sense of comfort that came just from having him near.

"You know," he murmured, "tonight got off to a bad start, but . . . I'm glad you decided to come."

"Me too." The words came out as a whisper. "I know it took me a while to come around to the idea, but now that I'm here . . ."

"Yeah?"

"Now that I'm here, I . . . don't think I'd want to be anywhere else tonight."

He smiled, and his arms tightened around my waist. Despite my anxiety about the crowded gym and the incident with Tara, I felt overcome with this sense of ease. This feeling that I was safe.

Before I'd realized it, I'd taken a step closer, bridging the last bit of space between us, and rested my head on his shoulder. The fabric of his jacket was cool and soft beneath my cheek. I could feel his breath in my hair. Could smell the fresh mint of his soap. And everything was perfect.

Which was the problem.

When the song ended, it yanked me back to reality. The poppy beat of a new song was a sharp reminder that this was exactly what I didn't want to happen.

I pulled away from Miles, and it was like stepping out of warm water and into the chill of winter. The sense of comfort faded away, and I was flooded with the fears I'd battled earlier that evening. It was all too overwhelming, moving from one extreme to another, and everything was swamped with fresh guilt.

"You okay?" Miles asked as I stepped away from him and pressed a hand to my forehead.

"I just need some air," I said, stumbling back another step. "I'll be back in a minute."

Before he could say anything, I grabbed my handbag from a nearby chair and headed toward the closest exit.

I ended up out in the parking lot, the night breeze raising goose bumps on my bare arms. I leaned back against the brick wall of the building and took a few deep breaths.

Out in the open, away from the crowd, it was easier to let that familiar anxiety slip away again. But all that did was make the muddled feelings about Miles clearer. I'd told myself we'd just come as friends, that I'd keep my boundaries up and everything would be fine. But when I was dancing with him, I'd wanted more.

I always wanted more.

But then what? I asked myself. *We date for a few months until I go to California, and he'll eventually find another girl who actually wants to sleep with him.*

I shook that thought away. It wasn't being asexual that worried me. It was that, if we did break up, be it because of sex or just distance and time, I didn't know what that would mean for us, for our friendship. I hadn't cared about someone this much since Sarah, and God, if I lost Miles, I don't know what I would do.

But this—getting close, pulling away, constantly building new, higher walls between us for safety—that could tear us apart, too.

I wanted to be with Miles, but I was scared. And I wanted Sarah there with me, to tell me what to do. I already knew what she'd say. She'd drag me back inside and tell me I was being ridiculous, that I should "kiss the boy already."

I almost laughed imagining it.

And then I wanted to cry.

My phone buzzed in my purse. I pulled it out and saw a text from Mom. She'd sent along one of the photos of Miles and me in front of our house. This one's my favorite, she'd typed. I took one look at the picture and closed the message. I needed to not think about Miles for a minute.

I found distraction in other text messages. I'd sent another to Kellie that morning, but she hadn't responded. A couple of days earlier, I'd also started leaving voice mails. I didn't even think twice about clicking her name and hitting the call button. Trying to get ahold of her felt so familiar at this point. Focusing on the letters, obsessing over collecting them, was easier than dealing with the issue right in front of me.

The call was on its third ring when the door next to me

opened and Miles stepped out into the parking lot. "There you are," he said. "You okay?"

I held up a hand, gesturing for him to wait as Kellie's voice mail picked up.

"Hey, Kellie. This is Lee Bauer. Again. I hope you're getting these messages. Listen, if you could give me a call back, I'd appreciate it. It's really important. Okay. Bye."

When I hung up the phone, Miles was scowling at me. "You're *calling* her now?"

"Texting wasn't getting me anywhere, so—"

"So maybe you should leave her alone. Give her space."

"I can't. I still need her letter."

He shook his head. "Let the letters go, Lee."

"What? No. Why would I do that?" I asked. "You keep saying stuff like this. What's your problem with the letters, anyway?"

"Nothing," he said, shoving his hands into the pockets of his dress pants.

Rage bubbled up inside of me. It was irrational, I know, but I was suddenly so furious with him. I was angry that he didn't understand why these letters mattered. Angry that he'd let me get so close to him when he'd promised we'd just be coming to prom as friends. Angry that every time I pulled away from him, the world felt a little colder.

"Stop doing that!" I yelled, because I just wanted to yell at him. "Stop being all cryptic and vague about why I should let this go. Why? What is your problem?"

"Drop it, Lee," he said. "Let's just go back inside."

"No," I snapped. "Why won't you write a letter?"

"Lee."

"Why won't you do it?"

"I'm going back in."

I grabbed his arm to stop him. "Not until you tell me what's wrong with you."

He shook me off and took a step back, his eyes flashing dark. "What's wrong with me?" he asked, his voice raised. "You're the one who is obsessed with these stupid letters!"

"Because they're important!"

"To who?"

"To everyone," I said. "The truth is important to everyone."

"No, it's important to *you*," he said, pointing a finger at my chest. His voice was so loud, so harsh, that I flinched away in surprise. "This isn't about the truth, Lee. It's about *you*. You and your guilt."

"I'm trying to make things better."

"Kellie doesn't want to talk to you!"

"She will once she understands what I'm doing."

"Not everyone wants to talk about it, Lee." He was shouting at me. He'd never shouted at me before. And even though I didn't feel threatened by him, it was still unsettling. "Maybe you and Denny and Ashley and Eden have stories you think the world should hear, but not all of us do. The truth isn't going to set all of us free. People don't want to hear my truth. Especially not you."

"Miles . . . What are you talking about?" I asked. He was

pacing now, his hands in his curly hair. I just stood there, staring. "I know what happened to you already. I know about the awful things those reporters wrote about you. How people misunderstood you. And you were the bravest of all of us that day. Why would you have a problem writing about that?"

"Because I'm——"

He was cut off by the exit door opening again. A couple of girls, dressed in purple and blue, came stumbling out, their arms intertwined. They looked between us, then began whispering to each other, giggling behind their hands, as they moved toward a nearby car.

When they were gone, I turned to look at Miles again. He was staring at his feet, hands shoved back into his pockets.

"Miles . . ."

"I'm gonna go."

"What?"

"I can't do this right now."

"Miles, you can't walk home. I'm your ride."

But he was already moving through the parking lot, toward the front of the school. And he didn't look back.

I stood in the dimly lit parking lot for a long time after he'd vanished. I couldn't go inside, couldn't look at Denny and Amber and try to explain what had just happened. Mostly because I didn't know *how* to explain. I wasn't sure how we'd gone from such a perfect moment, dancing together, talking about driving across the country together, to screaming at each other in the parking lot.

And now he was gone.

I didn't want to be there anymore. Not without him. So I pulled my keys from my bag and headed to my truck.

I drove around town with the radio blasting for a while. I knew if I went home too early, Mom would want to know what was wrong, and I was too tired to deal with her worry.

The lights were off when I finally did pull into my driveway. The windows were dark next door, too. I wondered if Miles had made it home, and how. I wondered if I should try to go talk to him or just let him have some space for the night. Part of me wanted to apologize, though I honestly didn't know what I had done wrong. Pushed him too much, obviously, but for a good reason.

I thought.

I'd just cut the engine when I heard my phone buzz. I lunged for it, certain it was him. Certain he was going to tell me we should talk. Certain he'd want to explain.

But the text message I'd just received wasn't from Miles.

It was from Kellie Gaynor.

It's funny how some parts of that March 15 come back to me so clearly, like a movie on a high-definition screen playing behind my eyes, but others are a blur or missing altogether.

Like, I don't remember which of us noticed the hickey on Sarah's neck, or how we convinced our biology teacher to let us both go to the bathroom at the same time. But the image starts to sharpen once we're standing in front of the mirror. I remember so vividly the look on Sarah's face as she peered at her reflection, tilting her head slightly so she could see the mark. It was an expression of mingled worry and annoyance, but I couldn't help noticing just a touch of pride.

Kellie was already there. I could see her in the mirror, standing off in the corner behind us, a shadow with a cigarette. She didn't say anything to us, and we ignored her. I always kind of thought of Kellie as the school's phantom, there if you looked closely, but easy to miss if you didn't look in the darker nooks and crannies.

The memory is silent at first. I know Sarah must have been saying something, talking about the mark on her neck as she pulled out some foundation and rubbed it into her skin, but the words are missing. It's like the movie is on mute, until the stall door opened behind us and Ashley stepped out.

"I was wondering where you've been the last few weeks," Ashley said. Her eyes were focused on Sarah, her mouth twisted into a sneer. It's funny, in some ways, remembering it now. Despite our current issues, the Ashley I know is kind and caring. Protective to a fault. This was a different Ashley. "I guess I have my answer."

"Oh God, Ash." Sarah turned away from the mirror to face her. The hint of pride I'd seen in her eyes a second ago vanished. "I'm sorry. I just—"

"Hey, I get it. Who needs Jesus when you have boys that'll suck on your neck?"

My hands balled into fists, but next to me, Sarah didn't even flinch. Things didn't hurt Sarah very often. Even at fourteen, she radiated this confidence I could never imagine possessing. When people insulted her—which, honestly, wasn't often—the words just seemed to roll off her. Like she knew she was better than any label they could have given her.

This was no different. She and Ashley had been friends—or, at least friendly—for a long time, but even when this girl she'd known all of her life tried to shame her, Sarah was unaffected.

I know in Ashley's letter she said Sarah's face went red, but I don't remember that. I do remember Sarah watching her as Ashley stepped forward to wash her hands in the sink next to mine. "You aren't going to . . . ?"

"Tell your parents?" Ashley asked. "No. If you're this comfortable with lying, why should I stop you? But remember, Sarah: Your parents don't know what you're doing, but God sees everything."

I glanced at Sarah again, and she rolled her eyes. A minute later, when Ashley had gone, she said, "I don't know if anyone ever told her, but as far as I know, Jesus likes nice people."

From the corner, I heard Kellie give a snort of laughter, and Sarah grinned wide, her braces on full display. Neither of us had ever seen Kellie Gaynor smile, let alone laugh. But if anyone could have done it, of course it was Sarah.

She picked up her foundation again and went back to work trying to cover the small hickey on her neck. "We should hurry, though. The bell is going to ring soon."

"You really think she won't tell your parents?" I asked.

"She won't. She's self-righteous, but she's not a narc. And honestly? I think she's just having a rough time lately. She hasn't always been that bad."

She capped the foundation and shoved it back into her purse. I had no idea how she managed to buy so much makeup and smuggle it to school without her parents noticing, but her collection just kept growing. Some mornings, after she did her own makeup at a cafeteria table using her phone's camera as a mirror, she'd turn to whatever girl was sitting closest and offer to do hers, too. Lots of freshman girls got mini makeovers courtesy of Sarah McHale's secret cosmetics stash.

Behind us, Kellie stepped into a stall and tossed the remainder of her cigarette in the toilet before flushing. Then she turned and started toward the bathroom door.

The next section of the memory feels like slow motion. Kellie walked out, Sarah zipped her purse, and then we heard the gunshots.

We didn't know what it was at first. My initial thought was firecrackers. I assumed some senior was pulling a prank. Sarah and I glanced at each other, then moved, together, to the door to see what was going on. By then, there was screaming.

We hadn't even taken a step out into the hallway when Kellie came rushing back in. She shoved us back into the bathroom with both hands. "Hide," she said.

"What?" Sarah asked.

But Kellie was already moving toward a stall. She was in such a panic that she hadn't even noticed one of her boots had come untied. She tripped on the string, landing hard on the floor. Both Sarah and I hurried to her, but she shook her head and pushed herself up. "Hide," she said again. "Now."

The gunshots had gotten closer. And the combination of the popping and the screams and the terrified look in Kellie's eyes finally registered with me. Something was wrong. Very wrong.

Sarah figured it out first. She grabbed me by the wrist and pulled me into a stall, locking the door behind us.

I don't know how long it was before he came into the bathroom. Realistically I know it was likely just a minute or two after we hid. But it felt like an eternity. Sarah and I stood facing each other, trying not to breathe. My heart started pounding so hard I could hear it in my ears. Sarah's fingers wrapped around mine and squeezed.

I heard him walk into the bathroom. Heard his heavy step on the tiles. Heard the creak of another stall door, a single gunshot, a yell.

And that's where the sound shifts again. Everything outside of the stall is muffled in my memory. I heard the shooter say something, heard someone—Kellie, obviously—respond, but their words were slurred and garbled. Instead, all I can remember hearing is Sarah. She was barely making a sound, her whisper so silent I probably wouldn't have heard it normally. Her eyes were squeezed shut as her lips mouthed a prayer.

I knew what was happening by that point, but it didn't feel real. It felt like a dream. Or like I was trapped in a video game. The most real part, the scariest thing of all, was the way Sarah's hands shook. She didn't get scared often. And when she did, she was the type to screech and run in the opposite direction, laughing at herself along the way. I'd never seen her face this white. Never heard her pray this desperately.

I don't want to go into the details of what happened next. You know them already. The short version is that he found us and shot twice over the edge of the stall. One bullet hit the wall, near my head, and the other hit Sarah, who was killed instantly, her limp body collapsing into my arms. He left the bathroom, leaving me unscathed. Physically, at least.

A minute later, the police arrived, and I heard more gunshots as he took his own life.

Things speed up again after that. The movie goes on fast-forward. An officer came into the bathroom and pulled me away from Sarah's body. Another officer was assisting Kellie, who was gasping. She'd been shot in the shoulder. In the hallway, EMTs were tending to people, but I couldn't see who. I remember asking about Sarah, asking over and over where she was and who was taking care of her, even though I think I knew she was gone.

Somehow, I ended up at the police station. Walking out of the school, riding in a cop car—those moments are gone. Because, in the next, I'm being questioned, still drenched in my friend's blood, and Mom bursts into the room and rushes to me. I'll never forget the way she hugged me. Like I was her life raft. Like holding me was the only thing keeping her from drowning.

And in her arms, I finally started crying. Because I knew for sure that Sarah—my best friend, my sister—wasn't going home. She'd never be held like this by her mother again.

I loved Sarah. I love her more than I'll probably ever love anyone else. And I hate that some of you reading this will think I'm just trying to tarnish her memory somehow by telling the truth. That is the last thing I want to do. I want Sarah to be remembered, but I want her to be remembered for the person she truly was, not the person the world wants her to be.

So, just in case I haven't made it clear enough: Sarah was not wearing a cross necklace that day; her last moments were not brave or heroic, we were scared little girls in a bathroom stall, and that does not change how much her life mattered; Kellie Gaynor was the one who spoke to the shooter, the cross the police found on the bathroom floor belonged to her.

She arrived at the café twenty minutes late. I didn't even recognize her at first. Not until she sat down at my table and pulled a pack of cigarettes from her purse in place of a greeting.

"Okay," she said, lighting one, right in the middle of the café. "So what do you want?"

It took me a minute to find my words. Her once long blue-black hair was now cut into a chin-length bob, bleached into an almost white blond. She'd replaced her thick eyeliner with a pair of black square-framed glasses. Her lips were painted a dark purple, and the black lines of a tattoo poked out from under the collar of her T-shirt. It also looked like she'd gained about thirty pounds, mostly noticeable in the new roundness of her face and fullness of her chest.

No one who had watched the news three years ago or reading the true crime message boards today would recognize this woman as Kellie Gaynor of Virgil County Massacre fame. And maybe, I thought, that was the point.

"Hi," I finally managed, once my surprise had worn off.

"Hi," she repeated, a hint of mocking in her voice. "Now what do you want, Lee?"

"Oh, I, um . . . I wanted to see how you're doing."

She took a drag from her cigarette, then narrowed her eyes at me as she let out a puff of smoke. "You sent me a dozen emails and left five voice mails—and I don't even want to count all of the text messages—so you could find out how I was doing? Really?"

I coughed and tried to wave the smoke away. Honestly, I don't know how she can still smoke those things. The smell reminds me too much of the bathroom. Of the moments right before the shooting started. Before the world changed. Sitting in that café, I could already feel my heart rate speeding up, and my skin began to itch as every movement out of the corner of my eye turned into something sinister.

When an employee came over to our table, it startled me so much that I nearly jumped out of my chair and bolted for the doors. I managed to keep calm, though, and I was relieved when he said, "Miss, you'll have to put that out. There's no smoking in here."

She sighed, took one last drag, and put it out without a word to the man, who glanced at me with an is-she-serious? expression. I wondered if he'd ever had to tell someone to put out a cigarette before. Smoking in restaurants had been illegal for so long, I couldn't even believe she'd tried it.

When he walked away, Kellie said, "So you want to know how I'm doing. Fine. I'm good. Aside from this weirdo who keeps harassing me."

"Someone's harassing you?"

She gave me a pointed look.

"Oh." I swallowed. "Sorry. I just really wanted to talk to you."

"About?"

I chewed on my lip and fiddled with the straw in my iced coffee. "Did you hear about Sarah's parents?"

"What about them?"

"They're writing a book."

She shrugged. "Good for them. What's that got to do with me?"

I blinked at her, baffled. "I mean . . . it's going to be about Sarah. About the shooting and what happened in the bathroom that day. You know, the necklace? I'd imagine it's going to mention you."

"Seems likely, yeah."

"Doesn't that bother you? That people are going to be talking about that again? That they'll think . . . that that story . . ." I was struggling to find the right words. Kellie was staring at me from behind her glasses, looking at me like I was the most annoying, foolish person on the planet. Maybe I was. Finally I blurted out, "Don't you want people to know the truth?"

She stood up. "I need coffee."

I watched her walk to the counter, listened as she ordered a large black coffee. Honestly, I was relieved to hear the same amount of disdain and exasperation in her voice when she talked to the barista as when she spoke to me.

When she came back and sat down, cup in hand, she ignored my last question. Instead, she said, "I go by Renee now."

"Uh, okay."

"It's my middle name," she said. "I also legally changed my last name. Hyphenated both of my parents' names. Gaynor-Marks. Mom went back to Marks when she and Dad got divorced. Anyway. Almost everyone knows me as Renee Marks now."

"I, um . . . I like it. It's a nice name."

Yes, I know. I sounded painfully ridiculous. But I had no idea what else to say to this. What is the protocol when someone tells you they've changed their name? Was I supposed to call her Renee now? Was that what she was trying to tell me? Still, if I hadn't been so anxious, I probably could have come up with a better response than "It's a nice name."

Kellie—Renee?—didn't even seem to hear me, though. She just kept talking, like I hadn't said a word.

"My friends know I'm from Virgil County," she said. "The close ones, anyway. Everyone else just thinks I'm from Illinois since that's where we moved for my senior year. But even the people who know, they don't know I was there. I tell everyone I moved before the shooting happened. They don't ask me questions about it. Why would they? I doubt most of them even remember who the hell Kellie Gaynor was. And if they did, well, they don't know her. The only person from Virgil County they know is Renee."

"You mean you haven't told *any* of your friends the truth?"

She took a sip of her coffee. "What *is* the truth, Lee?"

"I . . . I don't know," I admitted. "I just know the necklace wasn't Sarah's. I know that she didn't say anything to *him* and that whatever Ashley overheard—"

"Ashley? Is that bitch how that stupid rumor got started?"

I cringed a little. "She's not as bad as you think. She's actually a really good person."

Kellie rolled her eyes. "Yeah. I don't really care what kind of person she is. But you're right. It wasn't Sarah's necklace. And I am the one who talked to the asshole. That's at least part of the truth. But no. I haven't told any of my friends. I haven't told anyone—or talked to anyone—about it in three years."

"But don't you want people to know? What really happened?"

"I used to," she said. "I told everyone I could when I was sixteen, when I thought it actually mattered."

"It still matters, though."

"You didn't seem to feel that way three years ago."

"I . . . I know. Kellie, I'm sor—"

She raised a hand to silence me. "It's fine. I'm not mad about it."

"You're not?"

"I was back then," she said. "I was sure that if you'd spoken up, people would listen. They seemed more likely to believe you than me. I was sure that if just one person—the only other person in that bathroom who was still alive—spoke up, everyone would apologize to me. God, I was naive."

"But maybe they would have."

She shook her head. "No. That story was more powerful than either of us, Lee. And I get it. It's a damn good story. The sweet, pretty dead girl, dying a martyr for her beliefs, is way better than the angry emo chick, stuttering out answers in a panic because she doesn't know what the maniac with the gun wants to hear. Maybe if I'd died it would be a better story. Maybe not. Not sure I'm great martyr material."

"I still should have said something."

"Yeah. You should've. But then there'd probably be two families chased out of that hellhole of a town instead of just one. Like I said. It's a good story. And you know what people like way more than the truth? A good story."

She said all this so casually. No passion. No bitterness. Complete apathy, with maybe just a hint of resignation. These were the facts, at least as far as she saw them. No need to get worked up. Not anymore.

"I was so stupid back then," she said, almost laughing. "I tried to tell everyone the truth. Not because I wanted people to worship me the way they did Sarah. I didn't care about that. I just . . . I don't know. I thought the truth mattered."

"It does," I insisted. "The truth does matter."

"Why does it matter?"

"Because . . . because it's the *truth*." I was having trouble articulating what I wanted to say. I kept thinking of Miles, of our argument in the parking lot the night before. It seemed like such a simple concept to me. The truth was important. Facts were important. Why couldn't these people understand that? Hadn't we been told since childhood that you should always, always tell the truth?

I'd failed at that three years ago. I'd kept my mouth shut, and it was a horrible mistake. Why, now that I was trying to fix it, couldn't Kellie and Miles be on the same page as me?

She took another long sip of her coffee, her eyes turning toward the window off to our left. People were walking past the café. Mothers pushed babies in strollers. Couples held hands. Outside, no one knew that two of the survivors from a national tragedy were sitting in this rinky-dink café. Heck, they probably hadn't even thought about the shooting in ages. They had moved on so long ago that we were just . . .

A story.

"Did you know I used to go to church?"

I looked back at her, but Kellie wasn't looking at me. She was still watching the window.

"This tiny little Methodist church in the next town over. It's where my grandparents went, so I didn't mind making the drive. No one from school went there. I thought . . . I thought that made it safe." She pressed her lips together. "I told my preacher the truth. And the next week, he wrote a whole damn sermon about Sarah. Said we should all strive to be more like her. My grandma said it was the best sermon he ever gave."

"He didn't believe you?"

"Nope. And when I tried to tell Grandma the truth, she said, 'Now quit that, Kellie Renee. Lying to get attention is not becoming of a young lady.' Sometimes, I wonder if my parents even believe me. They said they did but . . ." She raised a shoulder and let it fall. "I have a feeling they were both relieved when I stopped talking about it after we moved. They got almost as much hell as I did, you know."

"I'm so—"

"Stop trying to apologize," she snapped, turning to glare at me. "That's not why I'm telling you this. I'm not trying to guilt you. I don't give a damn about your guilt, Lee. My point is that telling the truth hasn't done anything but make things worse for me. So while you're sitting there telling me the truth matters, I'm telling you—it doesn't. Not to me. Not anymore."

"But—"

"Every time I spoke up, I got shouted down. My voice was stomped out. I was turned into a freaking cartoon villain by my own friends and neighbors. That's what the truth did to me. They hurt more than that gunshot ever could. So Sarah's parents can write whatever book they want. That's their choice. Mine is to try like hell to put this behind me. And that's really freaking hard when you keep emailing and calling constantly just so we can sit here and talk about how important *the truth* is to you."

The weight of her words began to sink in, and a slow realization dawned on me. She hadn't just been avoiding me—the girl who didn't speak up—for the last few weeks. She'd been avoiding the past. She'd built a new life for herself, and here I was, harassing her, hoping to convince her to write a letter for my collection, hoping she'd share the truth with . . . whoever I decided to give these letters to when I was done. And that was the last thing she wanted.

Maybe I was no better than Brother Lloyd.

She stood up, grabbing her purse from the floor and taking a final sip of coffee. "I need to go. Campus is half an hour away, and I promised my friends I'd meet them to study for finals. So if that's all you wanted to talk to me about . . ."

I nodded. I had to work to bite back another apology. It kept creeping onto the tip of my tongue, nearly pushing through my lips, but I fought it. She didn't want an apology from me. She'd made that clear. And the least I could do now was to listen to her about what she wanted.

"Good. Then I'm going to go. I'd say 'See you later' but, let's be honest, I kind of hope I don't. No offense."

I nodded again.

And then she was gone. And I stayed in that café for another hour, staring out the window and wondering what I was supposed to do next.

I'm still trying to figure that out.

ROSI MARTINEZ

From Eden:

I guess I made Rosi sound kind of bad in my letter. We just didn't get along, which is hard when you are the only kids in a family that's as close-knit as ours.

There were a few times, though, when I think she tried to bridge the gap between us. Like when I showed up at Abuela's house one afternoon and found Rosi sitting on the couch reading a manga. The minute I walked into the room she tried to stash it away, but I'd noticed.

"What were you reading?"

"Nothing. It's stupid."

I rolled my eyes and started to walk past her, toward the kitchen, but she stopped me by clearing her throat.

"Actually . . . could you help me?"

"Help . . . with what?"

She held up the manga. "I borrowed it from my friend Jared. I know you're into this kind of stuff. But I don't understand how to read it. It doesn't make sense."

"You read the panels from right to left," I said. "The opposite of American stuff."

"Oh. Well, that explains a lot. Thanks." She hesitated. "Have you read this one?"

I looked at the cover, which had an illustration of a very tiny (but busty) woman wielding a massive sword.

"No, but it looks cool."

"It is," she said. "Well, at least I think it is. Even though I only just now figured out how to read it. But Jared says it's great. He says the girl in it is a real badass. Apparently they made a video game based on the series."

"Cool."

"Maybe . . . maybe you can borrow it from Jared after I finish," she suggested. "I bet he wouldn't mind."

"Maybe."

I wish I'd followed through with that. Even if I hadn't borrowed it from Jared, I could have checked it out at the library or ordered a copy online. I don't know why I never did. I guess I didn't take her suggestion seriously, or worried she was setting me up just to tease me or something. Looking back, I don't think she was, though.

As much as Rosi liked to shut me out and overshadow me when our family was around, I do think she wanted us to have something to talk about. Some common ground to share. Maybe if I'd tried a little harder, we could have been close.

Or maybe not. We were just so different that it's hard to imagine a world in which we were friends.

Still, I think about that day in Abuela's living room a lot, about Rosi clutching the manga in her hands, the popular cheerleader extending a geeky olive branch. And as much as I regret not taking it, that's a memory I want to hold on to.

I can't forget the bad things about her and pretend she was perfect the way people seem to want you to after someone dies. But I can remember little moments like this and believe that, maybe in some parallel universe, Rosi is alive and the two of us have worked things out over a stack of manga.

I needed to see Miles.

I stopped at a gas station on my way back to Virgil County and sent him a text message. I still wasn't entirely sure what had happened at prom the night before, why he of all of us wouldn't want to tell his story, but after talking to Kellie, I realized that maybe he'd had a point.

He sent me back an address. He, Denny, and Amber had gone to a party at some junior's house. I groaned and put my phone away before starting up the truck again. A crowded party was the last place I wanted to be, especially the night after prom, but I knew that if I went home now, I'd just end up sitting around, waiting for Miles and driving myself into a spiral of guilt and anxiety.

The sun had already set by the time I parked my truck down the street from the address Miles had given me. I texted him again, letting him know that I'd be at the house in a minute and that I wanted to talk. He didn't reply, and I was sure he was worried I'd just come here to pressure him into writing a letter again.

I ran up the front steps of the house, one of the larger ones in the county, and walked through the front door with a group of laughing girls. The local Top 40 station was blasting from a stereo in the living room. Some girls sang along while a group of boys sat on the floor around the coffee table, playing quarters.

I wove my way around furniture and past groups of friends standing in corners and piled onto couches, talking and shrieking with laughter. Like they weren't having to fight off the hum of death anxiety. Like they weren't worried about what might happen if someone barged through the front door with a weapon. Or what it felt like to stop existing.

I envied them.

Even when I'm having fun, that fear is always going to be there, even if it is just a quiet, fleeting thing. It will never leave me entirely, I'm certain of that.

I was sure that Miles and Denny had similar fears—at least the ones about escaping a confined space—so when I saw that the back door of the house was standing open and people were outside on the deck, I headed that way. It seemed likely that they'd be outside, where it would be easier to follow through with an exit plan.

I hadn't quite made it to the door yet when I heard someone shout my name. I jumped and spun around, only to see two older guys—ones I was sure had graduated a year or two before—moving toward me through the dining room. I didn't recognize one of them, but the other I knew, at least in memory. Peter McHale, Sarah's older cousin. And as you might expect, he looked furious.

Crap, I thought, and tried to walk a little faster, toward the back door.

But just then, Tara Chambers stepped through it. She saw me, then she glanced over my shoulder, and the guys headed my way. She gave them a nod and started walking to me herself.

I backed up and stumbled, my feet tangling with the leg of a chair. When I righted myself again, they'd come nearer. Closing in. Crowding me back until I was standing in a corner, surrounded by three angry people.

I could feel my throat starting to close up.

"We need to talk to you," Peter said, jabbing a finger at me. "You'd better shut your damn mouth about my cousin."

I wanted to make myself small. To shrink down to the size of a mouse so I could run past their feet. Or to evaporate, becoming a ghost and disappearing through the wall. But I was still solid, and very much human-sized, and they were too close. Sealing me in. Blocking my view of anything or anyone else.

For a minute, they weren't people anymore. They were walls. The walls of a narrow bathroom stall, and I was trapped there, waiting for the world to end.

"My aunt and uncle are a mess because of you," Peter was saying. "Haven't they been through enough? What the hell is your problem? Do you need attention this bad that you'll just come in and start a bunch of crap like this?"

I couldn't breathe. It felt like there was a hand clamped around my heart. I tried to rush forward, to push past them, but Peter caught me by the shoulders and shoved me back against the wall.

"Pete," I heard Tara gasp, like this—just this—was the first thing that had gone too far.

Peter ignored her. "Aw, are you scared, Lee?" he asked, his voice all menace and mock concern. "You should've thought about that before you started telling a bunch of lies. If you want attention, you're gonna get it."

His face changed then. Nose shortening, cheeks rounding, hair shifting from auburn to dishwater blond. Until he wasn't Peter McHale anymore, but *him*. Peering over the edge of the stall, gun pointed down at us.

I whimpered and sank to the floor, pressing my face into my knees and wrapping my arms over my head. I could hear screaming and the pop of gunshots. I knew it wasn't real. I knew this was just a panic attack, a flashback. But my body didn't seem to understand what my mind did. My chest ached and my lungs begged for air as I panted.

"Pete," I heard the other guy's voice whisper, "maybe we should—"

"Don't feel sorry for her," Peter snapped. "She's just being a drama queen. She's an actress, remember? She just wants us to feel sorry for her. Get up, Lee."

But I couldn't. I couldn't move. I couldn't even force out the words on the tip of my tongue, not even a feeble command for them to leave me alone.

"I don't think she's acting," Tara said.

And then there were more voices. Familiar ones.

"Is that Lee?"

"Get away from her!"

"What's going on?"

I raised my head slowly. Tara and Peter's friend had moved back, and in the gaps between their bodies I could see Denny, Amber, and Miles standing there, like they'd just come through the back door.

Miles looked furious.

"I said get away from her," he snarled at Peter.

Tara and the other guy kept backing up, as if to distance themselves from what had just happened. But Peter stood his ground.

"Or what?" he asked Miles.

Miles started to move forward, his arm already pulled back for a swing, but Denny threw an arm out to stop him.

"Or I'll have Glitter here bite your ass," Denny said.

"You're lying," Peter said. "Service dogs don't bite. They're trained not to."

"You want to test that theory?" Denny asked.

Peter hesitated, but I guess he wasn't as sure as he thought. After a second, he huffed and marched off toward the living room. "Whatever," he said. "You're all going to hell."

"Then we'll see you there," Denny called after him.

The minute he was out of the way, Miles rushed forward, falling to his knees in front of me. "Lee?" he said, but he didn't touch me, and I was glad for that. I didn't want to be touched. Not right now. Not even by him.

"Is she okay?" Amber asked. She was hanging back, next to Denny and Glitter. "Should we do something?"

"She probably just needs to go home," Denny said, his own voice a little shaky now.

"Would Glitter really bite?" Amber asked him.

"Nah. Not unless you're made of popcorn."

"Lee," Miles said again, his voice gentle. "Come on. Let's get outta here."

I nodded. I was still trembling, still not able to speak through my ragged breathing, but I managed to pull myself up on my own.

The boys had ridden with Amber, who promised to give Denny a ride home as we walked out of the party. People were still singing, still playing games and laughing. Completely ignorant to what had just happened in the dining room. No flashbacks. No panic attacks. They were free.

Sometimes, it feels like people who weren't there, who didn't witness the shooting firsthand, live on a different plane of reality.

When Miles and I reached my truck at the end of the street, I handed him my keys. The panic attack had mostly passed, but I still didn't feel like I should be driving. He took them from me without saying anything and we climbed into the cab, our usual positions swapped.

We were halfway home before I managed to say anything.

"I saw Kellie today."

He glanced over at me out of the corner of his eye.

"You were right," I said. "She doesn't want to write a letter. She doesn't want anything to do with me. I've been harassing her this whole time." I swallowed. "I'm no better than those guys at the party."

"Yes, you are."

"I'm not, though." I shook my head. "The only difference is that they want me to shut up, and I want her to talk. I'm such a jerk."

"Stop," he said. We pulled into my driveway then, and he cut the engine before turning to look at me through the darkness. "You're not a jerk."

"How can you say that?" I asked. "I've been harassing you, too. I'm sorry. I don't know why you don't want to write about it, but it shouldn't matter. You don't want to and I should've respected that. I just . . . I've been obsessed with this."

"I've noticed."

"I really did think I could make things better," I said. "But . . . I've just made things worse. For Kellie. For Sarah's parents. For Ashley."

"Maybe," Miles said. "But you helped, too. Denny told me tonight that he submitted that letter for a few different scholarships. He's already won two of them. And Eden . . . We were texting this morning. She told me what's been going on. Writing your letter helped her."

"I still should've stopped when you said no. I'm sorry, Miles. I care about you so much, and I was a crappy friend. I shouldn't have yelled at you last night. You don't have to write a letter if you don't want to."

He sighed. "Little late for that."

I looked at him, confused, as he reached into the pocket of his faded jeans and pulled out a square of messily folded pages and handed them to me. I could feel the frayed edges of notebook paper, and I started to unfold them, even though it was too dark in the truck to read.

"Don't," Miles said, holding up a hand. "Not . . . not in front of me. I can't."

He opened the door of the truck and slid out. I stayed put, watching his shadow cross the yard, weave around the fence, and disappear next door.

I waited a few minutes before climbing out myself. I wanted to make sure I was completely past the panic attack, that no lingering signs remained. I didn't want to freak Mom out. She'd be a mess if she knew the harassment had escalated.

Luckily, when I went inside, I found that she wasn't home yet. She must've been working a later shift at the store.

I went to my bedroom and stripped off my T-shirt and jeans, changing into the comfiest pajamas I could find. I climbed onto my bed, took a deep breath, and, when I was ready, unfolded the wad of pages Miles had given me.

They were handwritten, in his messy, scratchy penmanship. And it was addressed to me.

Dear Lee,

I didn't think I'd do this letter thing. I still don't want to. But . . . I don't know. I think I should. Not for the reasons you think it's important. You think it's better if the truth is out there, but for me, it'd be worse.

I don't want people to know the truth. Not my version of it.

No. I guess that's not right. I don't care that much about other people. I don't want *you* to know my story. The rest of the world can think whatever the hell they want about me, but you're different. I can't deal with the idea of you hating me. Which is why I never talk about what happened that day. But I can't keep dodging this. I can't handle lying to you anymore, so . . . I guess I'm writing a letter after all.

God, I hope you don't hate me after you read this.

So, you know how everyone thinks I'm some kind of hero? Because I supposedly tried to protect Ashley or something? Well, all of that is bullshit. I'm not a hero. Not even close. In fact, someone is dead because of me.

March 15 was my first day back from two weeks of suspension. I already knew I'd be repeating my sophomore year. I'd missed too much class, been in too many fights. Everyone was fed up with me by then. My grandmother, the principal, pretty much all of the teachers. The only person who wasn't was Coach Nolan. He was my US History teacher, and he'd been trying to get me to join the football team all semester.

"Might help you channel some of that aggression," he'd said. "You could even get a scholarship if you get your act together."

I just shook my head every time he brought it up. Sports, especially team sports, have never worked for me.

"Just think about it," he said. "It's not too late to turn things around."

For some reason, Coach Nolan believed I was more than just some punk-ass kid who couldn't stay out of fights. He really wanted to see me do well, even when no one else thought I could.

And I repaid him by getting him shot.

I was pissed that morning—the morning of the shooting. I don't remember why. I was always pissed about something. Coach Nolan had just given us a reading assignment, and everyone was opening their books, trying to get a jump start on their homework. Then some asshole senior behind me grabbed my beanie off my head.

I turned around in my seat to face him. I'd been in detention with him before. He was just some jerk, a slacker who'd failed US History enough times to be taking it again his senior year. The kind of kid who shoved underclassmen against lockers for no reason. The kid who cursed at teachers and threw punches over nothing.

I can't remember that kid's name now, but I remember that I hated him. Probably because I knew that, in two years, that'd be me.

I tried to grab my hat back from him, but he held it over his head.

"Hats are against the dress code, freak," he said.

"Give Mr. Mason his hat back," Coach Nolan said, barely even looking at us.

The kid rolled his eyes, but he did give it back. Because even if you didn't like Coach Nolan, you respected him.

I took my beanie and pulled it onto my head.

"That is actually against dress code, though," Coach Nolan said. But he gave me a quick smile, and I knew he wasn't going to ask me to take it off. No one cared if I broke dress code just as long as I kept my fists to myself.

"I was doing you a favor, freak," the kid behind me said. "Trying to keep you from looking like the white trash you are."

I wanted to ignore him, but he kept going, whispering low enough that Coach Nolan couldn't hear.

"I know you live with your grandma," he said. "Is that because your parents are in jail? Junkies? My guess is meth."

I know he was just trying to provoke me. He wanted a fight. He didn't know me. Had no reason to hate me. And he was just taking a wild guess about my parents. Because he knew if anyone would rise to the bait and give him the fight he wanted, it'd be me. And he was right.

I jumped out of my seat and threw a punch right at his face.

He ducked and I missed, but I tried again. He was starting to stand up when Coach Nolan came behind me and grabbed my arm. "Enough," he said before this asshole could get his swing in.

I shook Coach Nolan off and folded my arms.

He looked at me then. Completely disappointed. He didn't say anything, but I knew what he was thinking. I'd been back a day, and I was already in trouble again. He was wondering if he should even bother with me anymore. That look hurt worse coming from him than it had from anyone else.

"Come on, Mr. Mason," he said. "We're going to the office. The rest of you, keep reading until the bell rings. I'll be back shortly."

We never made it to the office.

I followed him out of the classroom. He glanced at me once as he walked, then turned to face forward again. "You have to cut this crap out, Miles," he said. "You're a smart kid. You've got potential. I keep trying to show you that and you just keep messing it up."

"Maybe quit trying, then," I said.

He sighed. "Maybe I should."

I shoved my hands into my pockets and stared down at my feet as we turned the corner.

We heard the gunshots a second later. They were coming from down the hallway, near the old computer lab. Coach Nolan saw ▮▮▮▮ before I did. For a second, we both froze. Then Coach Nolan started to run. Not away from the kid with the gun but toward him. He knew that kid had a gun. He knew he could get killed. But he ran forward anyway. To help.

Me? I just stood there.

Ashley was running at us. I still have nightmares about that moment. About the look of terror on her face. And how she fell, tumbling forward onto the floor. And the blood.

"Put down the gun!" Coach Nolan yelled. "Put it down! It's not too—"

It's not too late. I know that was what he was gonna say. It's what he always said to me. It's not too late to do better. To stop. To turn things around.

But it was, Lee. It was too late. Because before Coach Nolan could even finish that sentence, there were two bullet holes in his chest. I saw him freeze. Heard him gasp. I don't know if it was from shock or pain. And then I watched him fall.

And you know what I did?

I ran.

I was gonna run into the bathroom. I couldn't think of anywhere else to go. I thought maybe I could hide in a stall or something. But I'd only taken two steps when I tripped over Ashley and landed on top of her. He was still shooting, and I whispered to Ashley to shut up. I knew if I stood up, he'd probably shoot me, too. So I played dead on top of her.

I played dead while Coach Nolan bled out a few feet away.

I played dead while ████████ walked into the bathroom and started shooting.

While he shot at you, Lee.

Ashley told everyone I'd been trying to protect her. That's not true, though. I was just trying to run. The whole time I was lying there, my heart was pounding so hard I thought my ribs would break. I kept thinking about how I'd get away, even if it meant leaving Ashley, how I could move without him seeing me. I didn't hear what was going on in the bathroom. I didn't hear anything but the voice in my head screaming at me that I needed to get out.

I wasn't a hero. I was a coward.

And the worst part is, Coach Nolan would still be alive if I hadn't been such a screwup. If I'd just listened to him. If I'd just ignored that kid behind me and not thrown a punch. If I'd tried a little harder to stay out of trouble, he'd be alive.

He wanted to help me when no one else thought I was worth saving. And if I'd just let him, he would never have been in that hallway.

I got him killed.

But no one knew that. All they knew was what Ashley said. She thought I was a hero. And for the first time, no one was pissed at me. No one was disappointed. My grandmother told me how proud she was of me. She'd never said that before. She'd never had a good reason to. People started looking at me like I was worth a damn.

You looked at me like I was worth a damn.

I didn't want to be seen as a hero, but it was nice to not be seen as a lost cause for once.

I know I haven't really told you much about my parents or why I moved in with my grandmother. But there's a reason that kid in US History pissed me off so bad. When I was five, my mom overdosed. Heroin, not meth. She died and left me with my dad. You'd think after what happened to my mom, he'd want to stay away from drugs. And he did for about a year. Then we moved to Tennessee for a while and meth happened.

Dad was a dick whether he was sober or not. I got left alone a lot while he went out to get high or drunk or find some other way to spend the money we didn't have. The therapist I saw after the shooting thinks that's why I started fighting with other kids. Because

I wanted him to pay attention, and getting in trouble was the way to get him to notice or something. I think I was just angry. At him. At Mom for dying. At all the other kids at school for being happier than I was.

Then Dad got arrested. He beat the hell out of some guy at a bar, and when the cops came, Dad had drugs on him. So he got jail time and I got shipped off to live with a grandmother I hadn't seen in years. And the first time I got in trouble at school, I remember her looking at me and saying, "You look just like your father." And the way she said it, I knew that wasn't a good thing. He'd disappointed her, and now I had, too.

It didn't take long for everyone in Virgil County to know I was bad news. Sometimes just by looking at me. I know you thought so, too.

Don't be creeped out, but I remember the first time I saw you. I'd been living next door for a couple of weeks, but we'd never really crossed paths, I guess. Anyway, I was walking home. I'd been kicked off the school bus for cussing at the driver. You were sitting on your front porch with Sarah. Your hair was long back then, almost to your waist, and the wind kept blowing it in your face. You were spitting it out of your mouth while Sarah laughed. She reached up and tried to help you tie it back, and that's when I saw your face.

I don't think I thought anything that interesting. I don't remember thinking that you were beautiful. You are, but I don't think I saw it then. Pretty sure I just thought you were a girl. And you looked like a nice girl. The kind of girl who'd never look my way.

But then you did. You looked at me while I was walking up my driveway. And I stopped to look back at you. I was about to say something. Hi, probably. But then Sarah looked over your shoulder to see what you were staring at. And then she grimaced and whispered something in your ear as she finished tying the ponytail into your hair.

And then you frowned and shook your head and turned away.

I'm not saying I blame you. Either of you. I'm just saying that there was a time when you saw me differently. When you thought I was someone to avoid.

But that's not how you looked at me after the shooting. The first night I asked to come up on the roof, I thought you'd say no. I thought you'd want to stay away from me. But you didn't. Because you'd changed your mind about me. Just like everyone in Virgil County. Because you thought I was a hero. And I let you think that, because I like the way you look at me.

God, Lee, I've almost told you the truth so many times. Because I feel so guilty all the time. I'm a fraud. I'm the reason a good man is dead, and everyone thinks I'm a hero and I don't want them to think that, but I also don't want them to go back to being disappointed in me. I don't want to be my dad. I've tried to do better since the shooting. I've stayed out of trouble. I've tried to keep my anger in check. Mostly because I can't stop thinking about Coach Nolan. If I become a dirtbag like my dad, his death will be pointless.

It already is pointless.

But it feels like I owe it to him to do better. So a few weeks after the shooting, I got online and watched a documentary about the

American Civil War, and a few days after that, I picked up a biography of Abraham Lincoln, because . . . I don't know. Because it was the kind of thing that would have made Coach Nolan proud when he was alive. The kind of thing he never would have expected from me.

Turns out, I really like history. There's something about putting the puzzle together, figuring out how we got here, who and what led us to this point in time—maybe that sounds stupid. But you know how acting is an escape for you? I think history is that for me. I can get lost in the research for hours on end. Hours where I'm not thinking about the shooting at all.

Maybe if I was interested in other school stuff, college wouldn't seem like such a fantasy.

Maybe Grandma's right and I should go to vocational school. That's probably the most realistic option for me. But sometimes I think about what would happen if I could get into college, if I studied history. Maybe—and yeah, I know this sounds crazy—but maybe I could become a teacher.

Maybe I could do for other kids what Coach Nolan tried to do for me.

I don't know. All of that seems like such a long shot, and I'm just rambling. I hate writing.

But you keep asking for the truth, Lee, and the truth is that I'm scared you'll read this and hate me. That knowing I'm not a hero will change how you look at me. Because I'm pretty sure I can deal with the rest of this town hating me. Maybe I even deserve it because of Coach Nolan. But I can't deal with you hating me. I just can't.

Last night after prom, I called Ashley. I had her pick me up and we drove around town in her van for a while. She's the first person I've ever told any of this to. I didn't know what to do about you—about us—and I figured if anyone had a right to know the truth, it was Ashley. She's spent years thinking I tried to save her life when, really, I was just trying to hide. I thought she'd be pissed at me, but I knew she'd be the best person to ask for advice. She's always been good with advice.

Well, except when it comes to Kellie, I guess.

"You should tell her," Ashley said. She'd been surprised but not mad. If anything, she just seemed tired. "Look, I'm not too happy with Lee right now. With this whole letter thing. But . . . you love her."

I turned my head to look out the window. We were on our way back to my grandma's house. "I . . . uh . . ."

"That wasn't a question," Ashley said. "It's obvious. It's been obvious for a while. And if you're telling me this, it's because you want to tell her. You're just scared. You don't have to write one of her stupid letters if you don't want to. But tell her. I think you'll feel better once you do."

"She'll hate me."

"She won't. She'll be surprised, but she won't hate you." She paused. "Look, you don't have to tell her if you don't want to. It's no one's business but yours. Maybe a little bit mine. I mean, it's just one more thing I got wrong." She sighed and shook her head. "If anything, it's my fault you've felt like you had to lie about this. But I think you'll feel relieved once she knows."

"It's not just about you," I said. "Coach Nolan . . ."

"You can't blame yourself for that," she said. "You weren't the one with the gun."

"Yeah. But I . . ."

"Was a stupid kid," Ashley said. "We were all stupid kids. None of us handled that situation perfectly. Don't know if anyone could, really. But . . . we were kids who ended up in an awful situation. None of us asked for this." She glanced over at me before looking to the road again. "For what it's worth, I knew Coach Nolan. He wouldn't blame you. He'd just be happy you survived."

We pulled into my driveway a few minutes later, and I started to unbuckle my seat belt.

"Tell her," Ashley said. "Not because you think you have to. You don't. But . . . because it'll be a relief not to carry this around on your own."

I leaned across the seat and hugged her before climbing out of the car.

Then I stayed up all night trying to write this. Because I'm being a coward, again, and I can't tell you the truth to your face. I don't want to watch you turn away from me the way you did that first time I saw you.

Because Ashley's right. I love you, Lee.

I know that things are complicated with that. With romantic stuff. I know you're asexual, and I'm still trying to figure out what that means. I don't know what's going to happen when you move to California. I don't know what a future for us would look like. But I know that I love you. That I will do anything to keep you in my life.

I'll respect whatever boundaries you set. Even if that's just us staying friends. I'd follow you wherever you'd let me, as corny as that sounds. I just want to be with you.

And I don't want you to be disappointed in me.

So there you go. That's the truth you've been asking for. I really hope writing this wasn't a huge mistake.

Love,
Miles

× × ×

I dropped Miles's letter onto my bed and sprang up. It was past midnight by now, but I didn't care. I had to see him. I slid on some sandals and didn't worry about the fact that I was only wearing pajama shorts and a tank top. Then I hurried out of my room and down the hall.

"Lee baby?" Mom's voice, croaky with sleep, called from her dark bedroom. I'd heard her come in about thirty minutes earlier, before she'd headed straight for bed. "You okay? Nightmares?"

"Not this time," I replied. "I'm okay. I'll be back in a few minutes."

I jerked open the front door and sprinted down the front porch steps. All the lights were out next door, and as I crossed the yard, I hesitated. Miles had brought me home only an hour ago, but there was a chance he'd already gone to bed. And his grandmother was most certainly asleep by now. If I knocked, I might wake them both up. But this couldn't wait until morning. It couldn't even wait for me to go back inside and grab my phone so I could text him.

I swallowed my anxiety and stepped onto Mrs. Mason's front porch. I tapped on the door lightly at first. Then again a little louder. I was about to raise my hand to tap for a third time when the door swung open.

Miles stood there, dressed in a black T-shirt and boxer shorts. His hair was messy, but he didn't look like he'd been sleeping.

"Lee," he breathed, and I noticed the subtle shake of his hand as it rested on the door. The nervous twitch at the corner of his mouth.

Before he could say anything else—before he could move another muscle—I leapt forward and wrapped my arms around his neck. He stiffened at first, like I'd startled him. I almost stepped back, almost apologized. I knew better than to make those kind of sudden movements. But then his arms moved around my waist. He held me to him. Firm, but not too tight.

I pressed my face into his neck for a long moment. He was warm and smelled like a mix of mint and freshly washed clothes. I could have stood like that forever, just breathing him in.

But after a moment I pulled back. His arms loosened and I slid my hands to his shoulders, holding him still as I stared, long and hard, into his face.

"I read it," I whispered. "I read your letter."

His gaze lowered, but I squeezed his shoulders, urging him to look back up, into my face.

"Look at me," I said. "Please, Miles."

Slowly, he raised his eyes. And I tried to put everything in my expression. Every feeling I'd ever had for him. Every wish, every hope, every moment of calm that he gave me. I wanted him to see that I wasn't disappointed in him. I didn't see him as a hero. But I didn't see him as a monster, either. I just saw him as Miles. My best friend.

The boy I loved.

I think he understood. I watched relief cross his face, tempered with a new sort of nervousness. He swallowed, his Adam's apple bobbing. "So . . ." he said.

"So."

Then I did something I'd never done before. Something I'd never wanted before. I stepped closer to him again, and then slowly, gently, pressed a kiss to his lips.

He didn't tighten his hold on me. He didn't try to hold me to him or push the kiss any further. Instead, he just smiled. A broad, goofy smile that made a giggle rise in my own throat. A smile that assured me that that kiss, quick and chaste as it had been, was enough.

I eased away, squeezing his hand as I backed slowly off the porch. "I'll see you tomorrow," I said.

He nodded. "See you tomorrow."

"Miles?" I was off the porch now, standing in the grass. But I hadn't been able to turn away from him just yet.

"Yeah?"

"I love you, too."

I don't know what the future holds for Miles and me. Since that night, we've exchanged a handful of short, light kisses. I'm not comfortable with anything more. Maybe that'll change one day. Maybe it won't. Maybe there will come a time when he needs more than I'm willing to give. And maybe there won't. I don't know. Neither of us does. And I'm starting to think that's okay.

I've spent so long keeping him at a distance, scared of ruining the bond we have. And there's a good chance that once I leave this town, once I'm thousands of miles away, we'll have to go back to just being friends. But I'm starting to think that no matter what happens, we're going to be connected forever.

Not just Miles and me, but all of us. All of the survivors. No matter how angry Ashley is at me, no matter how much Kellie— or Renee or whoever she decides to be—wishes to be rid of us, we're tied together now. They are bonds of pain, sure, of a shared trauma. But they are also bonds of hope and comfort and an understanding that only the six of us will ever have.

No matter what happens with Miles, I'm comforted to realize that we'll always be connected. That he'll always be the one I can call when I'm at my most nihilistic. When the starless sky feels like falling into nothingness. Whether it's the fifth or tenth or thirtieth anniversary of the shooting, we'll be in touch. Even if this . . . whatever it is, between us right now doesn't last.

But for now, this feels right.

I'm writing this a few days before I leave for California. He's going to drive with me across the country with all of my things, then fly back to Indiana once I'm settled in. I'm dreading that part. The part where I won't live next door to him anymore. I won't be able to climb onto my roof and know he'll be there shortly.

But I think it'll be okay. We'll both be okay.

We've survived worse, after all.

THOMAS NOLAN

If you look up Coach Nolan's obituary you'll find out that he was forty-two, single (divorced almost a decade earlier), and had no kids. He'd coached both football and track, and a good chunk of the trophies in the glass cabinet near the front office of the school were thanks to him. When people in town talk about him, they mostly refer to his coaching, all the victories he led VCHS to. But they never mention him as a teacher.

Which, really, is pretty strange, since literally every student had to take at least one of his classes. We all knew Coach. We all cracked jokes about how formal he was, referring to all of his students by their last names, always wearing a jacket and tie in class. Pretty much everyone had done a Coach Nolan impression to amuse their friends at some point.

At the same time, though, almost everyone respected him. He was tough, but fair. I remember the first time I got back an essay I'd written for his class. There was a giant C at the top in red ink. I'd been mortified. I was no straight-A student, but I'd never gotten below a B before.

I went to his desk after class, nervously clutching the graded paper while Sarah waited for me by the door.

"Can I help you with something, Ms. Bauer?" he asked.

"It's, um, about my grade," I said, laying the essay on his desk. "Why did I get a C?"

"Because that's the grade you deserved," he said simply. He

could have dismissed me then and there, but instead he pulled the paper toward him and plucked a red-ink pen from the desk drawer. "Come here."

I hovered at the edge of the desk and watched as he marked up my paper, showing all of the places where I'd gotten dates or names wrong or where I'd repeated myself in order to meet the assigned word count. In the margins, he wrote out things I could have included, facts I'd missed. Then he handed the paper back to me.

"There was some good material in your essay," he said. "But not enough of it to warrant a better grade."

"Can I redo it? For a higher grade?"

He shook his head. "I'm afraid not. This isn't middle school anymore, Ms. Bauer. Things are going to be tougher. What you can do is use all of the information I just gave you as a road map for how to write a better essay next time."

At first, I was angry. It was the first semester of my freshman year. He was being way too hard on me, I thought.

But then, when our next essay was due, I did pull out the marked-up copy of my old assignment. I doubled-checked my names and dates, instead of repeating myself I found new material to work into the essay, and I actually used sources beyond just our textbook. And a week later, when Coach Nolan handed it back to me, he did so with a smile. There was a red A at the top of the front page.

Well, A-minus. His class wasn't going to be *that* easy.

I'd never felt so proud of myself for a grade before. And I think that was his goal. He made us work hard so that, when we succeeded, it was a real triumph.

Coach Nolan saw the potential in all of us, and just like with Miles, he tried hard to get us to be the best versions of ourselves. Sometimes that meant pushing angry boys to get their act together. Sometimes it meant staying after class to mark up an essay. He provided the map, but we had to reach the destination on our own, so that, when we arrived, it meant so much more.

Thomas Nolan was an award-winning coach.

But if you ask me—or Miles, or almost any of his former students—he was an even better teacher.

"So what are you going to do with the letters?" Denny asked. It was two days after graduation, and he, Miles, and I were sitting on the tailgate of my truck in our spot, way out in the woods.

"No idea," I admitted.

It had been a couple weeks since my meeting with Kellie at the café. After talking to her and then, that night, reading Miles's letter, I'd begun to rethink my whole plan. Not that it had ever been much of a plan to begin with. I'd been so sure that distributing the letters, getting the truth in front of people, was the only answer. It hadn't really occurred to me that those truths might cause even more pain for some of us.

"My mom saw Sarah's dad at the grocery the other day," Denny said. "He told her that the book will be out next spring."

My stomach clenched, the pain a mixture of dread and loss. I know Sarah's parents will never look at me as the same girl who used to have sleepovers at their house. No matter what I do with these letters, that damage has been done. In some ways, knowing that feels like losing Sarah all over again. I still care about them.

I never wanted to hurt them. But God, I really don't want that book published. Not just because of Kellie and my guilt over the part I played in what happened to her. But also because Sarah wouldn't want it.

I'm done pushing people into doing things they don't want to, even if I think it's better in the long run. We've all had our stories used to advance someone else's agenda in some way or another. I won't do that to my friends. Not again. Not anymore.

But that doesn't answer Denny's first question.

"I can't just destroy them," I said. "The letters. I don't know what to do with them, but . . . I can't let them go to waste, either. It just seems wrong."

"Did you write one?" Miles asked.

I shook my head. "No. Not yet. I don't know if I should bother now."

He shrugged and reached down to scratch behind Glitter's ears as the yellow dog sidled up to us, her tail wagging. She seemed just as happy to be back in our secret place as we were. I suspected her motivations came more from the freedom to track the scent of squirrels and pee on new trees. For us, though, it was bittersweet. None of us had said it out loud, but we knew this was likely the last time the three of us would be here together again now that we'd graduated.

I looked over at the tree Miles had carved the "6" into years ago. I could feel Miles watching me, could feel his eyes follow my gaze long before he reached out and wrapped his fingers around mine. "You should write a letter," he mumbled.

"I thought you were against the whole letter thing," I said.

He tilted his head at me. "It didn't turn out as bad as I thought."

I smiled, feeling the heat creep up my cheeks, only this time I reveled in the way he made me blush instead of fighting it.

Denny, either oblivious to this or pointedly trying to shut down the moment (I'm going to guess the latter), spoke up. "That's not a bad idea," he said. "Maybe writing your own letter will help you figure out what to do with the rest of them. It can't hurt."

He was right that it couldn't hurt, but here I am, the end of the summer, and I've written all of this down, hoping it would give me an answer, and I'm still just as confused as I was when I started.

Now I'm sitting here at my computer, staring at this massive document with all of our letters weaved in. Well, all of them but one. I don't have Kellie's letter, but her story is in here, too. Except, of course, that it's her story through everyone else's eyes. Just like it always has been.

If I try to publish this, then, sure, some of our stories will be out there, in our own words. Part of the story will be set straight. But I'll be taking Kellie's voice from her all over again. Even without her letter, I've depicted her, speculated. I have no more right to put her story out there than the McHales do.

But if I do nothing, if I hit "delete" on this document, then none of us get our story told. We'll all be forever stuck as the versions of ourselves seen in newspapers and TV movies. And hell, even if I do publish this, that might be the case, anyway. The world has mostly moved on from the VCHS massacre. It'd be hard to change the accepted version of the narrative that's been out there for years.

If it's going to happen at all, it's got to be soon. It won't be long before the McHales' book is out. People will be thinking about the shooting again. It's our chance to make people take notice. Our chance to be heard.

Maybe the reason I can't make a decision on this is because it's not my decision to make?

Whoa—wait. *That's it.*

It's not *my* decision. I shouldn't be the one making the choice about what to do with these letters.

But I think I know who should.

Dear Reader,

Damn it, I really didn't want to do this.

When Lee texted me in late August, asking me to meet her at the café on a Saturday afternoon, I almost didn't reply. I'd hoped our last meeting would be it—the last time I'd ever have to see anyone from that awful town ever again. But in her message, Lee promised that this would be the final time she'd ever contact me, and I don't know, I guess I was intrigued. So I went.

She was there with Miles, that quiet kid with the beanie. They were sitting side by side, looking at each other's face in that way that feels disgustingly intimate. When I pulled out the chair across from them, I made sure the legs scraped loudly against the floor, and they both looked up.

"What do you want?" I asked, sitting down and folding my arms over my chest.

Lee didn't bother with the small talk, which I appreciated. In fact, she didn't say a thing as she reached into her pocket and removed a small object. When she passed it across the table to me, I realized it was a dark blue USB drive.

"What's this?" I asked.

"Our stories," she said. "Denny, Ashley, Eden, Miles, and me. They all wrote letters, telling their stories, and I put them all together."

"And you're giving this to me why?"

"After I saw you in the spring, I didn't know what to do," Lee explained. "I had these letters, because I thought telling the truth would help. But then I talked to you and I realized that . . . that it maybe wasn't my decision." She looked down, shame coloring her cheeks a bright shade of pink. "I was confused, so I decided to figure things out by writing it all down—everything I'd done. I'd hoped putting it on paper would help me figure out what to do. And it did."

"Spit it out," I said.

"I figured out that I wasn't the person *to* figure it out," she explained. "You are."

I rolled my eyes. "You've got to be kidding."

"Believe me, she's not," Miles said. I almost didn't understand him at first. The kid really doesn't speak clearly.

"You can destroy it if you want," Lee said. "Or you can publish it. Or anything. It's yours now. I asked, and all of the others gave permission for you to use it—or not use it—however you choose."

"*All* of them," I repeated.

"Yes, even Ashley," she said, answering the question I hadn't asked. "She's still upset with me, but . . . I think she feels bad about what happened to you."

I rolled the drive between my fingers, watching the light from the café window gleam off its plastic casing. "Why do I get this? Why not someone else?"

"Because," Lee said, "of all of us, you're the one who has suffered the most."

"Don't pity me."

"I don't," she said. "But I do feel guilty. We all do. We saw you being silenced, we saw your voice get taken away, and we didn't do anything to help. So this is our way of trying to give you control of your story again. Use it or don't. We'll be okay with whatever you decide."

"Lee, we better get going," Miles said, checking the time on his cell phone.

"Right." She stood up, pulling her purse over her shoulder. "We've got a long drive ahead of us. We're making a road trip to California," she added to me, as if I cared about her plans.

I glanced out the window, at the old pickup truck I recognized from the last time we'd met here. Now the bed appeared to be loaded with what I could only guess were boxes and covered with a blue tarp. "You're driving across the country in that piece of junk? It looks like it might break down at the next exit."

Lee smiled. "It's tougher than you'd think."

As she and Miles moved toward the door, I called after her. "Lee." She turned and looked at me. "You said this was the last time you'd contact me."

She nodded. "I promise."

"Thank you," I said. "And . . . have a safe trip."

She smiled, waved, and stepped out into the parking lot with Miles at her side. I watched through the glass as her truck pulled away, fading into the distance as it headed west.

I'd thrown the thumb drive in a drawer when I got home and told myself to forget about it. I considered destroying it, smashing it with a hammer or tossing it into a fire in some symbolic gesture.

But I didn't own a hammer, and I wasn't sure if a hard drive would burn or how long it would take. So instead, it ended up in the drawer at the bottom of my desk, where the old batteries, unused cables, and slightly cracked cell phone cases went to die (because apparently I'm a hoarder who never remembers to just throw things away).

And I did forget about it. For a while.

Then, several months later, the fourth anniversary came. I'd been at Walmart the night before, buying food that I could stock-pile in my dorm room so I wouldn't have to go out in public the next day. I always skip classes on the anniversary. I tell everyone I have a cold. It's spring. The weather is changing. Sinuses are the worst. Etc., etc. So far, no one has noticed that my colds coincide with the Ides of March.

Anyway, I was buying groceries for my upcoming anxiety hibernation, and I saw that damn book.

It was there by the cash register, where all of the bestsellers go. Sarah McHale's face staring out at me. The face I'd seen only seconds before the monster killed her. And, of course, there was the cross.

Not *my* cross. Not the one they found in the bathroom—the one Sarah McHale had never even seen but somehow ended up being buried with. It was another cross. But that didn't matter, I guess. It got the point across, it sold the story, who cared if it was accurate?

I stared at that book for a long time. Long enough that the woman in line in front of me noticed.

"Have you read it?" she asked.

I looked at her, and for a minute a bolt of fear shot through me. Did she know who I was? Was she going to lash out at me? Spit on me? Scream at me in the middle of this Walmart checkout line? I could feel my body starting to fold in on itself, but I forced it to be steady.

You're fine, I thought. *She doesn't know. No one knows. You are Renee now.*

The woman was still looking at me, and I had to remind myself of the question she'd just asked. After too long a pause, I managed to shake my head.

"It's great," she told me. "The most moving book I ever read. I've already read it twice, even though it just came out last week."

"Just in time for the anniversary," I said.

The woman must not have heard the note of bitterness in my voice, because she just nodded vigorously. "It's so hard to believe it was four years ago. It was such a tragedy. I wonder how those other kids are doing. The ones who survived, I mean."

"Next customer," the cashier said, and the woman moved forward and began placing her items on the conveyor belt.

"Are you going to buy it?" the woman asked, looking back at me. "You should. It'll change your life. That girl was such an inspiration. It really reaffirmed my faith."

"Not today," I said.

But then, when the woman was gone and the cashier was asking for my items . . . I don't know why I did it. Self-destructive behavior. Morbid curiosity. Because part of me wanted to hate-read it. Take your pick. But I reached out, grabbed the copy at the front, and tossed it onto the conveyor belt.

"Glad you changed your mind," the cashier said as he scanned the book. "You won't regret it."

I already knew he was wrong.

When I got home, I barricaded myself in my room and changed into sweatpants.

The next day, I tried to do anything I could to keep my mind off the shooting. I tried listening to the happiest, most annoyingly upbeat music on my iPod. I tried watching some romantic comedy one of my friends had recommended to me. I even tried studying for my organic chemistry midterm. But nothing worked. My thoughts kept circling and circling, always coming back to that day four years ago. That bathroom. Those girls. That gunshot.

And then there was freaking Ashley Chambers.

When I logged into my email, I had a message from her. I don't know how she got my contact info. From Lee or Eden, I guessed. But she'd decided to reach out to me. On that day of all days. I was so furious, just at the sight of her name in my inbox, that I almost deleted it without reading.

Curiosity beat out indignation, and I opened the email.

It was short. Just a few lines. She said she'd been thinking about me since last year, when Lee started telling people the truth about Sarah. She said she was sorry, and that she wanted to reach out sooner but was nervous. She hoped I was doing okay, and she understood if I didn't want to write her back.

Well, that was good, because she wasn't going to get a response from me. I deleted the message and closed my laptop. Maybe it made Ashley feel better to apologize, but it made no difference to me. And I really wished she'd chosen another day to send that email.

I climbed back into bed and pulled the comforter over my head.

Maybe this sounds weird, but my shoulder hurt. A phantom ache left behind from a bullet wound four years old. It was faint, but there. A reminder that no matter how much that physical scar faded, the hurt might never end. I could go by Renee. I could craft a new history for myself. But this was something I could not escape. Not really.

Eventually I gave into the temptation and picked up the book. It was still in the shopping bag next to my door. It was the last thing I wanted or needed to read right then. But the pull was too strong, and I was weaker than I'd let anyone know.

So, yeah, I read it. I read every damn page. And it made me feel just as awful as you'd expect.

I was only brought up in the book a few times. A passing reference to "rumors" that Sarah's story wasn't true. No mention of my name. No mention of the abuse my family and I endured. I was barely more than a footnote.

Maybe you'd think that would be a relief. Better than having my name dragged through the mud again, right? But, no. It felt worse. So much worse. At least when people hated me, they heard me. They didn't believe me, but my voice was out there. They tried so hard to stamp it out, to silence me, but I'd kept yelling.

Until I just couldn't do it anymore.

But in this book, it's as if I didn't exist. As if that day didn't even happen to me. I'd rather have my name smeared all over those pages, to be condemned as some kind of devil-worshipping monster, than to have Sarah's parents tell her story as if I don't exist. As if nothing that I said, nothing that I survived, even registered with them at all.

I had no idea I'd feel that way until I read that book, until I threw it across my dorm room so hard that it bounced off the wall with a loud thud. I thought I'd been telling Lee the truth when I said I wanted to move on, that I didn't want my name or my story or anything out there. And I still felt that way. Still felt like the truth would bring me nothing but pain that I'd been fighting so hard to put behind me. If I had tried to speak up when she asked, tried to write one of her stupid letters, it just would have gotten me the same abuse I'd dealt with four years ago.

But there I was, being ignored, forgotten, pushed out of my own story entirely. And damn if that didn't hurt just as much.

I didn't know what I wanted.

I still don't know what I want.

For a long time, I just sat on my bed, staring at the book where it lay on my floor. And it was only then that I remembered that USB drive Lee had given me months ago, on her way to California. I'd actually managed to forget for a while. I hadn't wanted anything to do with it before, but all of a sudden, I had to know what was on there. I had to read another version of this story.

So I dug it out, plugged it into my computer, and read

everything Lee had compiled: her long letter, interspersed with shorter letters from the others. Stories I hadn't known. Stories from that day and the days, weeks, years that had followed.

Lee said I could do whatever I wanted with it. Write my own story, try to release it to the public, or just destroy the damn thing. Hell, I still have no idea which of those is the best choice.

But . . . screw it. Whatever. I don't know that it matters. I don't know if I'll ever let anyone else see this, but I can't get this stupid letter thing out of my head. It's been nearly a month since I opened the file she gave me, and I've opened it a dozen times since. And it's just going to keep driving me crazy until I write this down so . . . here you go. Here's my story.

I spent a lot of time in that particular bathroom. Always skipping class. Sometimes smoking. I *hated* school. I was that cliché angry girl with no friends and a great pair of combat boots. So I hid in a place where I could interact with as few people as possible. Boy, did that bite me in the ass.

So March 15, I was in the bathroom, as usual. I'd been in there, smoking in the corner so no one passing by would see, for most of the period. I'd told my geometry teacher I was feeling sick. I don't think she believed me, but she let me go anyway. I'm sure she disliked me just as much as I disliked her. I'd been in there alone all period, until Ashley Chambers walked in.

I knew Ashley. She was the kind of self-righteous Christian that I hated. The kind who acted like you had to do things her way or you were headed straight to hell. She was the reason I stayed away from things like the Fellowship of Christian Students. Well, that and my general disdain for most people. I know Lee says she's better now, and Ashley might have apologized to me in that email, but whatever. I'm not the forgiving sort.

Anyway, she didn't see me when she came in the bathroom. She was clearly distracted or else she would have noticed the smell of my cigarette. I was relieved. I didn't want to deal with her. So I pressed closer into the corner, hoping she'd leave without even acknowledging me.

But before she came out of the stall, two more girls hurried in. Freshmen freaking out about a hickey. They did notice me, and I expected them to give me a lecture about how I was breaking the rules. They looked like the kind of girls who would. But they didn't.

I didn't know Lee Bauer or Sarah McHale at the time. I mean, I knew their faces. Small school and all. But they were two years behind me and we didn't have any classes together, so I didn't know anything about them. Other than that, apparently, Sarah's getting a hickey was the end of the world and her parents were uptight, over-protective jerks.

I wasn't really paying attention to them until Ashley walked out of the bathroom stall and started pulling her holier-than-thou crap.

"Who needs Jesus when you have boys that'll suck on your neck?"

I rolled my eyes. It was so obvious she was jealous because no one wanted to make out with her. Not that I was one to judge. At sixteen, I still hadn't been kissed. Pretty much all the guys at VCHS thought I was scary, and I thought they were annoying. So no loss there, I guess. But still. Ashley's bitterness was so apparent it might as well have been written across her forehead.

By the time she noticed me, all of her snark had been used up on Sarah. She glared and I glared back and then she left.

"Someone needs to tell her that Jesus likes nice people," Sarah said.

Despite myself, I laughed. And I remember that she turned and grinned at me. Like I was in on the joke. People at school didn't look at me like that very often. But, I don't know, it was nice. For a second I thought that maybe Sarah McHale was kind of cool. One of the few people in this school I didn't despise.

The irony.

I glanced down at my watch—this clunky old thing that used to belong to my grandfather—and realized the bell was about to ring. I finished off my cigarette and tossed the butt into the nearest toilet, flushed, and headed toward the bathroom door.

That's when the world changed.

I heard the gunshots. It only took me a second to know what I was hearing. The screams made it abundantly clear. In some ways, I think I'd been expecting it. That sounds weird. But we'd been doing lockdown drills since I was in elementary school. I don't remember a time when I truly believed school was safe.

I've read the other letters. I know that everyone else was surprised or in shock. Maybe I'm just a pessimist or maybe I watched too many true crime documentaries. Either way, I knew it was an active shooter situation immediately. And I knew I didn't have time to get into a classroom before the school went into lockdown. So I ran back into the bathroom.

Lee and Sarah were in the doorway, and I shoved them inside. "Hide," I remember snapping.

"What?"

I was running toward a stall when I tripped. The laces on my boot must've come undone. I hit the tiles hard, knocking the breath out of me. I gasped and sat up. "Hide," I told the girls again. I was frustrated that they didn't seem to understand what I did.

Sarah must've picked up on it right after that, though, because she grabbed Lee by the arm and dragged her off toward another stall.

I got to my feet and rushed into the stall right ahead of me. I knew that if I locked the door, he'd know someone was in there. It'd be easy to shoot over or under. I also knew that if I didn't want to be noticed, I'd have to stand with my feet on the toilet so he couldn't see my boots under the door. Not to sound weird, but I'd thought about this before. In all the lonely hours I'd spent in that bathroom, I'd planned out a dozen nightmare scenarios and how I'd escape.

My mom calls me morbid. I call me prepared. Not that it did me a lot of good that day.

As I crouched on the toilet seat, my legs and back already aching, I raised a hand to my chest and reached under the neck of my T-shirt, but the little cross and the thin chain it hung on were gone.

Yes. You read that right. Cross necklace. The infamous cross necklace. The one that caused so many people to love Sarah McHale and hate me. That necklace was mine. I bought it with birthday money when I was eleven at a crafts fair, and I'd worn it pretty much every day since. Even after my parents split up and my mom stopped going to church. Even after at least three kids in my middle school asked me if I worshipped the devil because of the way I dressed. Even after I met girls like Ashley Chambers and realized why I kind of hated organized religion. I kept that cross on. And yes, despite all of that, I still believe in God. Regardless of whatever rumors you've heard.

But my necklace was gone. The chain must've broken when I tripped.

As stupid as this sounds, I almost went back to get it. I was thinking that if he saw it on the floor, he'd know people were in the bathroom, so I should go get it. But before I could move out of my crouching position, heavy footsteps entered the bathroom. I held my breath, thinking the words as I prayed.

But it didn't matter. I don't know if he saw me through the crack in the door or if he was just shooting at anything. I don't know if this was calculated or impulsive. I'm sure everyone has theories about why he did it and what his plans were that day, but I've tried to tune it all out. Like Lee, I just don't care.

Listen, I was an angry, depressed kid with a lot of hate for the people around me. And from what I've read in these letters, it sounds like Miles Mason had a messed-up home life. But neither of us ever shot at anyone. So I don't care how sad this guy's life was or how mean people supposedly were to him. Sorry, I just don't. He's the villain in my story.

One of them, anyway.

So he fired a couple of shots, one of which hit the wall and ricocheted back at me. I remember the pain bursting in my shoulder. Blunt and sharp at the same time. I screamed and fell forward, knocking the stall door open on my way down. From the floor, I could see my necklace, just a couple of feet away, but he was there, too. Standing over me as I bled onto the tiles.

And he saw the necklace, too.

"Whose ugly-ass cross is this?" he asked.

I gritted my teeth through the pain, but I was worried if I didn't answer him, he'd either shoot me again or think someone else was in the bathroom and go looking for Lee and Sarah. That sounds like I was trying to be a hero. I wasn't. I promise you most of my motivation for answering was selfish. I just didn't know what he wanted to hear.

"Mine?"

"Yours?" He sounded shocked and almost amused. Even the kid with the gun didn't believe I could possibly be the owner of that necklace. What foreshadowing of things to come.

"Yes," I gasped.

"You think Jesus is watching over you right now?"

What did he want me to say? I didn't know this kid. I didn't know if this was some bizarre right-wing Christian terrorism or something. The odds of him killing me if I said no seemed just as high as if I said yes. I wasn't defending my faith or being a martyr. I just wanted to survive.

"I . . . do. Yes."

But he wasn't listening anymore. Something from the other side of the bathroom must've caught his attention, because he was walking away, toward one of the other stalls. I crawled back into my stall and curled into a ball, trying not to listen to the next few gunshots. Trying not to think about how the girls I'd just told to hide were probably dead.

He left the bathroom then, and it wasn't long after that that the police came. I was rushed to the hospital and told that I was very lucky. The bullet in my shoulder hadn't done as much damage as it could have, and with some physical therapy and a lot of patience, it would heal. They told me I was going to be okay.

They didn't know that the bullet wound was the least of my problems.

I didn't tell people right away about what he'd said to me in the bathroom. Ironically, considering where we are now, I didn't think it mattered. As far as I knew, no one had heard that brief exchange. When there were two teachers and seven teenagers dead in a high school, who cared that I'd lost my necklace? Or that the asshole with the gun had asked me about it?

I didn't mention it to anyone until a couple of days after the shooting, when Detective Jenner stood in my hospital room, questioning me about what had happened. When I told him, he frowned and exchanged looks with the other officer.

"You sure that was your necklace?" he asked.

"Yeah," I said, annoyed. I had a shoulder wound, not a head wound. Of course I was sure. "Did you find it? The necklace?"

"It's . . . still considered evidence," he said. He left a few minutes later.

I never got that necklace back. It was buried with Sarah McHale.

My necklace. The one I'd worn every day. Was in another girl's coffin. And God, at the time, that made me so angry.

When I first heard the Sarah Story, I thought it would be easy to correct. It was a misunderstanding. It wouldn't be a big deal to just tell people the truth. But we know how that ended. With harassment and vandalism and my mother crying because the women in her office were making her life a living hell. My preacher at my church didn't believe me. My own grandmother died a year later, still sure I was a liar who just wanted attention.

Meanwhile, there were youth rallies in Sarah's honor, songs written about her, politicians telling "her" story as they lobbied either for or against whatever was on the agenda for that week. And hey, I get it. Like I told Lee, it's a great story. The girl who dies for her faith is much more compelling—and useful—than the goth loner who was so scared out of her mind that she would have done or said anything to survive. Plus, I lived. Where was the drama in that?

If you've read everything Lee wrote, then you know the rest. By the time VCHS opened up again, my family couldn't take it anymore. Mom packed up and moved us to another state, and Dad, along with his new wife, followed shortly after.

That's when I started going by my middle name, Renee, and stopped talking about the shooting altogether. They'd never have

said it, but I know my parents were relieved. Sometimes, I still wonder if they even believe me.

I don't think I want to know.

It's been a few days now since I wrote that last section. It's the
first time I've really explored the shooting in years, outside of my
own nightmares. It was painful, yeah, but it also felt good to write it
all down. To tell my story and not be screamed at or spat on.

I don't know what I'm going to do with this document. I keep
thinking about it. Circling the options over and over in my head,
weighing the pros and cons. And then I keep coming back to what
Lee said in the café last summer, when she gave me the thumb
drive. She didn't care what I did with the letters. It wasn't about
where they ended up, but about letting me have control of the
narrative.

I think I get that now.

I've realized that it's never going to be okay. The pain of what
happened to me—the shooting, the abuse after—it's not going
away, no matter what I do with these letters. I'm never going to be
able to forgive some of the people in my hometown. Honestly, I am
angrier at some of them—Brother Lloyd, Ashley, the preacher at my
old church—than I am at the boy who shot me. I don't know if that's
rational. But nothing about trauma is rational.

There's going to be hurt no matter what I decide to do with
these letters. But at least, for the first time in over four years, I have
the power over my story. Over all of our stories. Who and how and

when and if anyone reads this—it's up to me. Not a news crew look-ing for the best story. Not the heartbroken parents of a girl they need to believe was a martyr. Not even the well-meaning survivor determined to set the story straight and make amends.

It's *my* choice.

And I guess, if you're reading this, you know what choice I made.

Sincerely,
Kellie Renee Gaynor-Marks
and the survivors

ACKNOWLEDGMENTS

Writing *That's Not What Happened* was one of the most challenging experiences of my career, and I definitely wouldn't have been able to do it without a lot of incredible people. Without their expertise and support, this book would not be what it is today.

First, thanks to my agent, Brianne Johnson, and my editor, Jody Corbett. You two are the best team I could have asked for. You've been amazing champions of my work, and I will forever be grateful to the both of you.

Thanks to Stephanie Kuehn, S.E. Sinkhorn, Phoebe North, and Michelle Krys for taking the time to read and brainstorm with me. Your fresh eyes brought a valuable, new perspective to this story.

A huge thanks also goes out to the many fantastic people at Scholastic who have worked on and supported this book: Mary-Claire Cruz, Maeve Norton, Melissa Schirmer, Priscilla Eakeley, Rachel Feld, Isa Caban, Julia Eisler, Vaishali Nayak, Lizette Serrano, Emily Heddleson, Tracy van Straaten, David Levithan, Alan Smaggler, Elizabeth Whiting, Alexis Lunsford, Nikki Mutch, Sue Flynn, Jackie Rubin, Jody Stigliano, Charlie Young, Chris Satterlund, Roz Hilden, Meaghan Hilton, Tracy Bozentka, Jacqueline Bernacki, Barb Holloway, Barbara Synder, Dan Moser, Betsy Politi, and Alexis Lassiter.

Thank you as well to the team at Writers House, especially Alexandra Levick, you have all been so wonderful and helpful.

And thank you to my colleagues and students at Gotham Writers, for keeping me inspired and passionate about my work.

Thank you to the friends who have listened patiently to me talk about this book for the past three years and helped me brainstorm or aided me with research. Laurie, Lindsey, Amy, Alexis, Courtney, Debra, Kaitlin, Kara, Kate, Leila, Maurène, Samantha, Somaiya, Kristin, and Veronica, I love you guys.

Special thanks to Shana Hancock, Kate Lawson, and Wendy Xu for being exactly the sort of friends I needed during this venture. Hanging out with, texting, and skyping you all kept my spirits up even when I was diving into some dark territory with my research. I'm a lucky person to have met you all.

And, of course, to my family. There are far too many of you to name, but each and every one of you has supported and encouraged me for the past decade of my career, and I can't emphasize enough how much it means to me. You've been the best sort of cheerleaders a writer can have. Thank you all so, so very much.

And, finally, thank *you*. You, my readers, are why I am able to keep doing this, to keep doing the work I love. Whether this is the first book of mine you've picked up or you've read every one of them since I began publishing in 2010, I appreciate you more than you know. Thank you for your tweets, your emails, your kind words, and your time. I hope I can keep writing books for you for many, many years to come.

KODY KEPLINGER was born and raised in a small Kentucky town. During her senior year of high school she wrote her debut novel, *The DUFF*, which was a *New York Times* bestseller, a *USA Today* bestseller, a YALSA Top Ten Quick Pick for Reluctant Young Adult Readers, and a *Romantic Times* Top Pick. It has since been adapted into a major motion picture. Kody is also the author of *Lying Out Loud*, a companion to *The DUFF*; *Run*; *Shut Out*; and *A Midsummer's Nightmare*, as well as the middle-grade novel *The Swift Boys & Me*. Currently, Kody lives in New York City, where she teaches writing workshops and continues to write books for kids and teens. You can find more about her and her books at kodykeplinger.com.